Copyrighted Material

Rage of Night Copyright © 2020 by Variant Publications

Book design and layout copyright © 2020 by JN Chaney

This novel is a work of fiction. Names, characters, places, and incidents are either products of the author's imagination or used fictitiously. Any resemblance to actual events, locales, or persons, living, dead, or undead, is entirely coincidental.

All rights reserved

No part of this publication can be reproduced or transmitted in any form or by any means, electronic or mechanical, without permission in writing.

1st Edition

STAY UP TO DATE

Join the conversation and get updates on new and upcoming releases in the Facebook group called "JN Chaney's Renegade Readers." This is a hotspot where readers come together and share their lives and interests, discuss the series, and speak directly to J.N. Chaney and his co-authors.

https://www.facebook.com/groups/jnchaneyreaders/

He also post updates, official art, and other awesome stuff on his website and you can also follow him on Instagram, Facebook, and Twitter.

For email updates about new releases, as well as exclusive promotions, visit his website and sign up for the VIP mailing list. Head there now to receive a free copy of *The Other Side of Nowhere*.

https://www.jnchaney.com/the-messenger-subscribe

Stay Up To Date

Enjoying the series? Help others discover *The Messenger* series by leaving a review on Amazon.

RAGE OF NIGHT

BOOK 7 IN THE MESSENGER SERIES

J.N. CHANEY
TERRY MAGGERT

CONTENTS

The Messenger Universe Key Terms   ix

Chapter 1	1
Chapter 2	13
Chapter 3	23
Chapter 4	39
Chapter 5	51
Chapter 6	61
Chapter 7	81
Chapter 8	91
Chapter 9	103
Chapter 10	119
Chapter 11	135
Chapter 12	147
Chapter 13	161
Chapter 14	167
Chapter 15	177
Chapter 16	193
Chapter 17	203
Chapter 18	223
Chapter 19	243
Chapter 20	277
Epilogue	285
Stay Up To Date	293
About the Authors	295

THE MESSENGER UNIVERSE KEY TERMS

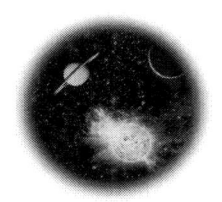

The Messenger: The chosen pilot of the Archetype.

Archetype: A massive weapon system designed for both space battle, close combat, and planetary defense. Humanoid in shape, the Archetype is controlled by a pilot and the Sentinel, an artificial intelligence designed to work with an organic humanoid nervous systems. The Archetype is equipped with offensive weaponry beyond anything known to current galactic standards, and has the ability to self-repair, travel in unSpace, and link with other weapons systems to fight in a combined arms operation.

Blobs: Amorphous alien race, famed for being traders. They manufacture nothing and are known as difficult employers.

Clan Shirna: A vicious, hierarchical tribe of reptilian beings whose territory is in and around the **Globe of Suns** and the **Pasture**. Clan Shirna is wired at the genetic level to defend and protect their territory. Originally under the control of Nathis, they are space-based, with a powerful navy and the collective will to fight to the last soldier if necessary.

Couriers: Independent starship pilots who deliver goods—legal, illegal, and everything in between—to customers. They find their jobs on a centralized posting system (See: **Needs Slate**) that is galaxy-wide, ranked by danger and pay, and constantly changing. Couriers supply their own craft, unless they're part of a Shipping Conglom. Couriers are often ex-military or a product of hard worlds.

Fade: A modification to the engine. It is a cutting edge shielding device that rotates through millions of subspace frequencies per second, rendering most scans ineffective. If the Fade is set to insertion, then the ship will translate into unSpace, where it can go faster than light. The Fade is rare, borderline illegal, and highly expensive. It works best on smaller masses, so Courier ships are optimal for installation of the Fade. One drawback is the echo left behind in regular space, an issue that other cloaking systems do not have. By using echoes as pathway markers, it is possible to track and destroy ships using the Fade.

Golden: A transhumanist race of beings who are attempting to scour the galaxy of intelligent life. The Golden were once engaged in warfare with the **Unseen**. They are said to return every 200,000 years to enact a cycle of galactic genocide, wiping out all technologically advanced civilizations before disappearing back from which they came. They destroyed their creators at some unknown point in the distant past and are remaking themselves with each revolution of their eternal, cyclical war.

Globe of Suns: A star cluster located in the far arm of the Milky Way Galaxy. It is an astronomical outlier. Dense with stars, it's a hotbed of Unseen tech, warfare, and Clan Shirna activity. Highly dangerous, both as an obstacle and combat area.

Kingsport: Located in the Dark Between, these are planetoid sized bases made of material that is resistant to detection, light-absorbing, and heavily armored. Oval in shape, the Kingsport is naval base and medical facility in one, intended as a deep space sleep/recovery facility for more than a thousand Unseen. The Kingsports maintain complete silence and do not communicate with other facilities, regardless of how dire the current military situation.

Lens: Unseen tech; a weapon capable of sending stars into premature collapse at considerable distance. The Lens is not unique—the Unseen left many of them behind in the Pasture, indicating that they were willing to destroy stars in their fight with the Golden.

Ribbon: Unseen tech that imparts a visual history of their engineering, left behind as a kind of beacon for spacefaring races.

Sentinel: A machine intelligence designed by the Unseen, the Sentinel is a specific intellect within the Archetype. It meshes with the human nervous system, indicating some anticipation of space-borne humans on the part of the Unseen. Sentinel is both combat system and advisor, and it has the ability to impart historical data when necessary to the fight at hand.

Shadow Nebula: A massive nebula possibly resulting from simultaneous star explosions. The Shadow Nebula may be a lingering effect from the use of a Lens, but it is unknown at this time.

Unseen: An extinct and ancient race who were among the progenitors of all advanced technology in the Milky Way, and possibly beyond. In appearance, they were slender, canine, and bipedal, with the forward-facing eyes of a predator. Their history is long and murky, but their engineering skills are nothing short of godlike. They commanded gravity, materials, space, and the ability to use all of these sciences in tandem to hold the Golden at bay during the last great war. The Unseen knew about humans, although their plans for humanity have since been lost to time.

unSpace: Neither space nor an alternate reality, this is the mathematically generated location used to span massive distances between points in the galaxy. There are several ways to penetrate unSpace, but only two are known to humans.

Pasture: Unseen tech in the form of an artificial Oort Cloud; a comet field of enormous size and complexity. Held in place by Unseen engineering, the Pasture is a repository for hidden items left by the Unseen. The Pasture remains stable despite having thousands of objects, a feat which is a demonstration of Unseen technical skills. The Lens and Archetype are just two of the items left behind for the next chapter in galactic warfare.

Prelate: In Clan Shirna, the Prelate is both military commander and morale officer, imbued with religious authority over all events concerning defense of their holy territory.

1

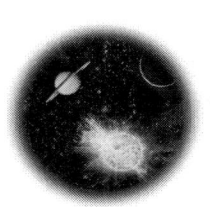

For once, Dash could simply fly.

He rested easily in the Archetype's cradle, watching the starfield on the heads-up. He flicked the view behind the Archetype and finally got a sense of motion, the Aquarian Ring getting smaller and more distant behind him. It had been a good visit with Al'Bijea; the dapper Aquarian leader had been keen to hear every detail of the massive battle they'd just won.

The Realm of Cygnus had fought against the Verity and the Bright at the shipyard, and the spinning wreckage told a story of chaos and death—and victory. Dash could tell Al'Bijea and his people got a real boost of confidence in their alliance with the Cygnus Realm, and that was important. It hadn't been that Al'Bijea was uncertain, just careful.

And against the Golden, nothing was a given.

"The starboard auxiliary stabilizer has gone offline," Sentinel said. "There seems to be a fault in the starboard power distribution system. I am attempting to isolate it."

"Should we turn back for the Ring?" Dash asked.

"That is not necessary. All of the redundant systems are still functioning."

Dash nodded and fully relaxed again. "Okay, then. Well, we'll loop back to the Forge to make sure that gets fixed." He eyed the threat indicator again—still blank—and then called up the Archetype's status board so he could get an overview of the mech's performance. It had taken a beating from a Harbinger that had been lurking near the Forge, either spying on them or planning an attack. Dash and the Archetype had finally won the fight, and the Harbinger was now glowing slag sluicing through the Forge's fabricators.

In the Cygnus Realm, enemies weren't just defeated. They were *useful*.

But the fight had reinforced something Dash had started to suspect—that the Golden were looking for ways to improve the combat abilities of their automated forces, and not just with better weapons or armor. It turned out that the Unseen, by effectively recruiting humans like Dash to their cause, had introduced a chaotic element—the natural spontaneity and unpredictability of the mercurial, passionate, *messy* creatures called people—into their war with the Golden, and the Golden were having trouble dealing with it. Whether the Unseen had done that deliberately or just lucked into it, Dash and his colleagues didn't know.

But the Harbinger he'd fought had been much more innovative and impulsive in its tactics; it took all of Dash's instincts, every move and reaction he'd learned from more than a few bar fights and ugly brawls, to finally defeat the damned thing. They'd definitely improved their AI, and had also started putting pilots into Harbingers—Verity pilots, like the ones he and Leira had fought right in the closing moments of the battle at the shipyard. They hadn't been very good, but their ever-better AI was a cause for serious concern.

"Dash," Sentinel said. "We are receiving a broadband distress call."

"From where?"

"Unknown. The transmission is fragmented and mostly incoherent, owing to interference from an intervening region of charged dust. I can only offer a direction and an estimated distance."

"This close to the Ring, it might be an Aquarian ship," Dash mused, then shrugged. "Eh, in any case, we'll go check it out. This is supposed to be a shakedown cruise to check out the repairs to this thing, after all. A few more hours of flying couldn't hurt."

Dash lined up the trajectory, boosted the drive, and headed for the closest safe translation point.

"May I make an observation?" Sentinel asked.

"Sure."

"You seem reluctant to return to the Forge."

"Huh? What makes you say that?"

"We completed all of the necessary tests and maneuvers to confirm that the Archetype is once more ready for combat before traveling to the Aquarian Ring. That visit was, itself, impromptu, as you hadn't planned it before contacting Al'Bijea regarding it."

"I just wanted to give him a full account of our fight at the shipyard."

"You could have done that just as effectively through holo-image transmissions."

"Not the same. Face-to-face diplomacy is—it's different. You get nuances, and—things. Details."

"You then planned a circuitous route back to the Forge, despite the fact that it is relatively close to the Aquarian Ring now," Sentinel went on. "And you further exhibited a physiological response suggestive of both relief and excitement regarding the distress call."

"It's a *distress* call. And I was *not* relieved."

"Your voice pattern and physiological response now suggests that you are experiencing shame and some anger. Am I embarrassing and angering you?"

Dash stared at the heads-up but didn't see the starfield and simply shook his head. "Look, I know you can practically read my mind. Hell, it's how the Archetype works. But seriously, this—" He shook his head again. "You're kind of getting into areas that aren't really your business."

"Is that because of some of the similarities between these reactions, and those you experience when you are in close proximity to Leira? Those are suggestive of attraction, both emotional and physical."

"Okay, you know what? This conversation is over."

Sentinel went silent. The quiet persisted until they were nearly at the translation point before Dash had to break it.

"Alright, fine. Putting aside the physical side of it—and I mean, seriously, let's *definitely* put that aside—what sort of emotional attraction to Leira are you talking about?"

"By comparison with your baseline levels of certain biochemical indicators, such as dopamine, cortisol, serotonin—"

"I think we can skip the biology stuff."

"I am simply observing that recently, and particularly since the battle at the shipyard, when you are in a position to observe Leira, all of these indicators change in a way that suggests you are both pleased and apprehensive, and this only intensifies with increasing proximity to her. I am, therefore, curious if this has some bearing on your apparent desire to remain away from the Forge."

Dash opened his mouth and took a breath to say, *No, of course not*, but he let the breath ease back out and closed his mouth again.

"Okay, Sentinel, let me ask *you* something. Why are you asking me about this?"

"As the AI responsible for oversight of the operations of the Archetype, it is vital that I am in close accord with you and your mindset."

"That the only reason?"

"You seem to be seeking a different answer from me."

Dash grinned. He'd have thought that Sentinel was just being cagey, if she was human. But she wasn't human, so she probably meant what she said.

"Am I staying away from the Forge?" Dash said. "Yeah, kind of. I'm not sure if you get this, being always on, never needing rest or relaxation, but being the Messenger is wearing. I'm in charge, which means I have to *be* in charge, making all sorts of decisions. And some of them are big decisions, with far-reaching effects. It's like everything I do has—ripples." His grin faded. "Sometimes, those decisions put a lot of people's lives on the line. Anyway, out here, I can just take some time to be me. Dash. Newton Sawyer. Not the Messenger."

"I understand," Sentinel replied. "And, be advised that I too benefit from periods of inactivity, even if I am *always on*."

Dash made a *huh* face. Sentinel liked having some downtime. He'd never realized, or even considered that. Of course, now he was wondering what she *did* with it.

"As for Leira," Sentinel said. "I gather that is a difficult subject for you, so I will not pursue it further."

"It's not difficult, it's more that it's—complicated." But he narrowed his eyes. "Wait a second. I know that you and Tybalt and

Custodian talk among yourselves. You haven't said anything about this to them, have you?"

"I have not. Custodian, in fact, recommended against any discussion of such personal observations regarding any humans with whom we interact."

"Well, good for Custodian. He's a smart guy."

"We will be clear for translation in thirty seconds."

Dash remained silent for about twenty of those seconds.

"So you haven't talked to Tybalt at all? He's—you know, not said anything about how Leira feels?"

"He has not. Do you wish me to inquire?"

"No," Dash said a bit too fast. "Of course not."

"We are now clear to safely translate."

"Yeah, okay." Dash initiated the translation drive but paused before activating it. "Don't say anything to Tybalt. Just—just forget I even said anything, okay?"

"Understood."

As the Archetype plunged into unSpace, Dash couldn't help thinking that Sentinel's final word, *Understood*, might have had just a hint of amusement in it.

"THIS IS THE *GRANITE*," the fuzzy, flickering image on the heads-up said. "We are under attack. Multiple hull breaches. And our last translation didn't work properly, so our translation drive is offline. Any ship, this is the *Granite*. We need your help!"

The *Granite* was one of their own, a former Gentle Friends heavy-cargo hauler, now a Cygnus Realm ship Benzel had brought into the fleet. She did general duties, including carting raw materials scavenged by the fleet back to the Forge. Dash had powered the Archetype up to full speed as soon as they'd received the first clear ID of the *Granite* from her flight transponder, and he now boosted to combat overspeed at the mention of attack.

"This is Dash, aboard the Archetype," he replied to the unsteady image of the *Granite's* captain, a man named Rosco. "I'm inbound to your location. ETA is twenty minutes, give or take."

"Glad to hear you, Dash, but I don't know if we're going to last that—"

The image flickered then cut out.

Dash looked at the sensors, his gut twisting at the thought the *Granite* may have just been destroyed. But they still showed her as being in one piece, and giving off power emissions, albeit fitful, unstable ones. "Sentinel, try getting him back."

"Unable. All usable comm channels have been flooded with extraneous noise, at least in the vicinity of the *Granite*."

"Natural, or are they being jammed?"

"There are no natural phenomena in the area that could account for this. Accordingly, I would suggest that—"

"They're being jammed, yeah."

All Dash could do was race on toward the stricken ship and hope that he arrived in time. He even considered trying to translate to get closer, but they were too deep into the gravity well of a nearby red giant-white dwarf binary system to do it safely. It probably explained why the *Granite's* translation drive had failed, in fact, though not why they'd dropped out of unSpace here in the first place.

It also didn't explain who was attacking them—although Dash could readily guess at that. Who else, besides the Verity or the

Bright? Or maybe some remnant of Clan Shirna that they'd somehow missed? Or the Golden?

No. Not the Golden. Those cowardly assholes seemed to be determined to have everyone else do their fighting for them.

"We are receiving another transmission," Sentinel said, as a brief, shimmering image of Rosco appeared on the heads-up. Dash thought the man looked utterly panic-stricken, but there was no audio—and then the image was gone. "High-power, directional, burst mode. It is encoded."

"Rosco must be trying to burn through the jamming. Can you decode it?"

"It will take some time, as there are gaps and errors that I will have to extrapolate around."

"Do it. Meantime, let's do a focused, max power transmission back. Rosco, this is Dash—"

The power emissions from the Granite suddenly spiked then dropped away. At the same time, a hard, fierce point of light flared in the middle of the heads-up, then it quickly faded and died.

"Based on the characteristics of its final power emissions, the *Granite* had just suffered a containment breach in its anti-deuterium storage. The ship has been destroyed."

"You've got to be shitting me," Dash hissed, anger percolating in every syllable.

Dash flew on anyway, but by the time he reached the *Granite's* last-transmitted location, they found nothing but an expanding cloud of atomic dust. There were no other ships nearby, and no evidence there ever had been.

Dash ordered Sentinel to scan anyway—full power, in all directions. Maybe broadcasting emissions from the Archetype like a beacon would attract whatever had attacked the basically defenseless *Granite*—and then he could kill it.

But nothing did, and Dash finally just slumped in the cradle. He no longer had any desire to be out here, alone, in space.

"Okay, Sentinel," he said. "Let's go home."

"SO ROSCO WAS RUNNING cargo on the side," Benzel said, leaning against a console in the Forge's Command Center. "I just confirmed that with some of our people. That's probably what got him into trouble."

"You think he was attacked by—what, someone he owed credits? Someone whose cargo he'd grabbed had come after him?" Dash asked.

Benzel shrugged. "Can't say. It's not like the *Granite* was a warship. She had one particle cannon, one missile launcher, and no armor to speak of. We were going to upgrade her, but—" He shrugged again.

"You don't seem all that surprised," Leira said, raising an eyebrow at Benzel.

For a third time, he shrugged. "Rosco was a good man, but he could never really get himself out of that privateer mindset. He always had an angle or a side gig going on." Benzel raised a hand. "Don't get me wrong, though. I'm not trying to excuse what he did. He got himself and three other good people killed. If we could bring him back to life, I would totally kick his ass from here to the galactic core and back—"

"Captain Rosco's encrypted message is now ready for you to review," Sentinel said. "There are still small gaps, through which we can extrapolate some, but not all, of the data. But it is largely complete."

"Go ahead, Sentinel, play it," Dash said.

The big holo-image that loomed over the Command Center came to life, filling with Rosco's face. The man had that same, frantic demeanor, but he managed to keep himself short of outright panic as he spoke.

"Dash, look," Rosco said. "We were running—on the side. I know—sorry. We picked up some cargo—the rim, planet called Terrace—jumped by a ship, not sure—imagery attached, but we can't shake them—for three days, keep translating, but—drive's out. I don't know if you're going to make—"

The imagery ended.

"It was at this point that the *Granite* suffered a containment failure in its anti-deuterium storage system," Sentinel said.

Silence followed. Benzel slowly shook his head. Wei-Ping muttered, "Damned fool."

"Okay, Sentinel, do we have that imagery Rosco said he sent with this transmission?"

"Yes. It is very brief."

The big holo-imager flicked to life again. It showed a sleek, smooth, teardrop-shaped ship, nearly twice the size of the *Granite*, based on the imagery's scale bar, and entirely midnight black. It zoomed into frame, fired a barrage of shots from rapid-fire pulse weapons, then nimbly zipped back out of view.

The image stopped. "A small amount of data was lost," Sentinel said. "But nothing that would add more information to the imagery."

"So we've got a new ship design out there," Dash said. "The question is, whose is it?"

"Those pulse cannons looked like Verity weapons to me," Wei-Ping said.

"I agree," Leira added. "They could be Bright, as well. But whatever it is, I'd say it's armed with Verity weapons."

"Okay, then," Dash said. "Let's assume it was a Verity ship of some new design. Something they were working on somewhere, though not the shipyard we attacked. That's right, isn't it, Sentinel?"

"We have not yet encountered this design, or any information about it, no."

"Okay. So, Custodian, let's see the most complete intelligence picture of the Verity we've got."

The big image changed to a star map, lit with thirty icons indicating known Verity-controlled systems, or ones that they were almost certain were.

"So there we go. Those thirty stars are what's left. We take all those out, and we end the Verity threat, new ship designs or not…"

Dash's voice trailed off as something suddenly jumped out of the star-map at him—something that hadn't occurred to him before, despite having seen this map many times now.

Leira noticed. "Dash, what is it?"

"Yeah, you look like you saw a ghost or something," Wei-Ping said.

Dash shook his head. "Not a ghost, but maybe something just as spooky. Custodian, zoom this image out. Make it, let's say, fifty percent."

The image shrank, the galactic arm abruptly receding, as though they were aboard an impossible fast ship far above the galaxy's ecliptic plane. The thirty Verity-controlled stars correspondingly crowded closer together, accentuating the pattern Dash had just discerned.

"There," he said, walking up to the image and pointing. "See it? These Verity systems—they become denser closer to the galactic core."

Benzel gave Wei-Ping a bemused glance, then shrugged. "Okay. So?"

"So, our understanding of the Golden so far was that they hung out outside galactic space, above and below the plane of the ecliptic. So why are the Verity, their allies, seeming to be concentrating their attention *toward* the galactic core—exactly the other way?"

Silence and shrugs followed.

"Maybe there's something in the core they want or need," Leira finally ventured.

"Maybe. Or maybe there's something in the core they're worried about," Benzel added.

Dash nodded. "Yeah. So the question is, which is it? And if there's something in the core they're more afraid of than us—" He turned back to the others. "What, exactly, the hell *is* it?"

2

"You know," Amy said, "now that I see it starting to come together like this, I'm starting to get kind of nervous."

She stood with Dash, Leira, Conover, and Amy in the fabrication plant, watching as still-glowing components for their new mechs, the Talon and the Pulsar, were hoisted out of molds and transported into a nearby assembly bay. Both mechs were in the final stages of completion and would be operational in a few days.

"How goes the simulator training with your AIs?" Dash asked.

"Hathaway is turning out to be a bit of a downer," Amy said. "Excuse me, *Doctor* Hathaway. He's all business, wants to keep getting into the science behind stuff, always blathering on about how I'm supposed to be furthering my education. I'm going to have to teach him how to be more of a free spirit, I can see."

"You should have mine, then," Conover replied. "Kristin is all bright and cheerful all the time. Like, she's relentless. And she likes to hum when she's prepping weapons or running diagnostics. She asked me if I liked musical theater and dancing. I mean—duh. *No*. Maybe we can trade."

"The AIs assigned to your mechs are specifically tailored to your respective personality profiles," Custodian put in. "Reassigning them would not offer any benefits, and would, in fact, degrade their performance during interactions with you."

"Mine's tailored to my personality?" Amy asked, putting her hands on her hips. "Really? He's nothing like me. Everything's so serious and factual. Sometimes I just want to scream at him to lighten up!"

Dash fought to keep from laughing. Leira couldn't, and had wandered a few paces off, staring away from them at another component being extracted from a mold. Dash could see her shoulders shaking.

"The selection criteria for the baseline personalities of your AIs were based on—" Custodian began, but Dash raised a hand and shook his head.

"It's fine. You'll get used to working with your AIs, don't worry. Believe me, when it comes to this sort of thing, these AIs really do know best."

Amy and Conover both frowned—again, Dash had to work really hard at not just bursting out laughing.

"Incidentally, the distortion lattice has now been fully implemented in the Pulsar," Custodian said. "It actually operates more efficiently than the versions retrofitted in the Archetype and Swift. The intent is to include a basic system in future mechs able to deploy it."

"But that doesn't include my mech, right?" Amy asked.

"That is correct. The Talon is intended as a light scout and skirmishing asset. Accordingly, it has been fitted with a stealth shield similar to that implemented in our reconnaissance drones. The Talon can generate sufficient power to operate the stealth shield, but as your AI will show you, its use will preclude operating most other systems while it is active, aside from drive, nav, and comm functions."

"Um...what about life support?"

"That will operate as well. It is always the last system to be taken offline because of power limitations, unless the pilot specifically overrides it."

"Okay, good." Amy clapped her hands together. "So I can be stealthed, or I can shoot. That sounds like an ambush to me!"

Dash turned to Conover. "As for the Pulsar's distortion lattice, you'll have to come up with some tactics for using that. Being able to generate a sudden positive or negative gravitational well around your mech sounds powerful, but you can only do it in short bursts."

"I've already started working on it. The Pulsar's not really a frontline mech, I'm thinking. It's more for supporting you guys and turning enemy assets against their own."

"Which means we need to get these new mechs integrated into the fleet training schedule as soon as we can," Leira said. "You guys should report to Benzel and Wei-Ping, and talk to them about it."

Amy and Conover both nodded, but any replies were cut off by a warning horn.

"Another shipment of Dark Metal harvested by our Aquarian allies has just arrived and needs to be moved to the feedstock processors through the area where you are now standing," Custodian said.

"In other words, get the hell out of the way," Dash replied, raising his voice over the growing hum and rattle of the Forge's machinery. "It's getting pretty noisy in here, anyway. Let's head back to the Command Center. There are a few things I'd like to talk over before we launch our next offensive."

THE COMMAND CENTER had started its own hum and rattle. The fleet was growing and exercising near the Forge while recovery and salvage operations went on at the former Verity shipyard, and in several other systems.

Space around the Forge was *busy*.

Along with the Realm navy, the Aquarians engaged in yet more operations, and coordinating it all had become a full-time job. They now had several consoles in the Command Center manned, including a duty Ops station that would run around the clock. Ragsdale, as it turned out, had experience running an Ops center from his own military days, and had taken on organizing and overseeing this one. It was a secondary duty, though, until they could find a suitable replacement because Dash really wanted the Security Chief to focus on security.

"So, in summary, we've no current security concerns among our personnel," Ragsdale said. "We had a few whose backgrounds we could properly confirm, and they've been taken off to go their own way. Everyone else who's left—I think we can rely on them. The emphasis, though, is on *think*."

"Do you ever completely trust *anyone*?" Amy asked.

Ragsdale gave her a thin smile and shook his head. "Not even myself. It keeps me sharp."

"Yeah, but what a way to look at the world, like everyone's a potential threat."

"Everyone *is* a potential threat," Ragsdale replied. "That's just being smart when there's a whole race of advanced aliens out there bent on eradicating us."

Amy opened her mouth but finally just shrugged. "Yeah, can't argue with that."

"Okay," Dash said, grabbing everyone's attention. "So that's the picture of where we currently are. The next big question is, where do we go from here?"

"We go and kick the Verity's ass into oblivion, the way we did Clan Shirna," Benzel said. "At least, that's been the plan so far. Did you want to change it?"

Dash shook his head. "No. We need to take the Verity out of this fight for good."

Wei-Ping cocked her head and narrowed her eyes at Dash. "But something's bugging you, isn't it?"

"Yeah, it is. Custodian, put that map you and I talked about this morning up on the big board."

The big holo-image flicked to the star map they were all starting to see in their sleep, the one depicting the bulk of the inhabited galactic arm. It was alight with a multitude of icons of various colors, depicting various events, in accordance with a key off to one side.

"What's missing from this?" Dash asked. "Rather, what thing isn't here that absolutely *should* be?"

For a long moment, they all just stared at the map, pondering Dash's question. It was Viktor who finally spoke up.

"The Golden themselves."

"Exactly," Dash replied, sweeping an arm towards the map. "We've had literally dozens of contacts, everything from remote-sensing signals from reconnaissance drones, or even the Forge itself, to pitched battles." He gestured at one cluster of blue points radiating out from the vast field of comets known as the Pasture, an ancient Unseen construct whose purpose they still didn't entirely understand. "This is—or was—Clan Shirna." Now Dash moved up to the map and pointed at a scattering of orange icons. "These are Bright. Most of the rest are Verity, aside from that smattering of green ones, ones we just don't have enough information about to say anything more than they're probably enemy activity."

He stepped back down. "The red ones are confirmed Golden contacts."

There were several near the Forge, reflecting battles they'd fought against Golden Harbingers and drones. A couple more at Burrow, where Dash had fought two more Harbingers. And there was one on Gulch, representing the crashed Golden battlecruiser they'd explored, with the help of Ragsdale and his people from nearby Port Hannah.

And that was it.

"None of those red ones are encounters with living Golden, either," Dash said. "They've either been things controlled by AIs or, in the case of Gulch, just bots aboard that crashed ship. We *did* actually find Golden there, but they were long dead."

"So the Golden are cowards," Wei-Ping said. "Don't want to get their own hands—or claws, or tentacles, or whatever they've got—dirty."

Benzel nodded. "Bastards do everything through others, not themselves."

"You could say the same about the Unseen," Viktor noted, then gestured around. "I don't see many of them around here helping us out."

Kai shifted uncomfortably. "The Unseen are nothing like the Enemy of All Life—"

"I don't think Viktor's suggesting they are," Dash cut in, heading off an argument. Kai had a lifetime of immersion in a mindset that saw the Unseen as something to be revered as gods, so any criticism of them would just get his shields up. "We don't even know if there are any Unseen left alive. Isn't that right, Custodian?"

"It is. There is no evidence, as yet, that any of the Creators have survived to the present."

Viktor offered Kai a nod. "Dash and Custodian are right. At least we have some hints that the Golden are still out there pulling the strings."

Dash turned back to Wei-Ping. "Anyway, you were partly right. The Golden obviously don't want to get their hands—pretty sure that's what they've got, hands, from their corpses, anyway—dirty. But I don't think they're cowards."

"Don't exactly see them spoiling for a fight," Wei-Ping shot back.

But Benzel crossed his arms and nodded. "I think Dash is right. I don't think it's about them being cowards." He looked at Wei-Ping. "What's the first rule of the Gentle Friends?"

"Don't take more than your cut?"

"Well—yeah, okay. The second rule, then."

"But if you can get away with it, take the biggest cut you can?"

"It's *violence is our last resort*," Benzel snapped. "Remember that one?"

"Oh, yeah. We want to avoid fighting as much as possible," Wei-Ping said. "But that's because we didn't want to hurt anyone, if we could get away with it, and *anyone* especially included us."

"Doesn't sound like that applies to the Golden at all," Viktor said.

"But it does," Benzel replied, standing and walking up to the big map beside Dash. Arms still crossed, he glared up at it. "At least the principle does. The Golden don't want to fight us—not because they don't want to get dirty, and not because they're cowards, but because it's more efficient this way. And being partly machines, they're all about efficiency." He glanced at Dash. "Am I right?"

"You are. *Exactly* right, in fact. The Golden are conning the likes of Clan Shirna, the Bright, the Verity, and probably others into attacking, disrupting, confusing, and generally just grinding away at us. They want to attrition us through allies—allies they don't give a shit about, remember, because they're sentient life and they'll eventually have to be exterminated, too. And they want to weaken everyone to the point where they can just come in and clean up. They're using the resources and blood of others to do their dirty work for them." He glanced at Benzel and nodded. "It's efficient."

"So we need to find the Golden and get them stuck into this war so we can fight them face-to-face," Leira said.

Dash nodded but looked back up at the holo-image of the star map. "I agree, but that's going to be tougher than I originally thought. I've been working off the assumption that the Golden are lurking just outside the galaxy, above and below the galactic plane, in isolated systems, on rogue planets, and the like. But the pattern of Verity-controlled star systems seems to hint at a real fixation on the galactic core. So is that where the Golden actually are? Or is there something else in there that the Verity are interested in?"

"Or scared of," put in Benzel.

"Yeah, and we've discussed this. So what we need to decide is where we focus our efforts. Do we start searching outside the galaxy? Or do we head inward, to the core, and start looking there?"

"The galactic core is a long way off," Viktor said. "And dangerous. The background radiation is a lot higher in there from all the stars jammed into it."

"Not to mention the effects from the supergiant black hole that sits in the very center of the core," Conover added. "We know it's there, but no one's been close enough to really get a good idea of what getting too close to it would be like. I mean, there could be time dilation effects."

"Wait, does that mean time runs faster for you when you get closer to the black hole? Or more slowly?" Leira asked.

"From what we know, more slowly," Conover replied.

Ragsdale narrowed his eyes. "If time *does* run more slowly closer to that black hole, could the Golden be using that? Could they be taking advantage of it to let time pass more quickly for us, compared to them?"

Dash raised his hands. "These are all great questions. And, frankly, they're getting into territory that leaves me kind of staring blankly and just nodding along. Anyway, we don't have to answer this right now, but we do need to think about it." He looked back at the map. "The bottom line is that we've never seen a Golden in the fight, at least not yet. And I agree that they're not cowards, and just using…let's call it cheaper life, to do their dirty work for them—"

Custodian cut in. "That may not be entirely true. I have further processed the *Granite's* combat footage and resolved more detail. I believe there is something you should see."

"Put it up here," Dash said.

A window popped open in the big holo-image, revealing a snippet of footage from the attack on the *Granite*. Once more, the massive Verity ship rotated in the weak starlight, its smooth hull black from end to end. But in this zoomed and obviously cleaned-up imagery, another craft rested on its upper surface. It was lean, with a silvery glint, and configured more like an atmospheric fighter, with delta wings completely unnecessary for space combat.

"What the hell is that?" Leira asked.

"I will enlarge the image further," Custodian said.

The small ship zoomed even closer. The imagery now showed a small shape standing next to the delta-winged craft—a suited figure. It waved lazily at the fighter, and a hatch irised open. The figure stepped into the opening; a few seconds later, the engines fired and the small ship streaked away at a right angle, leaving the field of view entirely in less than a second.

"That was one hell of an acceleration," Amy said.

Dash exhaled when the imagery stopped, but his body stayed tense. "Okay, guess I was wrong."

"About?" Conover asked.

The rest of them said nothing, their eyes were burning as they stared at the screen. *They know*, Dash thought. *They know what we just saw.*

"The Golden. We just saw them, and they *are* in combat, after all."

3

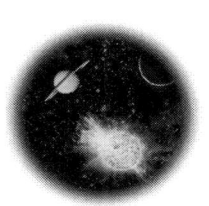

As Dash strode across the docking bay, heading for the Archetype, Amy turned away from the nearly complete Talon and grinned at him.

"Got your big boots on?" she asked.

Dash shot back a scowl. It had somehow become a running joke—that he was both the Messenger and a farmer, because he "farmed" Dark Metal. He had to admit that most of the Archetype's flight time had been devoted to recovering precious Dark Metal, a pretty mundane task for one of the most powerful military assets in known space. But it was a necessary one and, considering that a lot of the Dark Metal they scavenged came from remote, isolated systems, a potentially very dangerous one.

"*Hah,*" he shot back at Amy. "That joke is far from cutting edge, but...man. This design *is.*" He paused, though, to admire the sleek the lines of the Talon. Custodian had moved it here for final refinements and tweaks now that the heavy fabrication and assembly was done. It had meant displacing the *Slipwing*, which had used this docking bay as its home ever since they'd first encountered the Forge, and that gave Dash a bit of a pang. But having another mech join the fleet more than made up for it.

"She's looking good," he said to Amy.

"Yeah. A few more little jobs, and then Custodian says he can load up the AI and we can take it out for its first test flight." Her smile faded. "Like I said before, I have to admit, it makes me kind of nervous."

"You'll be fine. And I mean that, you will definitely be fine. Custodian, Sentinel, and Tybalt know what they're doing. If they didn't think you were going to work out as a pilot for the Talon, they'd have said so. Isn't that right, Sentinel?"

"Correct. Amy has all of the attributes needed for an effective mech pilot."

"I agree that she will be entirely adequate," Tybalt added.

Amy frowned at that, but Dash just grinned. "Coming from Tybalt, entirely adequate is a glowing compliment."

"Dash, I'm out here with the *Rockhound*, ready to get going," Leira said over the comm. "You joining us or taking the day off?"

"Be right there," he said, giving Amy a wave and mounting the Archetype. Once settled in the cradle, he powered the mech up, launched it, and eased into formation with the Swift and the *Rockhound*.

"Okay, so everyone's good with the nav data?" he asked.

Both Leira and the pilot Jacobi acknowledged, and they set off, heading for a remote system with one of the strangest Dark Metal signals they'd yet detected.

"Brown dwarfs are weird," Leira said, once the mechs and the *Rockhound* had dropped out of unSpace and headed starward in their destination system. "Always seemed to me that they should just make up their damned minds—be a star or be a planet. Choose one, you know?"

Dash smiled. This system was, indeed, an oddity, it's primary star a brown dwarf—a large, hot sphere of mostly hydrogen that sat poised forever on the brink of nuclear fusion and turning into a star. This one was vast, but diffuse, having less of an actual surface and more just a fuzzy, gradual transition from *brown dwarf* to *not brown dwarf*.

It still looked like a star system, though, with a trio of rocky planets hurtling around the primary wannabe star. The Dark Metal signal emanated from one of them, and now Dash saw the explanation for its strangeness, the fact that it waxed and waned on a repeating cycle of almost exactly forty-one hours. The second of the two planets had an orbital period of precisely twice that, which meant that the Dark Metal was regularly occluded behind the brown dwarf relative to the Forge. For some reason, this brown dwarf seemed to be acting as a barrier to the ceaseless streams of neutrinos that normally made Dark Metal visible.

"Okay, so this Dark Metal signature is on that second planet," he started, then narrowed his eyes at the heads-up. "No, wait. It's on a moon orbiting that second planet."

"Either way, it means getting awfully close to the brown dwarf," Leira said. "That might be okay for us in the two mechs, but all that radiation is going to be hard on the *Rockhound*."

"Yeah, I haven't had kids yet," Jacobi put in. "Still might want to someday."

Dash nodded. The brown dwarf was hot, but nothing like a star.

As a result, its planets all orbited very close to it, and fast. If it ever did manage to light itself up as a star, all three of these planets would puff away to vapor. In the meantime, though, they swung like mad around the almost-star, bathed in the infrared rays and hard radiation streaming from it.

"Sentinel, can we reconfigure the Archetype's shield to protect the *Rockhound* while we're in close to that thing?"

"Yes. It will diminish the protective effect of the shield from a combat point of view, but it will still be more than capable of blocking virtually all of the most dangerous radiation. It will not block the infrared emanations, but the *Rockhound*'s cooling systems should be capable of dealing with that."

"Good news, Jacobi, you can have a dozen kids if you want," Dash said over the comm to the *Rockhound*'s pilot. "And get all hot and bothered while you think about the process, you randy old spacer."

"Don't need infrared rays for that!" Jacobi replied, and Dash laughed.

In close formation, the mechs and the *Rockhound* started in-system, heading for the second planet.

"So what, exactly, was this supposed to be?" Leira asked.

Dash stared at the imagery on the heads-up for a moment, then shook his head. "Beats me. We've got Dark Metal—a lot of it, it seems, with some of it jammed down in that crevasse, and the rest lying on the surface in that—what the hell is that, anyway?"

"Didn't I just ask that?" Leira said.

Dash stared at the broken…whatever it was. It looked like the remains of a gantry of some sort that had once risen from the barren, radiation-scoured terrain of the moon. Risen a long way, in fact, now that Dash traced the debris across the cracked, rocky surface and saw it dwindle off into the far distance, maybe even to the horizon.

He checked the heads-up to make sure the Archetype's shield still enclosed the nearby *Rockhound*, then he checked the threat indicator, which was blank. He turned his attention back to the debris. "Sentinel, have you got any idea what this might be? Or was, more like, since it looks wrecked now?"

"It would appear to be a symmetrically stabilized orbital tower. The more popular designation, taken from your own archives, would be a skyhook or a beanstalk, the latter used in some space-faring cultures from Old Earth."

"Ah, okay." Dash let out a low whistle. Skyhooks were enormous towers, with one end anchored on the surface of a body, on its equator, and the other far above, in geosynchronous orbit over that anchor point. The tower would, in theory, rotate in perfect sync with whatever body—moon, planet, whatever—to which it was anchored. That meant that, from the perspective of someone standing at its base, it would just be a vast tower reaching up into space. Elevators attached to it could then lift payloads into orbit for a fraction of the effort or cost of achieving escape velocity with a ship.

"I'd always heard that these things were unstable," Dash said. "I know they've been tried in different places, but they've never worked out. They're hard to keep aligned properly, and they need to be made of really strong stuff—oh. That's what all the Dark Metal here is for."

"So it would appear. Dark Metal-infused alloys would be more than sufficiently strong to resist the powerful forces that would act on such a structure."

Dash nodded at the wreckage. "Yeah, well, looks like it didn't work out too well regardless."

"The bigger question is why was it here?" Leira said. "What were they planning on lifting into orbit from this rock? Especially since it's not a very big rock, so lifting with a ship is no big deal in this gravity well."

"No idea," Dash replied. "Maybe it was a prototype and they were testing it, or the stuff it was made of, or something. And doing it in a place with low grav so it didn't need to be as big."

"All reasonable assumptions," Sentinel said. "Indeed, they were observations I was about to make myself."

"Hah! I beat the super-advanced, hyper-fast alien AI to the punch," Dash said, grinning.

"You did. An impressive achievement."

Dash kept his grin but narrowed his eyes. "Was that sarcasm?"

"Of course not."

"Uh, Dash?" Jacobi cut in. "That shield of yours is blocking most of the radiation here. *Most*. Remember how I said I'd still like to have kids?"

"I hear you—that's enough sightseeing. Okay, folks, let's get to work gathering up all this Dark Metal."

"THAT WAS a true pain in the butt," Leira said.

Dash gingerly placed the last piece of debris into the open hold of the *Rockhound* then backed the Archetype away. A suited figure inside the ship waved at him, and the clamshell cargo doors began to cycle closed.

He had to nod at Leira's comment. The skyhook, for all its designed durability when it, crumbled like wet tissue as they went about retrieving it. Sentinel offered that it was something about how it had been made; skyhooks needed to resist tremendous tensile forces, from gravity at the bottom pulling it down, to the angular momentum of its orbiting, geostationary top, yanking it up. Those, when perfectly balanced, kept the skyhook in place and in one piece. But the design of this one meant it was weak to lateral, shearing forces, so it had been like a cable—hard to pull apart when stretched taut, but easy to push and deform from the sides. Maybe that's why it eventually failed, Dash thought.

He withdrew the Archetype from the *Rockhound* far enough to keep the sturdy little ship enclosed in the shield, then turned—

The threat indicator lit up.

"Multiple missile launches," Sentinel said. "Impact in ten seconds."

Dash swore. How had enemy ships managed to get so close without them knowing?

No—these weren't ships. They were weapons platforms, installed on this moon but far enough away to be below the horizon relative to the skyhook debris. The missiles raced in, leaving barely enough time for the point-defense batteries on the two mechs and the *Rockhound* to react. They managed to swat all but three of the missiles out of space, but two straddled the Archetype, near hits, while one detonated close to the *Rockhound*. The shield, configured to enclose the ship against the radiation hazard, only blunted some of the resulting blasts. The Archetype's armor shrugged off the sudden pulses of raw energy and the following blast of plasma, but the *Rockhound* reeled, debris spalling off her port flank.

"Dash, we don't have a line of sight to those missile launchers!" Leira said. "We have to get further away from this moon!"

"Understood, out to you—*Rockhound*, what's your status?" Dash asked.

"Moderate damage to our port hull—one breach, but not a bad one. But our main drive is offline, so thrusters only."

"Got it," was what Dash said, but inwardly, he cursed. On thrusters only, the *Rockhound* would take forever to get up any sort of velocity. That meant the Archetype was effectively tethered to something that could barely accelerate. But if he pulled away to engage the missile platforms, he'd leave the *Rockhound* and her crew fully exposed to the hurricane of radiation pouring off the brown dwarf.

The threat indicator lit again. "Another salvo of missiles is incoming," Sentinel intoned. "Impact in ten seconds."

Dash just let the point-defense system do its automated thing and focused his attention on the broader battle. "Leira, go, attack one of those platforms. See if you can—"

Another missile got through the point-defenses and detonated. Fortunately, the Archetype's bulk blocked much of the blast from reaching the *Rockhound*. "—see if you can take it out while we try to sort this out here!"

"On my way." The Swift powered up and soared away from the surface of the moon. Dash turned his focus back to the *Rockhound*.

"What's the status of your drive?"

"The fusion monitor is stuck in a reboot cycle and we can't get it unstuck. We're kind of jammed in safe mode until we can."

The fusion monitor was a basic safety system, monitoring the performance of the reactor, making constant adjustments and corrections to the magnetic shield that bottled up the stellar heat of the fusing deuterium. All ships had them, and if they stopped operating properly, the reactor was designed to cut off its own fuel and stop the fusion reaction. If the reactor remained shut down for more than a few minutes at most, though, it would have to be put through its whole restart sequence, which would take many *more* minutes.

Another salvo of missiles launched from the unseen platforms. Dash saw Leira fire a barrage of her own, then follow up with blasts from the Swift's nova cannon. But the platforms, or whatever was guiding their fire, seemed to have sensed the predicament the Archetype and the *Rockhound* were in and concentrated on them.

Dash added the dark-lance to the weight of fire from the point-defense systems, but a missile still managed to sneak through, searing the Archetype and stripping more chunks off the *Rockhound*.

Through all of this, they'd managed to move a single klick. The *Rockhound* burned her thrusters as hard as she could, but it was just far too slow.

Dash's mind raced—could the Archetype just grab the *Rockhound* and accelerate with her? No—and he didn't need Sentinel to tell him that the ship's mass was great enough that it would slow their acceleration. If the Archetype pulled too many g's, the mechanical stress could rip the *Rockhound* apart.

He could think of only one thing.

"Can you guys bypass the fusion monitor?" he asked.

There was a pause—during which yet *another* salvo of missiles was launched at them—then the pilot came back. "We'd have to keep the reactor in tune manually, Dash. We're good, but I don't know if we're *that* good."

This time, Dash risked using the distortion cannon. They were still close enough to the moon that it caused a flurry of rocks and dust to suddenly start tumbling up from the surface, but it also threw enough of the incoming missiles off that point-defense could take the rest. The tug from the distortion effect also gave them a bit of a boost, so Dash reoriented the weapon's targeting and fired again, using the abrupt surge of gravity to boost them even more.

It still wasn't going to be enough. Leira was slowly degrading one of the bunker-like platforms, now that Tybalt had shared the image and she could see it. It was a toroid, partly buried in the moon's rock surface. Besides missiles, it also sported rapid-fire pulse cannons of its own, and these were now firing at Leira, eating away at the Swift's shield.

"Sentinel," Dash said. "Can you take control of their fusion reactor? Keep it working without, you know, going boom?"

"I can, but to ensure a reasonable safety margin, it will be necessary to run it considerably below full power—missiles incoming."

"Damn it—okay, do it. *Rockhound*, Sentinel is taking control of your reactor. As soon as you can, light up that drive!"

"Will do. Shit, missiles incoming."

Again, thanks to the dark-lance, the distortion cannon, and the point-defense batteries, they again suffered only one near-hit. However, it still hurt the *Rockhound*, forcing her to fall back on emergency power for life support and other critical functions.

"Dash, got to be honest here," Jacobi said. "I'm not sure we can survive one more of those."

"Understood. Leira, status!"

"This damned bunker thing is tough. It's got shields and heavy armor. And it hits hard. We're landing hits back, but we could really use you in this fight."

Dash took a breath and let it out. Once again, the reality of being a leader slammed home. If he left the *Rockhound* to join the fight, they could probably clean up the Golden missile bunkers—because they almost certainly were Golden, they were too sophisticated for even Bright or Verity installations. But that could kill the *Rockhound*'s crew. If he didn't, he might be risking one or both mechs. Logic told him that the right answer was to sacrifice the crew to ensure the safety of the mechs—

But logic sucked.

"Sentinel, we could really use—"

"I have the *Rockhound*'s reactor back online," she cut in. "I have throttled it back to forty percent power, however, to account for damage and ensure a safety margin."

"Good, fine—*Rockhound*, go!"

The ship answered by lighting its main drive, a searing tongue of fusion plasma that flung her away from the moon. Dash powered up the Archetype in tandem with it, keeping pace.

They maintained that pace, accelerating as hard as the damaged *Rockhound* safely could. More missiles launched from the bunkers, but their longer flight time, as they chased after the *Rockhound* and its guardian mech, made it easier to deploy countermeasures against them. Ten minutes later, Sentinel judged the radiation flux. Though still worrisome, it no longer posed a fatal risk to the *Rockhound*'s crew, who had also gotten the balky fusion monitor working again.

Dash ramped the Archetype up to full power, somersaulted the mech, and drove back toward the moon.

"Okay, Dash, I think that bunker's finally dead," Leira said. "Took a bit of a beating doing it. Did you want to take out the other one, or just scoot, now that the *Rockhound* is flying again?"

Dash glared at the image of the second bunker. "Oh, I want to take out the other one alright. I don't want to leave anything Golden intact, ever, if we can help it."

"Okay, on my way—"

"Don't bother," Dash said. "I've got this. Sentinel, power up the blast cannon."

A low thrum ran through the Archetype as the wing-like accumulators spread from its back and began to flicker with building energy. The weapon was easily the most powerful in the mech's arsenal, but it was slow to fire and carried a risk of knocking the Archetype basically offline. Once they managed to get it fully powered-up—a goal to which they seemed to be forever inching closer, but never quite reaching—that would change. But now, it was a weapon to be used only when it was *really* needed.

Or when Dash *really* wanted to blow the hell out of something.

"If you break your mech, Dash, Tybalt doesn't know if we'll be able to tow you—" Leira said.

The firing solution confirmed, Dash triggered the blast cannon.

A colossal burst of energy erupted from the surface of the moon, and it was as strong as an asteroid collision. A huge gouge opened in its surface as rock was turned to incandescent vapor and glowing slag. Chunks of debris, some as big as the Archetype, were flung into space.

"—home," Leira finished. "But I guess you're not worried about that."

Dash flicked his eyes over the Archetype's status display. A few glitches, but nothing serious. He instructed Sentinel to stow the blast cannon then fixed his attention on the toroidal shape of the bunker.

Or, rather, what was left of the bunker. The rock around it had vaporized, and it had toppled into the resulting crater, its wreckage protruding from quickly darkening magma.

"Take *that*," Dash said.

"Well, I guess we're finally done here," Leira offered, but Dash shook his head.

"Not quite. We've still got a couple of Golden bunkers to pillage. After all this trouble, I'm not going to pass up on denying another few hundred kilos of Dark Metal to the Golden and taking it for ourselves."

"Waste not, want not," Leira said. "I saw that in an *olllllld* vid. Some grandmother type said it."

"Smart lady. And I certainly *want*."

When they finally arrived back at the Forge, the *Rockhound*'s crew immediately came to Dash and thanked him personally for sticking by them the way he had. He brushed it off, but Leira, watching from a discreet distance away, came up to Dash when they'd gone and rolled her eyes.

"You've learned an awful lot of humility," she said. "The Dash I first met was a lot more full of himself."

He shrugged. "That Dash wasn't jammed into making life-and-death decisions over and over again—and on behalf of other people, at that. I guess it's easier to be full of yourself when *yourself* is all that really matters to you." He gave her a sidelong glance. "Sorry if that disappoints you."

"The old, full-of-himself Dash was actually something of an ass. I think I like this new and improved version better."

"Huh. All it took was becoming the leader of an entire realm, immersed in an interstellar war for the survival of all sentient life, to gain some respect. Hell, if I'd known that, I would've done it years ago."

Leira laughed, and Dash laughed along with her—but it faded as their eyes met.

A moment passed, the only sound the distant background hum of the Forge permeating the docking bay. Then Leira opened her mouth—

"Messenger," Custodian said. "If I may, I require a moment of your time."

Leira closed her mouth again and smiled.

Now it was Dash's turn to roll his eyes. "What is it, Custodian? Is it about those wrecked bunker components we brought back? Look, we didn't really want to hang around that system, trying to strip out the Dark Metal—"

"No, it is not that. Although, as an observation, it is interesting that they were toroidal in shape."

"Uh—okay. How so?"

"A toroid is fundamentally a circle. And circles are very useful."

Dash frowned at Leira. "Custodian, what the hell are you talking about?"

"Again, a moment of your time, please."

He sighed. "Looks like duty calls yet again. I'll catch up with you later."

Leira nodded, offered a final smile, then withdrew, leaving Dash able to offer a *moment* to Custodian.

"Okay, so what's so urgent—and secret? Is there something secret you want to talk to me about?"

"If you will don a vac suit and proceed outside the Forge, onto its surface, I will explain, Messenger."

"You want me to go—"

"Outside, yes."

Dash had been starting to get irked at having to put off showering, eating and generally getting some down time, but this was intriguing.

"Okay," Dash said. "I'll go get a vac suit and step outside."

"I will be ready when you do."

4

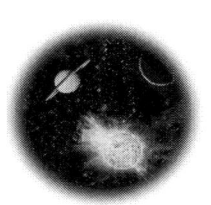

Dash felt the maintenance remote start to slow. He'd been riding it—actually, clinging to it felt more accurate—across the surface of the Forge, the spherical device racing over the vast hull as it dodged protruding sensor masts, the bulky domes of point-defense batteries, and towering shield generators. Those were just the things he recognized, as there were a multitude of other devices and constructs whose purpose Dash could only guess it. It had been both exhilarating and terrifying.

Now, the remote slowed to a running pace, then a walking pace, and then it stopped. A few meters away was a small airlock Dash had never seen before. That wasn't surprising, though; he'd never seen the vast majority of the Forge's hull, except from far away. He tried doing the mental mapping required to figure out where this airlock would be, but the trip on the remote had left him a little disoriented. About halfway between the Forge's pole and its equator, maybe? In a section that was mostly powered-down hab? Or was this closer to the Command Center?

"If you would dismount and enter the airlock, Messenger, we can proceed," Custodian said.

Dash suddenly realized he'd just been sitting here, lost in trying to figure out where he was. "Oh, right—sorry," he said, and clambered down from the remote. Custodian must have applied artificial gravity, because there was no sense of weightlessness at all. Dash just walked to the airlock, which opened as he approached. He stepped inside, and the direction of the gravitational pulls slowly changed, reorienting him so instead of the airlock opening below him, at his feet, it now stretched ahead of him. It cycled closed once he was inside, then it pressurized and the inner door slid open. Dash stepped through and found himself in a darkened corridor. As soon as he took a couple of paces, lights flicked on, revealing another door at the other end.

"This feels like our first day on the Forge all over again," he muttered, remembering how parts of the Forge would power up at his approach, then power down again as he left them. But the station was running at far lower power levels then—so why was it necessary here and now?

"Custodian, where am I? And did I have to come in through the outside? Couldn't I have just entered from inside the Forge?"

"No. This portion of the Forge is isolated from the rest and is intended for the exclusive use of the Messenger."

"Really. Huh." He unclipped his helmet and removed it, and then he walked toward the door ahead of him. It opened as he approached and, again, the lights flared on in the compartment beyond.

It was a spacious chamber, probably a little bigger than the lounge they'd repurposed as their War Room, but much smaller than the Command Center. Displays came to life as he entered. The one that snagged his attention immediately depicted a star chart, but this one was far more expansive than the one they'd normally used for their planning; it included most of the galaxy. At this scale, the inhabited arm occupied only a small portion of the display, and the area of Verity space into which they were steadily advancing was just a blip. The overlay highlight—perhaps thousands of star systems under Verity control, sprawled across much of the galaxy's breadth- was small. Their empire was inconsequential.

Dash just stared. The scale on this map was incomprehensible. Moreover, it showed detailed data for most, if not all of the Milky Way galaxy, that simply wasn't available—well, anywhere except in this room.

"Okay," he finally said. "I'm impressed all over again. I mean, I thought the Forge had lost that wow factor for me, but this is—" He shook his head.

"Why am I here?" he asked. "And alone? What's this all about?" He glanced around at consoles holding what seemed to be a plethora of new information that they'd never had available before. "And why haven't you let us in on *whatever* the hell this all is before now?"

"This is the beginning of the next phase of the Messenger's role in the war against the Golden. It has been initiated by circumstances. Prior to this, this part of the Forge, and my knowledge of it, were both dormant."

Dash looked at another console, this one showing details of celestial phenomena that, as far as he knew, were entirely unknown to humanity, and the other races inhabiting the galactic arm. Many of them lay far outside known space and were probably just distant smudges and specks on astrophysical surveys. It was yet another trove of stuff that would fetch untold prices if it ever hit the market.

"Okay," he finally said. "I get it. You couldn't tell us about something that you didn't even know about." He glanced back up at the main display. "So what is the *next phase* of my role as Messenger?"

"So far, you have been laying the groundwork for the war against the Golden. You have located the Archetype, become aware of the Golden and their intentions, activated the Forge, begun production of new assets, and begun recruiting allies. Now, it is time to begin fighting the war in earnest."

"What does *that* mean?"

"You will note the expanded star chart, showing a large zone of influence extending through portions of the galactic core, this spiral arm, and the one adjacent."

"Yeah, I see that. Whose zone of influence was that? The Unseen's?" He peered at the chart. If it was, they had a big empire, or realm, or whatever the Unseen would have called themselves. As in, unthinkably big. At her best speed, it would take the *Slipwing* years—*decades*—to cross from one side of it to the other.

"No. That is the territory that was controlled by the Golden at the peak of their incursion into the galaxy."

Dash stared for a moment. "Wait. The Golden controlled all that territory? All those systems? There must be thousands of them."

"Eighty-six thousand, four hundred, and sixteen, to be exact, although the Creator's acknowledge uncertainty in that number of up to five percent."

"Were they still bent on killing all sentient life when they held all this territory?"

"Yes."

Something dark, profoundly deep, and terribly vast began to nudge its way into Dash's thoughts. His voice became quiet.

"So are you saying that's what they did? Exterminated all life in these systems?"

"To the best of the Creators' knowledge, yes. Or, to put it another way, there is no reason to believe they did not."

Dash wasn't sure how long he just stood there, his gaze wandering around the galaxy, his stunned outrage growing. The map didn't show a zone of influence, it showed a zone of extermination. A zone of genocidal horror.

Eighty-six thousand star systems. No doubt many of them were lifeless, but how many weren't? How many races had there been two hundred thousand years ago? How many had survived the Golden rampage?

How many beings had the Golden killed? How could such a number even be contemplated, much less understood?

But something hard, sharp, and immediate hit Dash. "Custodian, when this happened, two hundred thousand years ago—my own people, humans…we were sentient, right?"

"Based on the Creators' archives, and data from your own two hundred thousand years ago, humans were in a primitive form, having originated in a region on your origin world known as Africa, and were beginning to spread into neighboring regions. They lived in loose, family-based tribal groups, and were using basic tools made of stone, wood, and bone."

"Okay, would that count as sentient?"

"By any reasonable standard of the concept of sentience, yes."

"So we would have been a target for the Golden. They would have exterminated us, too."

"Almost certainly."

Dash walked up to the large map. "Show me where Old Earth is on this."

A blue point of light appeared, far out in the remote reaches of the galactic arm.

"Zoom that in."

The image swelled, with Old Earth remaining in the center.

Dash studied it. The nearest Golden controlled system was a little over eight light-years away from Sol, the star around which Old Earth revolved. It had a standard stellar catalog number, but the imagery also gave its human designation, *Sirius*.

Dash had to take a step back. Two hundred thousand years ago, while Dash's ancestors were still perfecting the use of stone tools, genocidal aliens were lurking less than nine light-years away. In celestial terms, that was nothing.

Nine light years—as little as a half-day of travel in an early ship—had been all that separated all of humanity from sudden extinction.

An image came to him of primitive people, clad in animal skins and clutching tools of rock and wood and bone, suddenly looking up at the sky as it turned to a sheet of incandescent plasma.

"Messenger? Are you alright?"

Dash blinked. Again, he had no idea how long he'd just been standing there, contemplating oblivion.

"I—" He nodded. "Yeah. Or—actually, no. No, I'm not alright. I just learned that my entire race came within a few hours of being obliterated." He let a long sigh deflate his lungs. "Sorry, but these sorts of ideas take a little while for me to process."

"Understandable. Your brain is capable of remarkable feats, but in some respects, it is extremely inefficient. I will wait while you continue processing and storing this information."

That actually made Dash chuckle. He knew Custodian had gotten it wrong, thinking Dash was literally processing and storing data—and doing it really slowly—but he'd also gotten it right, because that kind of *was* what he was doing, wasn't it?

He finally walked back from the map and told Custodian to zoom it back out to the original image.

"Okay. So, obviously the Golden don't control all those systems anymore. Was that thanks to the Unseen?"

"The Creators' war against the Golden was a long and costly campaign, fraught with much uncertainty. But, yes, they were able to eventually drive the Golden back."

"Including from Sirius, thankfully."

"Indeed. That system was itself the site of a battle. A large one, according to the Creators' records, in fact."

"The Unseen fought the Golden at Sirius," Dash said. "Huh. Well. I guess we humans literally owe your Creators our lives—hell, our *existence*."

"So it would appear."

Dash stared for another moment then shook his head, like he was trying to clear away clinging cobwebs. This was all fascinating, but he had to get back to more immediate concerns.

"Okay, so what is this supposed to be telling me about my next phase as the Messenger?"

"The Forge was never intended to be a front-line battle asset, although it is capable of functioning as one. Rather, it was intended to be the nucleus of a much larger war effort. The Cygnus Realm is an embryonic version of that."

"You mean, we need to start controlling more territory."

"Yes, but not for the sake of simply controlling it. The war effort so far has concentrated on Clan Shirna, the Verity, and the Bright. As you have observed, the Golden have remained largely apart from this. It would seem that they are employing a different approach than they did two hundred thousand years ago. Then, they simply attacked, conquered, and exterminated systems and races directly. Now, they are using a more insidious approach, working through intermediaries. The question therefore is, what are the Golden themselves doing now?"

"Yeah, don't think I haven't been wondering that myself. So we need to bulk up the territory we control to—what? Gather resources? That's fine, but even the Forge, as the nucleus of all this, can only produce so much, right? Meanwhile, while we're farting around fighting their minions, the Golden themselves could have whole factory planets pumping out weapons and Harbingers and who knows what. It's all going to suddenly descend on us like a nova blast, and that'll be it. They'll get *way* past Sirius this time around."

"That is true. And that is why your strategy cannot rely solely on the Forge. Rather, the Forge will, as noted, be the nucleus for an expanding Cygnus Realm, which will itself be based on establishing approximately concentric spheres of military forces and installations, and advanced manufacturing facilities known as Anchors. Each Anchor will essentially be a smaller version of the Forge, functioning as factory, command center, and base, all in one."

"Concentric spheres," Dash said. "Circles. That was what that cryptic comment of yours back in the docking bay was about, wasn't it?"

"I found the occurrence of circles regarding the Golden missile bunkers interesting."

Dash had to grin. "You know, Custodian, it's taking you longer than Sentinel, but I think you're starting to show a few signs of humanity—like appreciating an interesting coincidence."

"I have no difficulty recognizing a coincidence. It is a simple concept."

"Not what I mean. The fact that you could make that remark about it, being all mysterious like that, added nothing to anyone's understanding of the coincidence, did it?"

"No, it did not."

"So you made that comment just *because*, right?"

"Just because of what?"

Despite the raw horror of the things he'd learned in this secretive compartment, Dash laughed. "Don't worry about it." The laughter soon faded into a thoughtful frown.

"Alright," he finally said. "So how does this work? How do we build these Anchors? Have to be honest, this doesn't sound like it's going to happen very quickly."

"It will not. Construction of the Anchors, their deployment, and securing the systems around them will be an ongoing, progressive endeavor. It will not only involve a great deal of time and effort, but also likely considerable combat."

"And that means a lot of casualties."

"Undoubtedly."

Dash sighed. "Shit."

Custodian said nothing—because there was nothing to say to that, Dash knew. It was what it was.

"Okay," he said, reaching to scratch an itch on his arm and realizing he was still clad in his vac suit. "Okay. So each of these Anchors is going to be like a little Forge. But there's only one me. This can't all fall on the Messenger."

"Of course not. Each Anchor will require a capable, competent commander who is able to operate independently, in accordance with the overall strategy that you devise."

Dash really wanted to scratch that itch, but he had to settle for scrubbing a hand through his hair instead. It was just something to do while the enormity of what lay before him really began to settle in.

"I suspect you have an opinion about who will command these Anchors," Dash finally said.

"I believe my opinion mirrors your own. You have capable commanders right now, and more who are developing. In time, they will be ready," Custodian said.

Dash thought about the roster of people he'd come to count on. Leira could command an Anchor. So could Viktor, and Ragsdale. Benzel and Wei-Ping, definitely. Amy?

Amy might not be a good fit.

Conover? But he was still just a kid.

Still, he had to voice it. "Even Conover?"

"Conover has abilities that, given time, will develop and allow him to thrive as a commander," Custodian said. "In fact, he may have the greatest potential of all of your current allies."

Dash let out a long sigh and closed his eyes in resignation. "This war really is going to be an awfully long one then, if you can see Conover in independent command of an Anchor, and everything that goes with it."

"Yes. I am sorry to say so, but you are undoubtedly correct."

Dash pushed himself away from the wall and peered at the map again. "Then it's time to get back to work. I need a couple of days to ruminate on all this, but in the meantime, tell me about that section of skyhook we found. It didn't look like any other lift system I've seen."

"That is because it was not designed by humans," Custodian said.

"So it was a Golden thing, then?"

"Almost certainly."

"Hmm. Golden. Which leaves me with one question. What were they lifting into orbit, and where? Surely it couldn't have just been stuff from that barren moon."

"I do not know the purpose of that particular construct. It may have been a prototype, or a test of a new concept."

"Okay, so did they try it anywhere else? Do we know?"

A single star brightened on the map. "The only record I have of a potential Golden orbital facility is here, in the highlighted star system," Custodian said.

Dash leaned in, staring at the map. He touched it and it expanded, popping open a window with astronomical details. "Aw, crap," he finally said. "A gas giant?"

"Yes."

"Of course it is."

5

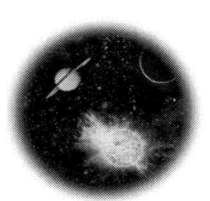

"It's a gas giant all right," Leira said. The Swift hung in orbit next to Dash and the Archetype, massive, pastel bands of clouds swirling in torrents under the turbulent shear of supersonic winds.

"Okay," Dash said. "I'm assuming we're not going to the surface because there probably isn't one—"

"Actually, this planet does have a solid core," Sentinel said. "Likely made of exotic matter, such as metallic hydrogen."

"Well, yeah, okay. And what, exactly, would the conditions be there?"

"A temperature of approximately twenty-four thousand degrees Celsius, and a pressure of—"

"Some really, *really* big number, I know. Anyway, like I said, we won't be going there. So, if there's anyone here, they'd need to be higher up in the atmosphere, right? Like helium-3 miners working on gas giants I've heard about. Sentinel, scan for something like that."

"There are several artificial constructs in orbits, the atmospheric depths of which would conform to approximately standard temperatures and pressures," came the instant reply.

"Okay, then. Are they Golden, or Verity, or otherwise likely to be hostile?"

"Broad-spectrum emissions from the gas giant introduce some uncertainty, but no, it is unlikely that these facilities are constructs of the enemy."

"They're probably more helium-3 miners, or something-miners, anyway," Leira said.

Dash pushed up his lower lip and nodded. "Alright, then. Let's go pay them a visit, shall we?" He decelerated the Archetype, letting it fall toward the clouds beneath. Leira didn't immediately follow.

"Leira," he said. "You coming?"

"Yeah, yeah. Sorry, this takes me right back to when we were falling into that gas giant on board the *Slipwing*. You know, come to think of it, I've almost died on board that ship of yours a few times."

"*Almost* is the most important word in that sentence."

She sighed over the comm. "Go ahead on in, Dash. I'll be right behind you."

"How many of these places are there?" Leira asked, as another of the stations came into view. They all seemed to be based on a standardized design, like huge, inverted teardrops, with the rounded top truncated and replaced by one or more transparent domes. They were technically in orbit, but also well into the atmosphere, so a complex array of mag-drives both kept them boosted against atmospheric drag, while also blocking the worst of the particle radiation from reaching the habs inside.

"Not sure," Dash said. "This is, what, the sixth one we've seen?" He glanced at data on the heads-up. Have to admit, they orbit in a pretty nice zone up here. A little over one standard atmosphere pressure, and the temperature out there is a balmy twenty-five degrees Celsius. Too bad the air's made of poison."

There actually was oxygen, Dash saw, along with the usual components of breathable air, like nitrogen, carbon dioxide, and water vapor. But most of the atmosphere was methane and ammonia, so breathing it would make a human very quickly dead.

Still, they'd die in relative comfort, choking their life out on what amounted to a warm, cloudy day.

It wouldn't be fatal to *everything*, though.

A huge, broad arrowhead rippled into view. It was alive, that much was clear. Alive, probably a good hundred meters across, and moving with lazy undulations that pushed it along through the air. It wasn't flying, as much as it was floating, which Sentinel said was how it had probably managed to grow so big.

And it wasn't the only native life form they'd seen. Something like a jellyfish, with dangling tentacles hundreds of meters long, seemed to drag them through clouds of methane, feeding on the stuff. They also glimpsed something like an enormous ribbon, with what looked like eye stalks; they never did see the entirety of that creature and could only guess at its size.

The arrowheads seemed to be the hunters. They saw one suddenly dive, slam into one of the jellyfish, then stop and begin absorbing it like water being soaked into a sponge. One actually came to investigate the two mechs; a few warning shots from the point-defense batteries convinced it to back off.

"I did not expect so much wildlife," Leira said. "Kind of fascinating, and I've never been into xeno-zoology."

"I wonder if it would be considered sentient," Dash mused over the comm.

Sentinel replied. "There are tests that could determine that. Why do you ask?"

Dash pressed his lips together. "Doesn't matter. We're here to talk to the colonists, not the natives."

For no reason other than it was the closest, Dash told Sentinel to open a comm channel to the nearby floating settlement. An immediate reply came back.

"Wait—you're human? Those are ships you're in?"

"Yeah. They're not human ships, though. And I'll be happy to explain all of it, but I'd rather do it face-to-face."

A moment passed, then a new voice came on. "This is Vincent Powell, Commander of Pan-Alagus station. You said your name was Dash?"

"Well, my full name is Newton Sawyer. But I prefer Dash, yeah."

"And you're from the Cygnus Realm? Never heard of it."

"Well, now you have. And like I said, I'd be happy to explain all of this to you, but I'd rather not do it over a comm."

"How do we know you're not Marauders?"

"Marauders?"

"Yes. We haven't encountered any ourselves, but we've been getting reports of ships going missing, settlements being attacked, all by this group called the Marauders."

"Oh. You must be talking about the Golden, and their lackeys, the Verity."

A long pause, then Powell came back on the comm. "Okay.

Going to be up-front here. As you've come within scan range of other stations, they've all been sounding the alert. We've got a dozen fighters on standby here."

"I know," Dash said, glancing at the heads-up. "I can see them."

"You can—wait, how? They're a thousand klicks away, behind about two dozen major storms."

"That is part of what I want to explain to you. And then, I'm hoping you can help *me* with something—and that'll help you at the same time."

"What do you mean?"

"There's a good chance that your Marauders are already here, somewhere in this planet's atmosphere. They're our enemies. We want to find them and stop them before they can do any harm to you, or anyone else."

Another long pause. "Alright," Powell finally said. "We'll take a chance and trust you. You can land those ships, or whatever the hell they are, on landing platform three. You'll see it, it'll be the only one open, with its anti-collision lights flashing."

"I see it now. We'll be there in a few minutes."

VINCENT POWELL WAS A STERN, middle-aged man with a severe haircut. He simply stared until Dash finished talking. Powell did a good job of being unreadable; his face could have been that of a statue etched in stone. But Dash sensed a keen mind at work behind those blue eyes, turning over all of the remarkable claims he'd just made, examining each like it was a problematic piece of some bigger machine.

Dash waited.

Finally, Powell leaned forward on the table filling much of the conference room in the Pan-Alagus Station. "I've always understood the Unseen to be a myth. Or, if they ever did exist, they died out thousands of years ago."

"Well, they're not a myth. And they might have died out thousands of years ago, yes. What you're seeing here is their tech, which is partly controlled by some pretty sophisticated AIs."

Powell tapped a control. A holo-screen holding a bunch of hand-written data about helium-3 and deuterium processing quotas vanished, replaced by an image of the Archetype and the Swift, standing side-by-side inside the hangar opening onto landing platform three. He leaned back.

"You know, I'd have just written all of this off as bullshit—at best, you guys being delusional crackpots, and at worst, some sort of scam." He looked at the two mechs. "But then I've got those things sitting in my hangar. I had our techs take a discreet look at them—"

"We know," Leira said. "Tybalt asked me if they should be considered a threat. I told him no."

"Who's Tybalt?" Powell asked. "You have other crew on board those things?"

"In a way," Dash replied. "Remember those AIs I mentioned? Sentinel, Tybalt, say hello to Director Powell."

"Hello, Director Powell. I'm Sentinel, an artificial intelligence aboard the Archetype. That is the larger of the two mechs you see."

"And I am Tybalt, the AI aboard the more flexible and agile of the two mechs you see."

Dash glanced at Leira, who grinned. "I think Tybalt's feeling a little outclassed in some ways."

"I am most definitely not feeling outclassed."

"Yeah, guys, let's not air out our dirty vac suits in front of our hosts," Dash said, then looked Powell straight in the eye. "Anyway, yeah, it's all true. The Unseen are real, and they are dedicated to fighting the Golden—who are dedicated, themselves, to killing all sentient life everywhere. We obviously don't want that to happen." He smiled and shrugged. "Like I've told others, believe me, if I was sitting in your chair right now, I'd probably think this might be a scam or something, too. But it's not. There's a war being fought, the most important one ever."

Powell leaned forward, placed his elbows on the table, and laced his fingers together. "Okay. I'm an open-minded guy. I'm going to believe all this, at least for now. What do you want from us?"

Dash nodded. Powell fell into the *I like this guy* category—straightforward, no-nonsense, skeptical without just being a denier. He reminded Dash of Ragsdale.

"Well, we came here for one reason, but actually, now that we're here, I think we have a second one," Dash replied. "You collect and refine helium-3, right?"

"We do, along with deuterium, methane, and ammonia, all into the interstellar commodities market. Why?"

"We—the Realm of Cygnus—have an ongoing need for helium-3 for our fusion fuel for some of our ships. We've been collecting it ourselves, but if we can free up the resources that are doing that, we could put them to use doing other things. In return, you guys probably have to import a lot of your food, I assume?"

Powell nodded. "We produce about sixty percent of what we need here, on the station, but we can't afford the space for more without eating into our gas-handling capacity." His eyes narrowed. "You're suggesting a trading agreement?"

"Yeah, I am. Helium-3 in exchange for food. We've definitely got a surplus. Also, I think you'll be pleasantly surprised by some of the things we can provide to you."

"Let me guess—the Unseen were also amazing farmers."

"In a way," Leira said. "Yes, they were. And so were the Golden. We've captured a bunch of their tech, and some of it is about food production."

"Okay," Powell said. "We can work on that. What's the other thing that brought you here?"

"Well, Leira mentioned the Golden and, like I said, they might already be here somewhere. Our archives record the presence of a Golden orbital facility somewhere on—or in—this planet."

Now Powell frowned. "Here? On Gale?"

"Gale?"

"It's what we call the place. Its official name is just a string of letters and numbers."

"Okay—then, yes, somewhere on Gale, there is, or at least was, an orbiting Golden installation of some sort."

"We tried scanning for it," Leira said. "But there's just way too much interference from the planet itself."

"Damned right there is," Powell replied. "We have to deal with it every day. That landing platform you used has a superconductive grid embedded in it to drain away the electrostatic charge on your —mechs, you call them? Anything flying through Gale's atmosphere picks it up. If you don't ground it away in a controlled way, then it'll ground itself the first time something—or someone—comes too close. We had three people killed before we realized how much of a threat that was."

"So that's our second thing. We're hoping you can point us at whatever Golden thing might be here."

"Assuming it's still here," Leira put in. "The record of whatever it is, or was, is pretty old. It could have been swallowed by this gas giant long ago."

"Or the Golden could have come along and removed it," Dash added. "That's why we came to you."

Powell looked from one to the other as they spoke. Finally, he stood, moved to another display, and called up an image of Gale. He touched a part of the flat surface, highlighting a broad band across the planet's lower hemisphere, about halfway between its equator and south pole.

"If there is anything alien here, on Gale, then it won't likely be anywhere outside this zone, because we'd have almost certainly detected it."

"So what's special about that one zone you've outlined?" Dash asked.

Powell smiled. "Allow me to introduce you to the Roaring Forties."

DASH SETTLED himself into the Archetype's cradle as the platform on which it and the Swift stood was eased back out of the hangar and into Gale's unforgiving grip. The moment the big doors had slid open, noxious fumes poured into the hangar; now, winds gusting up to two hundred kilometers per hour slammed into the mechs, roaring around them with ferocious howls that Dash could feel through the Archetype's structure as fitful vibrations.

Three hundred klicks per hour was a lot—enough to flatten any structure not designed to take it. But that paled in comparison to the wind speeds Powell described in the Roaring Forties.

Two *thousand* kilometers per hour.

The platform finished extending. Dash checked over the Archetype's status on the heads-up, saw everything was nominal, then powered up the thrusters and backed the mech into space. When he was clear, Leira followed in the Swift.

"I have to admit," Powell said over the comm. "Those mechs of yours look rather alien—and lethal."

"I've been flying the Archetype for a long time now, and sometimes, I feel exactly the same way," Dash said.

He saw three icons approaching on the tactical display. Three sleek, gleaming arrowheads zoomed into formation with the two mechs. Powell himself flew one of the atmospheric fighters, with two of his most experienced pilots in the other two.

"We don't go anywhere near the Roaring Forties, as a rule," Powell said. "Not unless we really have to. Even then, I'd only trust—oh, maybe five or six of my pilots to make the flight. I hope those mechs of yours are up to it. They don't look very, well, aerodynamic."

Dash smiled. "Considering what the Archetype and Swift have been through, I think they'll be fine."

"Something about being made by a hyper-advanced bunch of aliens, from tech we never even imagined existed," Leira had added.

"Okay, we all set?" Powell asked. He'd sent an array of commands, assembling the plan with a decisiveness born of competence and experience. With a final tap, their path was set.

"We are," Dash replied seconds later. "Sentinel and Tybalt have both received the flight plan you sent over. Any time you're ready."

"Okay, then. Let's go see if we can find some of your alien baddies."

6

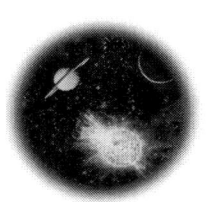

The Roaring Forties lived up to their name. Even the mechs, as powerful as they were, were flung about like toys when they eased into the zone of ferocious wind shear marking the northern edge of the phenomenon. Powell had explained that the Roaring Forties were—as far as any of the scientists knew--a perpetual storm triggered by the planet's axial tilt, the amount of heat energy received from its primary star, the effects of a nearby moon, and—other stuff.

That *other stuff* covered essentially all of the terrifically complex dynamics of Gale's vast, turbulent atmosphere, which were so chaotic that even the best computer simulations could only *hope* to get half-assed close to accurate.

In fact, shortly after they'd left Pan-Alagus Station, they witnessed some of that chaotic power firsthand. As they set a steady, angular course toward the Roaring Forties, slowly easing themselves ever further south, but otherwise trying to travel with the prevailing winds as much as possible, they encountered what Powell called a *thermal*. Somewhere far below, deep in the searing, crushing depths of Gale's atmosphere, something had happened, triggering a sudden upwelling of superheated gas. It plowed up through the atmosphere like a nuclear explosion, but much, much larger than even the biggest-yield warhead.

"Sentinel," Dash asked. "How much energy do you think we're seeing here?"

"I would estimate approximately four times ten to the nineteenth joules of energy equivalent."

"Uh, okay. Can you express that as something other than a stupidly huge number?"

"If you fired the dark-lance continuously for about forty-eight hours, you would approximate that much energy release."

"Oh. Okay. That's *way* clearer." And considering a single, five second dark-lance shot could blow apart an unprotected frigate…

"I'm assuming we're not going to fly through that," Leira said as the vast, glowing plume of incandescent gas billowed up ahead of them, blotting out the rest of the sky.

Powell laughed. "Well, you guys and your fancy alien mech things might be able to do it, but our ships would be puffed away to smoke."

Dash chuckled back. "I think we're okay not finding out."

They saw no more thermals, but that was fine—the Roaring Forties were more than enough for Dash.

Terrific gusts of wind slammed into the Archetype, wrenching it from side-to-side, up-and-down, and back-and-forth, at all once. The inertial dampers, designed for much higher accelerations, kept Dash from feeling it. But the heads-up tracked every one of the sudden spins, twists, and wobbles. He frowned; if the Roaring

Forties were like this throughout, then the chance of finding anything—even Golden tech—was pretty remote.

Without warning, the hard surges of sudden movements stopped as the Archetype broke into clear air.

"There's no way that was the Roaring Forties," Dash said. "They looked thousands of kilometers across on that map you showed us."

"Oh, hell no," Powell replied, laughing. "That was just the first boundary layer. This is the second boundary layer—the winds here aren't turbulent, they're nice and smooth."

"And over a thousand klicks per hour faster, I notice," Leira said. "We're moving along at a terrific clip for being inside an atmosphere."

"And as long as we travel with them, it'll stay that way. We'll ride this boundary layer to the only place I can think of where your Golden thing, whatever it is, might be hiding. It's called Big Eddy."

"Big Eddy?"

"Yeah. It's literally an enormous eddy—a calm spot, in the middle of the core zone of the Roaring Forties."

"Do you have a name for that, too?"

"We do. We call it *keep the hell out*."

"Well, that was interesting," Dash said.

They left the innermost zone of the Roaring Forties—a place to, indeed, keep the hell out of. It had actually been far easier for Dash and Leira, because the formidable power of their mechs were able to overcome the worst of the hypersonic turbulence. Still, they hadn't been able to completely avoid being flung about by the colossal cyclones, titanic gusts, and vast wind shears. At one point, they clocked a blast of wind at nearly three thousand kilometers per hour. They'd also seen another of the violent thermals come rushing out of Gale's depths and get immediately ripped into racing streaks of glowing gas.

It had been alarming, even safely cocooned in the Archetype. And that was saying something, considering the things Dash had experienced piloting the mech. But what that dwindled into was almost trivial compared to what Powell and his pilots had gone through.

They'd flown like they were, themselves, sophisticated AIs, throwing their little arrowheads of ships through abrupt climbs, dives, and turns that seemed to anticipate the next battering ram of air rushing up or down or across their flightpath. It was a display of skill that impressed even Sentinel.

"They are very accomplished pilots," she observed. "I have noted at least seventeen instances in which one or more of those ships came within a second or two of catastrophe."

As soon as they entered Big Eddy, though, it *all* changed.

They might have been flying on a pleasure cruise, passing through a stable zone of absolutely clear air a thousand klicks across, floored far below by lightning-lit, brown and violet clouds, roofed above by a pinkish sky holding a dazzling sun. Incredibly, they found things living here—more of the jellyfish-like gas-bags and undulating deltas, and things like huge birds that seemed to just perpetually soar through the open sky.

As soon as Dash said, *that was interesting*, Powell laughed.

"Yeah, interesting is the word. Flying across the Roaring Forties and back is a thing that pilots will do to prove they're—you know, *all that* as a pilot."

"So you put yourselves through incredible danger, where even a little mistake can easily get you killed, just for bragging rights?" Leira asked.

"Well, when you put it that way, it sounds stupid," Powell replied.

"No, no, don't get me wrong—I've been a pilot for years, I totally get it. Just making sure I had it right."

"No, Leira," Dash said.

"What do you mean?"

"No, you may not borrow one of their ships and try to fly back and forth across the Roaring Forties to gain credibility. With anyone."

"You're no fun."

"Not when it comes to the pilot of one of our two operating mechs, I'm not, no."

Even as he said it, Dash found himself wincing a bit. He was being a killjoy? Really? Flying across the Roaring Forties for fun would have been something he absolutely would have tried, and not that long ago. Hell, he'd have raced Leira—

Who he really, really didn't want to see get hurt.

Dash sighed and shoved the thought away. Now was not the time.

"Okay, Sentinel, are we scanning anything that might be Golden tech?" Sentinel said.

"Within the volume of atmosphere defined by this feature, Big Eddy, no. However, there is a sporadic Dark Metal signal emanating from directly below us."

Dash studied the heads-up. Indeed, there was something beneath them, somewhere below the lightning-shot clouds.

"Leira, are you detecting this?"

"We are. Tybalt suggests that we move to opposite sides of Big Eddy and try to triangulate on the signal, see if we can get an approximate depth."

"I gather this means you found something," Powell put in.

"So it seems," Dash answered. "We're not sure what yet, though. And whatever it is, it's way down in those clouds below us."

"Okay, well, we'll cruise up here while you do whatever you need to do. Oh, and if whatever this is, is a threat—" Powell started to say, but Dash interrupted.

"You've got the two things most capable of dealing with any Golden threats in—well, pretty much the whole galaxy, at least for now, right here." Dash spoke with the confidence of a mech pilot who hadn't lost a fight. Yet.

"Good to know. Just don't poke something so it wakes up later, unless you're prepared to settle down here," Powell warned.

"We will not leave you hanging, Director. That's a promise."

"Good, because I'm going to hold you to it."

Dash studied the cloud tops, now just a thousand meters below the Archetype. The electrostatic charge in the gases around the mech had amped up to mind-boggling levels, so much so that the Archetype acted as a lightning rod, huge blasts of lightning leaping out of the clouds and crackling across its armor. Fortunately, the mech had been designed to withstand far worse, but it still made Dash flinch every time one of the searing flashes erupted around it.

"So Tybalt says whatever that is down there, it's about two thousand kilometers down, give or take five hundred or so," Leira said.

She held the Swift on-station about a thousand klicks above Dash, ready in case he needed assistance.

"Sentinel, can we try and go that deep?" he asked.

"Inadvisable. Conditions at that depth, in a gas giant of this size, would likely exceed the Archetype's safe limits for pressure."

"Okay, so that's out. I guess we just gather as much data as we can then head out."

"So there's no risk from whatever's down there," Powell said.

"I seriously doubt it," Dash replied.

"That's not a, *no, there's no risk*, then."

"I can't *guarantee* that there isn't a whole fleet of warships down there," Dash replied. "But, Golden tech is about on par with the Unseen, so if the Archetype won't survive long down there, nothing of theirs is likely to. It's probably either a wreck or something that wouldn't be affected by the pressure and heat."

"Like a stash of Dark Metal, maybe," Leira said.

"Dark Metal. You keep talking about that," Powell said. "What is it, exactly?"

"You know what, Director—?"

"Vincent."

"Okay. You know what, Vincent? I'd be happy to explain it all to you. So why don't you grab a ship and come back to the Forge with us, let us be your hosts for a while. It'll be a lot easier to tell you all about it there."

"Fair enough. We'll have to go back to the Station, though. There's not really any way to get aboard your mech out here."

"Sorry, these things aren't built for passengers. If you have a ship you can take, we'll meet you in orbit. We're about done here, anyway."

"Sounds good. I'm assuming you're just heading straight up from here, so we'll see you in space in a few hours."

"Roger that."

It took most of their time waiting in orbit for Sentinel and Tybalt to process the data they'd collected in Big Eddy, which now sprawled far beyond them, a vast, unblinking eye in an omnipresent, planet-scale storm. When the filtered and refined data finally appeared on the heads-up, Dash was—

Unimpressed.

"That's it?" He narrowed his eyes and tilted his head, trying to make sense of what he was seeing. Part of it looked vaguely like the skyhook wreckage they'd recovered from the moon orbiting the brown dwarf. But other parts of it—knobs and protrusions extending away from it, with no apparent rhyme or reason—didn't look like anything Dash had ever seen before.

"This imagery is a top-down view of an elongated structure that extends even deeper into the planet's atmosphere. It depicts approximately the uppermost thousand meters of a much larger structure, the length of which is unknown."

"So probably a skyhook, extending from depths that are already too deadly to reach, to even *deadlier* depths. Why?"

"The Golden wanted to lift something up from down there, or transport it down, or both," Leira said.

"Well, yeah. But *what?* And *why?*"

None of them—Dash, Leira, nor the AIs—could come up with anything but wild speculation.

The arrival of Powell in orbit, aboard a business cutter called, fittingly enough, the *Roaring Forties*, prompted them to end their guessing game. Forming into a tight formation, they broke orbit and started back to the Forge. Once there, with Viktor, Conover, Custodian, and all the others working on it, maybe they could come up with answers. Because, when it came to the Golden, Dash hated mysteries. Golden mysteries could get many, many people killed.

Dash crossed his arms and looked at the skyhook wreckage from the moon, now laid out in the main fabrication bay. The original plan had just been to smelt it down, but once the mysterious construct on Gale had come up, he'd put in a hurried call back to the Forge to preserve whatever was left. Fortunately, it was virtually all of it.

"I anticipated that it might be useful to retain the remains of this skyhook until the matter involving the gas giant was resolved," Custodian said.

"Good work," Dash said, then he glanced around at the others—all of his senior officers, plus Powell, who was only just starting to *not* look utterly stunned. He happened to catch the man's eye and smiled.

"Believe us now?"

Powell looked around. "Yeah, I think there might be a little substance to your claims." He took a deep breath. "Holy shit, this is—I don't know. *Impressive* just doesn't seem to do it justice. And you're this—Messenger, commanding all of this?"

"Guilty as charged. Although I don't like *commanding*. *Leading*, maybe. What we do around here is entirely a team effort.

"Does that mean the beatings will stop, at least while Vincent's here?" Amy asked with a sly grin.

Dash shook his head. "Nope. I'll just move them behind closed doors. At least until morale improves."

There was laughter all around, and Powell shook his head. "Hard to believe you guys are able to keep a sense of humor, considering all of"—he gestured around—"well, again, *this*."

"It's either that or go insane," Dash said. There wasn't as much laughter this time, though, so he just moved on.

"Anyway, just a quick comparison with whatever we found on Gale seems to show it's something similar to this, but scaled up and a lot more complicated." He gestured at the image representing the processed data from the gas giant, which was the best view they'd likely ever have of whatever it was—at least, without something that could dive far deeper into a gas giant's atmosphere than any of their current tech would allow. Dash rubbed his chin. There *must* be a way.

"So the Golden want to lift something in and out of a dense, heavy atmosphere," Conover said. "The question is, what?"

After a moment of thoughtful silence, Dash gave the shrug they all eventually would. "Good question. No answer, unfortunately." He looked at Powell. "And I don't think the good folks from Pan-Alagus can add anything, because they didn't even know that the Golden construct was there."

"All due respect, but you could hide entire fleets of ships inside Gale, and no one would ever know they're there," Powell replied. "We just assumed that below the Deadline there was nothing but superhot, super-pressurized weirdness, certainly not that somebody had stored something down there."

"The Deadline?" Viktor asked.

"Sorry, that's the absolute depth limit for our toughest craft. It's about five hundred kilometers deeper than Pan-Alagus Station itself. Believe it or not, there still seem to be things living deeper than that, but when you're nothing but a methane and ammonia eating gasbag, I guess you can get away with it."

"And you've never seen any evidence of what might be Golden activity?" Ragsdale asked. "No strange ships, transmissions, or emissions, that sort of thing?"

Powell shook his head. "I had my people comb through our records while we were making the flight back here. We have no records of any ship traffic we can't explain as, well, not genocidal aliens. And as for emissions, Gale is nothing but. The planet blasts energy out in pretty every part of the EM spectrum from one place or another, and the particulate radiation is pretty fierce."

"And there's so much static electrical build-up," Leira put in. "You can't trust a lot of the readings anyway. Even Tybalt was having trouble keeping the real data sorted out from the artifacts caused by the electrical charge on the Swift."

As Leira spoke, Powell's face took on a thoughtful cast. "There are old stories about ghost ships vanishing into the deeps, below the Deadline, and things moving around down there that seem to have no explanation. But, hell, every planet has those, right? Ghost stories?"

"They do," Dash said. "But some of them might amount to actual sightings of Golden or, for that matter, maybe even Unseen activity. Have you met Kai?" Dash gestured to the monk.

Powell introduced himself, and Dash went on. "How about sitting down with Kai and his people over a glass or two of plumato wine and telling him whatever ghost stories you can think of?

They're absolutely brilliant when it comes to teasing out the ore from the asteroids in information stores."

"A lot of what we deal with is written records of our Order," Kai said. "Which are more like stories and legends than hard data. We often have to interpret what we're reading."

Powell nodded. "Be happy to. Love to try out this plumato wine I keep hearing about."

"Well, if you like it, you're going to want to make it part of our trade deal," Dash said, grinning. "Oh, and you can speak to Harolyn about that. She's in charge of all of our non-military activities, like diplomacy and trade."

Harolyn gave a wave.

"As for the rest of us, we need to try to figure out what's going on with this." He waved a hand at the wreckage of the skyhook. "What's it for? Why was it built?"

"Not only that, but we've found two of them, now," Viktor said. "And if there are two—"

Dash nodded.

"There might be more."

THE WRECKAGE of the skyhook was big, awkward, and complicated, and although Custodian could scan it for hard data—things like dimensions, materials, and the like—there were still subtle nuances that remote sensing just couldn't discern. For that, Benzel had a solution: a wreck-crawler.

Dash assumed that by wreck-crawler, Benzel meant some sort of device, like a drone or a remote. When he returned to the bay, though, he'd had a woman in tow.

"Meet Dayna," Benzel said. Dash greeted her, having to look up to do it. She stood a good quarter meter taller than him; that, together with her preternatural leanness, told him she was probably from a low-grav world.

"I've seen you around before, but not much on the Forge," Dash said. "Are you okay with the gravity here? I can get Custodian to reduce it in this bay if you'd like."

She smiled. "Thanks, but not necessary." She pulled open her jacket, revealing a belt sporting a series of small black boxes. "Benzel had Custodian whip this up for me. It's a grav belt. It helps offset the effects of the Forge's gravity." Her smile widened. "These would fetch a fortune on my home planet."

Dash grinned back. "Yeah, that and hundreds of other things just in our *current* line of sight. No smuggling, though."

"Wouldn't think of it. I know the rules, and I happen to agree with them."

Dash nodded, gratified. It was too easy to fall too far into Ragsdale's mindset of *everyone is a potential risk* and forget that the vast majority of their people were good, honest, and dedicated to what they were doing.

"So I assume a wreck-crawler crawls around on wrecks?"

"Yeah. There used to be a bunch of us in the Gentle Friends. After we took a—" She hesitated, and Dash just waved a hand.

"After you took a ship as a prize, yeah. It's not exactly a secret, what you guys used to do."

"Okay. Well, after we took a prize, someone needed to go through it, and over it, in detail. You'd be surprised how many things you can find hidden in, or even outside, a ship. Found a stash of some pretty hardcore immersive imagery hidden in the base of a sensor array on the hull of a gas tanker once."

Dash laughed, thinking about the places he'd hidden things aboard the *Slipwing*. For that matter, there might still be a few of them there; he should look into that. In the meantime, though, he left Dayna to do her work and went back to conferring with his senior officers.

While Dayna crawled the wreck, her experienced eye scrutinizing every square millimeter, Dash mused over what they'd actually found. This really bothered him. He didn't like mysteries when it came to the Golden, and he couldn't help but think this one was the most mysterious they'd encountered so far, so it might be something particularly big.

"But it might not," Viktor countered. "It might be something unimportant."

"Yeah, like maybe the Golden hide their porn down inside gas giants," Amy put in.

Dash smirked at her and glanced at Dayna, remembering her story about the stash in the sensor array. "Funny you should mention that. Anyway, yeah, I know, it might be absolutely nothing and we're wasting our time. *Not* knowing is kind of what makes it, you know, a mystery."

"It might even be a failed experiment," Conover said. "That thing in Gale's atmosphere might have just sunk down there, and this wreckage from the moon just shows how this version of their skyhook doesn't work."

"Except the one on Gale is bulked up with a lot more components," Amy replied, gesturing at the grainy image still projected in the bay. "It looks like they might have modified it, maybe improved it."

"What we need is to find another one," Dash said. "One we can actually get at—"

He broke off suddenly, eyes narrowed.

"What is it?" Leira asked. "I recognize that look. You're up to something."

"Not really up to something. Just an idea. Custodian, could you do a scan for signals that are similar to this one, and the one from Gale, and from that, give me a list of the *smallest* gas giants that display it?"

"What are you thinking, Dash?" Viktor asked, but it was Leira that answered.

"I know what he's thinking, and the answer is no way," she said, glaring at Dash.

"What's he thinking?" Amy asked.

"He wants to find the smallest possible gas giant containing one of these things so he can dive down and access it directly." Her glare hardened. "And remember how you told me no, I couldn't fly the Roaring Forties for sheer fun? I wasn't being serious, and you knew that. But this is serious, Dash. You can't do this."

"Just relax. First of all, we'd need to find a suitable candidate," he replied. "And there might not even be one. Second, I'd only do it if—"

"I have found a suitable candidate," Custodian announced.

They all stared. Dash blinked. "Already?"

"The intersection of the data sets was quite limited. You specified similar signals that corresponded to gas giants, and then the smallest of those. That is, by definition, a single candidate, since only one can be smallest."

"Yeah, okay, we get it. Where is it?"

A new holo-image opened, showing the familiar star chart of the arm. One system, about thirty-two light-years core-ward of their present location, had been highlighted. A second window popped open, showing a dazzling blue planet streaked with pale wisps of white.

"This imagery is taken from your own archives, copied from the *Slipwing*."

"Really? I had this on my ship?" Dash asked.

"Yes. You did not know?"

"Well, no. I subscribed to an astrogation database-update service for a while, but I kind of missed a few payments. Anyway, I'm not going to know every bit of data in the *Slipwing's* archives off the top of my head."

"In some respects, you humans are extraordinarily limited," Custodian said.

"Hah, well, try drinking some plumato wine, Custodian," Amy shot back. "Bet you can't do that!"

"You are correct, Amy. I cannot. I guess you've got me there."

Her eyes went wide. "Was he just *sarcastic* to me?"

"I'm telling you," Dash replied. "We're definitely rubbing off on these AIs. Anyway, what can you tell us about this planet?"

"One of your astrogation surveys imaged it three years ago, so these data are quite recent. It is at the lower limit of what would be considered a gas giant, and it is extremely similar, in almost all respects, to a planet in your origin system named Neptune. Technically, it would more properly be termed an ice giant, as it is much colder than Gale."

"And this is the smallest gas—er, ice giant that gives off the signal we're looking for?"

"Yes."

Dash stared at the image, and at the data portrayed with it. Like most planets in uninhabited systems, this one had no name, just the catalog designation of its primary, followed by a *4*, so it was the fourth planet outward from the star. It was about one-fifth the size of Gale, so it was small enough that they could penetrate much deeper into its atmosphere, with considerably less risk. But *less risk* was relative; the Deadline for this planet might be more forgiving, but dropping more than a short distance into its roiling, wind-whipped envelope of gas would only *probably* be fatal, instead of definitely so.

"I'll say it again, Dash. No," Leira said.

"I am not going to take stupid chances, Leira, believe me," he said. "But if we could just figure out a way to drag whatever is there *up*, maybe we could access it safely."

"So lasso it."

They all turned to the speaker—Wei-Ping.

"What?" Dash asked, voicing the question they were all probably wondering.

"Lasso it," Wei-Ping repeated. "You know, tie something to it and pull it up out of the atmosphere."

Benzel snorted. "We'd need more tow cable than we could possibly carry—hell, than we could possibly imagine. And then we'd never be able to lift the weight of the cable."

But Conover spoke up. "Custodian, I seem to recall an entry in the fabrication database for a monomolecular filament cable. It was described as literally unbreakable, even though it was only one molecule wide."

"Yes, it essentially is a single molecule, made of carbon atoms arranged in a chain, interspersed with a repeating sequence of Dark Metal."

"We don't need all the details," Dash said, suddenly intrigued. "Just tell me how strong it is and now much it would weigh."

"As Conover indicated, its tensile strength is virtually infinite. In reality, that is not the case, of course, but the forces required to break it vastly exceed anything not generated by a stellar-scale phenomenon. That said, it masses approximately one-fourth of a kilogram for every kilometer of length."

"Holy crap, why are we not making this stuff already?" Benzel asked.

"And can you imagine how much something like that would be worth?" Wei-Ping put in.

"We are not manufacturing it because no need for it has been identified," Custodian said. "It is also a hazardous material to work with."

"I'll bet, being one molecule wide," Viktor muttered. "Talk about sharp."

"And as for how much it is worth—" Custodian began, but Dash cut him off.

"Not really important right now. How long would it take, say"—he looked at the data for the ice-giant, particularly the pressure and temperature versus depth curves—"five thousand kilometers of the stuff."

Someone whispered *shhiiiit*, but if Custodian thought the amount to be unworkably large, his usual, smooth tone gave no sign of it.

"The maximum fabrication rate attainable by the Forge, in its current state, is approximately one kilometer per day."

"So five thousand days?" Benzel said. "Yeah, I don't think we want to wait around, what, something like twelve *years*?"

"Thirteen point-seven years, in fact," Custodian said.

Dash deflated. "Well, that's a non-starter, then. Too bad, too, because the Archetype, together with the *Slipwing* should be able to do the job of pulling whatever it is out of that ice giant." He shrugged. "It was a nice idea while it lasted."

"Not so fast," Harolyn said, and everyone turned to her. She normally attended meetings like this but didn't say much during discussions about military strategy, or detailed debates about engineering. "Maybe we can't have the fancy, indestructible, Dark Metal-infused sort of this stuff, but there is a human-made variety that's pretty damned strong. It's used by asteroid miners for towing rocks around."

Dash perked up again. "Custodian, does the *Rockhound* contain technical specs for this stuff in its database?"

"Yes. The monofilament cable in question is manufactured on a planet named Kapok, which happens to be located in a system with an unusually large asteroid field. Presumably, it is made there because it is close to where it is going to be used. It possesses about one-third the tensile strength of the Creators' version, and is somewhat more massive, at about one kilogram per kilometer of length."

"So if we tripled it up, we'd have about the same strength as the Unseen stuff," Dash said. "

"If you're going to Kapok, I'll come with you," Benzel said.

"Why?"

The former Gentle Friends leader gave a thin smile. "Let's just say that I have friends there."

7

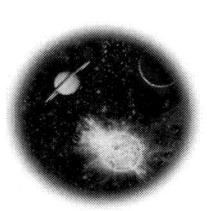

They brought the Archetype and Swift to Kapok, along with the *Snow Leopard*, but left the mechs in orbit and shuttled down from Benzel's ship. "It'll be better if we just leave these up here," Dash said.

"This orbit is pretty high," Leira noted, as she pulled off her vac suit aboard the *Snow Leopard*'s shuttle. "Any reason for that?"

"Yeah. I'd like anyone on the surface to just be able to make out that they're something special, but not be able to get any more detail than that," Benzel replied.

Dash exchanged a *whatever* look with Leira; Benzel seemed to know what he was doing. So they just settled back to enjoy the ride to the surface.

The shuttle fell out of orbit, passed through a searing entry into the atmosphere, then decelerated as it plunged surface-ward. They punched through a dreary overcast, then flew through periodic rainstorms across a landscape dotted with gaping pits and slag heaps from industrial operations. Eventually, a sprawling, grimy city came into view, wreathed in clouds of mist and vapor that mingled with the constant rain. It all had a bleak, industrial look to it, a place where manufacturing was the only thing that mattered, and clean air and water and an orderly landscape all came much further down the priority list.

Benzel briefed them; the factory producing the monofilament cable they sought was owned by a cartel whose principles he knew from past dealings—by which, he meant, of course, the buying and selling of pirated goods. "They're good people, though," he quickly added. "Once you get to know them, you'll find out they're really just businesspeople, like anyone else."

"Yeah, the thief-y, murder-y kind of businesspeople," Leira muttered.

Benzel shrugged. "Only some of the time."

Now, as the shuttle deployed its landing gear and set down on a platform a short distance away from the factory that was their destination, Benzel made sure to check over his equipment—including his pulse-pistol. Dash noticed that.

"I thought you said these were friends of yours."

"No, I said the factory was owned by friends—really, more business associates—of mine. I'm not sure who actually runs this particular factory, though."

"That's comforting."

"Just being realistic—and prepared," Benzel replied.

The shuttle touched down in a swirl of dust and grit that dispersed when its thrusters shut off. The airlock cycled open and they disembarked into a dreary, industrial cityscape with drab, boxy buildings squatting under the unbroken grey sky. A pervasive hum and rumble of machinery at work vibrated the air, which itself held a slightly acrid, chemical tang. A persistent, cold drizzle made the whole gloomy picture complete.

"Charming place, this Kapok," Leira said.

"These people definitely aren't big into environmental protection, that's for sure," Dash replied, nodding.

Benzel led them across the landing pad to a bridge that connected it to the bulk of the nearest factory complex. At the far end of the bridge, a wide door rolled open and a group of figures exited.

"Wonder if they have anything to do with us?" Leira asked—

Just as the group of figures fanned out and opened fire.

Slugs snapped past them; a couple clanged off parts of the bridge with flashes of sparks. Dash and the others took whatever cover they could find.

"Yeah, I'd say they have something to do with us," he shouted, yanking out his pulse-pistol. "Benzel, what the hell?"

"How do you know this is about me?" Benzel snapped back, raising his pulse pistol. "You've probably still got a few people out for your head."

Leira winced and ducked as far behind an upright girder holding up the bridge's railing as she could. A slug ricocheted off the alloy-mesh decking a few centimeters from her foot. "How about we just say, for now, this is directed at all of us?"

Dash, pushing himself behind a girder opposite Leira, glanced quickly around. The shuttle was, per their standard procedures, lifting off, the pilot taking it to a safe distance and staying ready to come back fast to evacuate them. They could go back to the flat, open expanse of the landing pad to do that, or they could push ahead along the bridge. As for trying to jump over the handrails—

He peered down between metal-mesh panels. It had to be at

least a ten-meter drop to a paved alley between the factory and whatever building was topped by the landing pad.

"Are we going to try to talk," Leira shouted. "Or are we going to shoot?"

A slug banged against the girder Dash was using as a shield, its fragments making bright little spots of pain against his arm. He winced. "Start with shooting but use low-power. We'll see if that'll encourage talking."

As one, they aimed and fired the pulse-pistols. The searing bolts lashed out, flashing against the nearest wall of the factory with loud cracks.

The incoming fire immediately slackened as the shooters sought their own cover behind railings and a pile of scrap beside the factory door. Dash took the brief lull to pick a target, line it up, and double tap a pair of shots. One went wide, but the other struck the man in the shoulder as he tried to acquire a target. The man fell back. Another cried out when Leira landed a pulse-shot cloud close enough to concuss him.

The incoming slug fire intensified a bit, but it also became sporadic and much less well-aimed. Slugs snapped and buzzed all around them, as they snapped out return fire. Even set to their lowest power, the pulse-pistols far outclassed simple slug-guns in terms of both firepower and the intimidation factor. Benzel took a woman down with a hit to her leg, then all of their attackers, except for the one Dash had shot, backed off and ran back inside the factory.

"Come on!" Benzel shouted, as he charged for the now-closing door.

Dash and Leira exchanged an exasperated glance then ran after him.

The door had almost closed by the time Benzel reached it, but he grabbed a chunk of alloy rod and shoved it into the gap, jamming them open. Dash glanced at the man he'd shot, who'd been left behind by his friends—mid-twenties, a little on the gruff side of plain looking, clad in unremarkable clothes. He groaned as they approached, and his eyes widened.

Dash picked up the man's slug pistol and shoved it in his pulse-gun holster. "Just stay down and you'll be fine," he snapped, then turned back to the doors in time to see Benzel shoving his way through the gap between them.

"Again, Benzel, what the hell?"

Leira rolled her eyes. "I can't help feeling he knows more than he's letting on."

"I suspect you're right. I'm having that pirate-y sensation I get every time we run into an old *business associate* of his. Come on, let's go make sure he doesn't get himself killed."

Dash followed, pushing through the gap between the doors. It was a squeeze, and it gave him a momentary pang of fear—what if the rod broke and the doors slammed shut on him, or he was shot the instant he entered? Neither terrible thing happened, though; Dash just found himself in a cavernous room lined with crates on cargo-pallets—a warehouse, presumably for goods ready to be carted across the bridge to the landing pad for loading and shipment. He made his way along the widest path left that led straight from the door to the far wall. Leira followed. Any second, he expected the firefight to resume, inevitably leading to a gut-wrenching and deadly cat-and-mouse thing among the stacked crates.

But they made it to the far end, where a metal staircase switched back and forth up the corrugated wall to a door near the high ceiling. Benzel crouched at the base of the staircase, looking up.

Dash moved in beside him. "Benzel, what the hell is going on?"

The former Gentle Friends leader shrugged. "Okay, I might have heard a rumor about who was running this place."

"Who?"

"Someone with whom I've been involved in some—um, *business disputes*."

Dash sighed. "Leira and I are both couriers. We know all about *business disputes*."

"Yeah, it's code for, you screwed someone, and now they want to kill you," Leira snapped.

"Exactly. Would have been nice if you'd told us this *before* the shooting started," Dash went on.

"Like I said, it was just a rumor." He tried looking contrite. "Guess it wasn't just that, though. Sorry."

Dash just shook his head. *Contrite* on Benzel just made him look more fiercely defiant.

"Anyway, we want to get up there." Benzel nodded at the door at the top of the stairs.

"That looks pretty freakin' exposed," Leira said, eyeing the stairs. Each of the seven or eight flights had a hand railing, and that was it for cover.

Dash pressed his lips into a thin line and gave Benzel a hard stare. "Is this getting us any closer to scoring our monofilament cable?"

"Well, crouching here definitely won't," Benzel said.

"Okay, and where are the guys who were shooting at us?"

"Not sure. They didn't go up these stairs, I know that." Benzel made a vague gesture at the massive warehouse around them. "Out there somewhere, I guess." He hefted the pulse-pistol. "Although, these things probably made them shit themselves enough they're still running."

"That another rumor?" Dash asked.

This time, Benzel actually did look a little contrite. A little.

Dash curled his lip. "Fine. Two of us will stop on each landing and give cover, while the third goes up to the next one."

Benzel and Leira nodded, and Dash raced up the first flight of steps, his feet metallic thumps on the runners. He made it to the first landing and crouched, his pulse-pistol raised. He felt incredibly exposed, to the point of actually feeling naked. It was a far cry from the *cocooned-in-virtual-invulnerability* feeling he got from being ensconced in the Archetype.

"This five-centimeter pipe just ain't giving me a good feeling," Dash muttered, glaring at the upright stanchion holding up the railing. Leira pounded up the steps and crouched beside him, then Benzel raced past them, up to the next landing.

One flight at a time, they made their way up the stairway. By the time they reached the top, they'd taken no fire; indeed, scanning across the warehouse, a now lofty vantage-point, Dash couldn't see anyone in the warehouse at all.

"Guess we did scare them off after all," Leira said, clutching her pulse pistol.

Dash nodded. "Sometimes the pay just isn't worth it."

Benzel reached the top landing behind them and grabbed the door latch. "Ready?"

"Yes, definitely, anything to get off these damned stairs," Leira snapped.

Benzel flung the door open. It revealed a short, gloomy corridor that led to another door. Two side doors were locked; Dash resolved that if the one at the end was locked, they'd just get the hell out of here and approach this a different way.

But it wasn't. He shoved it open, and found himself in a spacious, palatial office. He had a brief impression of a thick carpet, walls paneled with swirls and whorls of red and pink wood grain, overstuffed furniture—

But the woman sitting behind the massive desk, holding a wicked-looking gun on him, snagged and held his undivided attention.

"I don't want to shoot *you*," she said, looking annoyed.

"Glad to hear it," Dash said. "Because I don't want you to shoot me, either."

"No, it would be me she wants to shoot," Benzel said, pushing past Dash. Leira came up warily behind but stayed out in the hallway, watching to their rear.

"Friggin' pirates," Dash muttered.

"Right? So shifty," Benzel admitted.

"Nice to see you, thief." The woman's voice was like cool water over stones, her face even less emotional. The gun was now pointed at him, so it made sense that he was being addressed. "Do you remember me?"

"Um, sure." She narrowed her eyes and he shrugged. "Okay, I remember the name, but not exactly why you're threatening to blow a hole in me."

"The *Silvertide* and the *Western Nova*. Sound familiar?" she asked.

"Ahh." Benzel flicked his eyes toward Dash and Leira, whose weapons were now trained on the woman. "I do remember now. May I introduce Katerina Vensic, whom I've worked with—"

"Don't," Dash said, as Katerina's hand twitched.

"Worked with?" Her words were a hiss. "You stole the two most important ships in my fleet. I would not say we worked together, you pig."

Benzel ran his hand through his hair, embarrassed. "Yeah, it's all coming back to me. Guess I should say sorry all around."

"Apology accepted. May we sit down, Katerina? We have business with you—the paying kind. And we can discuss righting previous wrongs as well," Dash said.

Katerina's pale blue eyes narrowed. "If one lie comes out of your mouth, I shoot him. If two lies are spoken, I shoot you all. Understood?"

"And if you fire that weapon at all, I'll bring this factory down around your ears. I don't make idle threats," Dash said.

She inclined her head toward the sumptuous chairs, lowering her gun—which Dash recognized as a powerful, albeit short-ranged laser pistol—but not very far. "You have one minute."

"That's good enough," Dash said. They all sat down. "I need every meter of monomolecular cable you have, and I'll pay."

"How—how much cable?" Katerina's eyes went wide. It was a large factory, and the cable was thin.

"All of it."

"All?"

"That's what I said. Can we move past the concept of *all?*" Dash asked.

Katerina leaned forward and tapped at a terminal on her desk "That's nearly forty thousand klicks worth of cable as of this morning. You're sure?"

"Quite. Let's talk price," Dash said.

"Ten percent of whatever it is you're doing with it."

"Three, or we walk."

"Done," Katerina said. She stood, offering her hand. "So what bizarre, no doubt super-valuable thing are you going to lasso from its current owner?"

"What makes you think we're stealing something?" Leira asked.

"Well, you're not miners, and Benzel is pirate scum. That means you're stealing something," Katerina said.

"Not exactly stealing, but close enough," Dash said. "Have you heard of the Realm of Cygnus?" Dash asked her, watching her eyes closely.

He saw that she recognized the name. "The Realm—wait, you're the ones with those—the big robotic things. Mechs, right?"

Dash glanced quickly at Leira and saw that she, too, appreciated the significance of the moment; for the first time, someone recognized the name, which meant word was getting around. "We do. Would you like to see them?"

"Yes." Katerina stood. "But I'm more interested in what you're doing with them. We know something of the Golden around here."

This left Dash staring. That was more recognition than he'd expected.

"Care to take a little trip?" she went on.

"While the cable is prepped?" Benzel asked.

"Shut up, Benzel. You still owe me ships," Katerina said. "But yes, close by. We can take your shuttle. It's to the east, about a hundred klicks."

"What is it?" Dash asked.

Katerina paused, her eyes going distant, momentarily looking into memory. "A near miss."

8

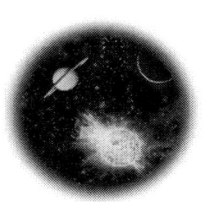

THE PILOT BANKED the shuttle over the marshy landscape. Dash saw flat, sodden terrain out to the misty horizon in all directions. It was definitely different from the polluted sprawl of the industrial city called Hub, but just as dreary.

"Is there any part of this planet that isn't depressing?" he asked.

"For that matter, does the sun ever come out?" Leira added.

"I hear there are some nice, forested mountains on the southernmost continent," Katerina replied. "But they're also all volcanic and tectonic and the like, so you risk being blown up, buried, incinerated, or crushed if you go there."

Dash nodded. "Nice."

"There," Katerina suddenly said. "See that big round lake? Let's land close to it—but not *too* close."

The pilot grounded the shuttle about a hundred meters from the lake. They dismounted and walked toward it. Dash felt the mossy ground sink under his feet, and saw it slowly spring back behind him when his weight came off it. Leira looked at her feet with a frown.

"Is there actually solid ground under us?"

"Somewhere," Katerina replied. "Just don't stand in one place for too long or you might sink. It's drier just ahead of us."

The ground did indeed rise slightly as they approached the lake, which was obviously a crater of some sort. It also became firmer and drier. Katerina led them to within about ten meters of the edge of the round lake and stopped.

"I'm a little antsy about getting any closer," she said, blinking drizzle from her eyes. "We don't know what's actually in there, but whatever it is, it's killed everyone and destroyed everything that's entered the water to find out."

"Defensive drones or something?" Leira asked.

"Some kind of automated system, anyway. But I've got a simple solution," Dash said. He looked up then gave Katerina a brief smile. "You wanted to see our mechs?"

"Of course," she said.

"Sentinel, Tybalt, can you join us down here please?"

"We will be there shortly," Sentinel replied over the comm.

They didn't have to wait long. Sonic booms came echoing out of the east; a moment later, two massive shapes punched out of the overcast and quickly approached.

"Here they are," Dash said.

The Archetype and Swift streaked downward, braking hard to settle on the ground ten meters away. Their enormous bulk blotted out the pale, watery light of the system's sun. They still radiated the heat of their entry into the atmosphere.

"Sentinel, Tybalt, say hello," Dash said.

Both mechs snapped off jaunty salutes, prompting both Dash and Leira to grin. They introduced themselves, while Katerina simply stood, mouth slack, staring in awe up at the alien war machines towering over them.

"Um," she said—and that was all.

"Yeah, that was about all I had to say about them, too," Dash said. "At least until I got used to them. Sentinel, scan this crater and tell us what you find."

"There is a strong signal, including indications of Dark Metal. The crater itself is shallow, as the sides have collapsed," Sentinel said.

"Benzel, would you take Katerina back to the shuttle and tell the pilot to get ready to lift in case this gets complicated? We're going in," Dash said.

Leira followed his lead as both mechs lowered themselves, opening their cockpits so they could clamber into the cradles. By the time the mechs had enclosed and sealed them, Benzel and Katerina crouched in the shuttle's open hatch. Dash led the way, walking the Archetype into the water on one side of the crater, while Leira lifted the Swift with its mag-drive and lowered it into the crater ninety degrees from the bigger mech. That way, if they had to shoot, they didn't risk hitting each other.

Katerina, in the meantime, cupped her hands, shouting. "Dozens of people have—"

The Golden drone exploded out of the water, weapons blazing in a wild spray of rapid-fire pulse bolts. Some slammed into the Swift, while a single missile caromed off the Archetype's armor, then streaked away to explode hundreds of meters overhead with a dazzling flash and a heavy, rolling boom.

"Clear to fire!" Leira said, letting Dash know he was in the clear. The Drone tried to climb, opening the distance so its missiles had time to arm properly, and Dash fired the dark-lance at what amounted to less than point-blank range. The drone simply disintegrated and plummeted back to earth in a spectacular shower of glowing slag. The debris rained onto the mechs with a rattling series of clangs, followed by sharp hisses as it bounced into the water.

"And... we're done," Dash announced.

Katerina still crouched in the shuttle, hands over her ears, eyes wide enough to show their whites all around. Dash saw Benzel, grinning, pat her on the shoulder and say something that was probably along the lines of, *it's okay, it's all over now.*

"What. . .what the hell was that?" Katerina asked, her voice coming over Benzel's comm.

"That was a little something the Golden left behind," Dash replied, his voice booming from the Archetype's external speaker. "They tend to do that, leave behind automated defense systems. Now, let's check out whatever it was guarding—you know, the loot."

The two mechs waded further into the crater, into ever deeper water. Eventually, they were completely submerged. While Leira remained alert for other threats, Dash grabbed whatever had embedded itself in the muck, yanked it free, and then withdrew. When the Archetype emerged a moment later, its massive hands held a twisted piece of junk that looked rather familiar.

He placed it on the ground, where it rocked to one side and then lay there, dripping. It was ten meters of metallic structure that resembled a construction crane or gantry, but far too heavily built for the local gravity planet. Empty sockets on the bottom were clogged with mud, but a tap from the Swift's left hand made the muck fall out with a wet plop.

"Huh." Dash zoomed the heads-up imagery, examining the sockets.

"Huh?" Leira asked.

"You know something?" Benzel asked, as he and Katerina picked their way back toward the mechs.

"I know what this is. Rather, I know what it attaches to, and I have a few ideas," Dash said.

Tybalt chimed in over the external speaker. "If you have not made the connection, allow me. The bracketing indicates this is a section of an orbital lifting system, not unlike the others we have found. A skyhook, to use your limited parlance, but it is also compatible with the Shroud. I believe the two to be related in purpose, if you can grasp such a concept."

Katerina looked askance at the mech then turned to Benzel. "Is that robot always such a—you know, tight-ass?"

Benzel grimaced. "You have no idea."

"I would point out that I am not a robot," Tybalt said. "I am an artificial intelligence, tasked with assisting Leira to operate the Swift, which is a mechanical construct."

Benzel's grimace became a broad grin. "See?"

KATERINA DECANTED amber fluid from a bottle into glasses. Dash caught a whiff of something that reminded him of old school chemical rocket fuel, or something like it—potent and probably not very pleasant, anyway.

Taking one of the glasses, Katerina sat back behind her desk and gestured at the others she'd poured.

"Please. It was a very good month."

Leira picked a glass up, sniffed it, and recoiled a bit. "Um, thank you? I think?"

Katerina laughed. Dash and Benzel each picked up a glass. It struck Dash that he'd been spoiled by Freya's plumato wine; not that long ago, he'd have happily drunk something as acrid and potent as this promised to be without a second thought. Was his palette getting *refined*?

Before he took a sip, he glanced at the chrono. The monofilament cable they'd purchased wouldn't be loaded aboard the heavy-lift shuttle sent down from the *Snow Leopard* for another hour or so, according to the crew doing the loading. That left them time to sit and get to know Katerina Vensic, probable ex-pirate and definite criminal, now manager of a large manufacturing operation.

She'd listened as Leira explained how she and Dash had met. "Ooh, a daring rescue," she said with a grin.

Dash had tried sipping at the drink Katerina poured but immediately realised, as something like a tiny plasma blast shot across his tongue before it gave up and went numb, that this was not a sipping drink. He took a breath and slammed back the whole shot. He had to remember to exhale afterward, because his body seemed to have forgotten how. Leira finished speaking and looked at Dash; he took a few seconds letting the liquor burn away before speaking. When he finally did, his eyes were unfocused, but not from the shot this time.

He picked up the thread of the story, describing how he'd stumbled on the Archetype. He then segued into what had happened next, and then next after that, and that was why his eyes had gone distant. So much had happened, all over a very short time. He ended up just delivering a *very* brief thumbnail of what had happened since he became the Messenger, because the whole story, he knew, could have taken him hours to tell.

In fact, he had to record this. Start capturing a personal log.

When it was all over, and assuming the Golden hadn't won, he'd have one *hell* of a story to tell.

Assuming the Golden didn't win.

"So the Cygnus Realm is a real thing," Katerina finally said. "We've heard lots about it through the back channels, and I mean *lots*."

Dash exchanged glances with Leira and Benzel. "Really? What have you heard?"

"Well, a huge pile of what's obviously complete bullshit, and a few nuggets of something that actually sounds like facts. I mean, did you know that you guys are actually a front for a secret cabal of the most rich and powerful people in the known worlds, and your goal is to set up a one-arm government?"

Dash chuckled and looked at his companions again. "Hey, look guys, we're the Illuminati!"

The others grinned, then Benzel spoke up. "We need to start collecting all these rumors. It'll make for good laughs around the fleet!"

"What have you heard that's not obvious bullshit then?" Leira asked.

Katerina looked at her glass and shrugged. "That you seem to have discovered some alien tech. We've heard rumors about those mechs, but I thought it was really more like, I don't know, engine technology, or fuel, or something." She shrugged again. "Frankly, I just assumed you were really another pirate gang"—she turned and glared at Benzel—"like the Gentle Friends, and whatever tech you'd found had just, you know, powered you up."

"Yeah, piracy is the last thing on our minds," Dash said.

Benzel scratched an ear and smiled. "Believe it or not, that's actually true. These ships we use, like our flagship, the *Herald*, would seriously kick ass as privateers. But that's not what they're for."

"What they're for, is fighting the Golden," Dash said. "And I mean that literally. All the tech we use, all made by the Unseen, was intended for one thing and one thing only: defeating the Golden so that they can't wipe out all life everywhere."

"All life not being wiped out would be a good thing, yes," Katerina said. "Although, I must admit, until that little display out at the crater, I assumed *that* was all overblown, too. Even the fact that everyone who tried to explore the lake died— well, we'd learned a couple of years back that it might be something belonging to an alien race called the Golden, but I don't actually believe that. Part of me figured it was just a dangerous lake, with some sort of hazard in it, like it was toxic, or had some sort of weird layer of acid in it, or maybe something big and hungry lived in it. There are so many stories around the arm about alien this, and Unseen that—"

"Who told you it might be the Golden?" Dash asked. "Who actually used that name?"

"Lizard-like guy with funny patches on his neck that changed color with his mood. He came looking for monofilament cable. Said he needed to tow some comets somewhere. When that crater came up in conversation, his patches had turned kind of blue, and he'd said not to worry about it." She narrowed her eyes. "Said the Golden would take care of us if we helped him out."

"Clan Shirna," Dash said, nodding. "Figures."

"Yeah, the Golden would take care of you, alright," Benzel muttered.

"They wanted to lasso some comets out of the Pasture," Leira said to Dash, who nodded again.

Katerina sat forward. "That's right. Clan Shirna. I take it you know them."

"We did," Dash replied. "And then we wiped them out."

There was a moment of silence as Katerina sat slowly back. "You're not joking, are you?"

"No. Wish I was, but I'm not."

"So this is real. The Golden are an actual, real thing, and they have an actual, real hate on for us—"

"And an actual, real desire to destroy us, yeah," Dash said.

"Okay, then. Again, after that display at the lake, I guess I believe you. Those mechs alone—I've definitely never seen anything like them. And then there's this thing called…the Forge, was it?"

"Yeah. The Forge."

"It's a space station."

"A space station, a huge hab, an enormous military base, a super high-tech factory."

"And, since we've arrived on it, the place that makes some of the best booze in the galaxy," Leira said, putting her mostly untouched glass back on the desk. "Sorry, Katerina, but with all due respect, this stuff is awful."

Katerina laughed. "It's definitely an acquired taste. Right, Benzel?"

Benzel drained his glass, made an *aaaaah* sound, then plunked it down and gestured for a refill. "I was actually going to say it's a little on the watery side."

She laughed, poured a refill, then shaped her face into a glare. "I'm still pissed about those ships you stole from me, but finally confronting you about it when you're what seems to be a key player in an interstellar war for the survival of, well, everyone, kind of gives me some perspective."

"So you're not going to shoot me."

"I didn't say that," Katerina replied, smiling sweetly as she refilled the glass. "However, I know it wasn't personal, so I'm not going to shoot you right *now*."

Benzel picked up the drink and raised it in a toast. "Good enough for me."

Katerina toasted him back then turned to Dash. "So what, exactly, was that thing you pulled out of that crater? I heard mention of a skyhook, but that didn't look like any skyhook I've seen—not that I've seen many, them being super tough to build and keep working properly and all." She smirked. "Which means I've actually seen none, outside of concept images. But those are all way chunkier than what you yanked out of that water."

"Yeah, that's alien tech for you," Dash said. "Thanks to an exotic type of material called Dark Metal, things that are basically impossible for our tech are no big deal for the Unseen or the Golden."

"Dark Metal? Never heard of it."

"Neither had I, until I found the Archetype and became the Messenger. And I still don't really understand what it is. It's a solid, but it's also a liquid; it's strong beyond belief and can resist temps that would puff anything else to vapor, but it's really easy to work; it's metal, but it also seems to be ceramic, and plastic, and sometimes I swear the damned stuff is also organic."

"It's weird," Leira said. "But it makes things like the Forge, and those mechs—and these Golden skyhooks—possible."

"Okay, so the Golden once had an honest-to-goodness skyhook here? Why?"

Dash shrugged. "No idea. We've been finding more evidence of them lately, but they seem to mostly be involved in some Golden scheme about gas giants. That's why we want your monofilament, in fact. We think we've found one intact, in a place where we can probably get to it."

"So you want to tow it out of—what, the inside of a gas giant?"

"Sounds kind of stupid when you say it out loud, doesn't it?" Leira asked, glaring at Dash as she did.

Dash pointedly ignored her. "Yeah, that's the plan. We want to snag one of these things intact and find out whatever the hell the Golden are up to with them."

Katerina gave Dash an appraising look and a slight nod. "If a scoundrel like Benzel—"

"Hey!"

"—can find it in his greedy pirate heart to join this cause, I might be able to too," she said.

"That's great," Dash replied, but gave her a quizzical look. "So, just you? Don't get me wrong, we're not going to say no—"

"I did not become manager of this factory because I'm a smart businessperson—although I am," Katerina shot back, giving Dash a thin smile. "I have an organization—"

"A criminal syndicate," Benzel muttered.

"—and it's linked to, other organizations—"

"More, and bigger, criminal syndicates."

Katerina shot Benzel a hard glance. "That's the fusion drive calling the kettle hot, now, isn't it?"

Benzel raised a hand. "Not denying it. Hell, criminal syndicates could be really useful for our cause."

"They could," Dash agreed. "I've had my own fair share of dealings with them—hell, I might have even done some wheeling and dealing with yours, Katerina. And, frankly, we need all the allies we can get. Remember, as we were telling you all about the Golden, we mentioned Clan Shirna, the Bright, and the Bright's especially terrible subsidiary, the Verity? Those are all Golden allies. We've got Benzel's people, the Aquarian Collective—"

"They're pretty regular customers of ours, yeah, I know them," Katerina put in.

"—and the folks who've come to the Forge as refugees. That puts us a little behind the curve compared to our opposition."

"Yeah, that Forge of yours. I'd really like to see it."

"And I'd like to show it to you. But before we'd be able to bring any of your people there, I'll be honest, we'd have to be able to dig into their backgrounds and skills."

Katerina narrowed her eyes. "Some—no, a lot of the people working for me might not like you checking too deeply into their backgrounds. I'm pretty sure you can guess why."

But Dash shook his head. "Knowing their skills is just so we know how to best employ them. As for the background stuff, we sincerely don't give a damn about their criminal histories or anything like that. We're more concerned about what sort of security risk they might pose."

"We've had some problems with collaborators—you know, spies and saboteurs," Leira said.

"Wait—regular humans? Fighting for the Golden?" Katerina's face tightened with a mix of genuine shock and disgust that, right there, convinced Dash that she, at least, could be relied on.

"Yes," Leira said.

"And what happened to them?"

Dash gave her a flat look. "They aren't problems anymore."

Katerina returned his gaze squarely.

"Glad to hear it."

Yup, this formidable woman was *definitely* someone Dash wanted on their side.

9

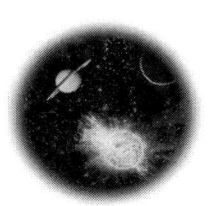

"Incoming, and hot," Benzel snapped. "Four hostiles just sub-luminal, straight in from the star." He ordered the helm to throw the *Snow Leopard* into a series of hard turns, employing every defensive tactic he knew. The ship responded with an acceleration and agility that clearly surprised Katerina; Benzel had told her the *Snow Leopard* had been upgraded with Unseen tech, but not exactly how. "You wanted to see the mechs in action," he said to her. "Well you're about to get the chance."

Katerina stared at the heads-up display filling the forward wall of the *Snow Leopard*'s bridge. It was glittering with what seemed like nothing but bad news. To her credit, she only went a little pale.

"How far until the Forge?" she asked.

"Too far. But the bogies'll be scrap pretty quickly anyway if I make my mark—and there they go," Benzel said.

"Let's split 'em up, Leira," Dash said over the comm. Benzel watched as the Archetype surged ahead, breaking right with a wrenching acceleration that probably looked suicidal to Katerina. A second later, the nova-gun—newly installed in the Archetype, giving it another firepower option—fired, and the enemy count immediately fell by one.

Benzel saw Katrina gape at the heads-up; she'd winced at the dazzling flash of the Archetype's shot, the raw power of the energy discharge recorded on the *Snow Leopard*'s sensor board.

"What the hell did he just fire?" Katerina asked, her eyes now goggling at what had, just a few seconds ago, been a massive enemy… thing, but was now just an expanding and cooling cloud of gas.

"Called a nova-gun. Pretty damned blunt instrument," Benzel said. "It somehow squirts its shot through unSpace, so it actually detonates inside any protective shields. And that slag used to be a Harbinger, although these are a bit beefier. We're starting to suspect the Golden have as many shapes and sizes as there are things alive." He nodded and tapped the comm. "Good shooting, Dash. Usually takes more than one hit to bring a Harbinger down."

"Got lucky with that one. It's a good show for Katerina, though. Tell me, is she impressed?"

"I passed impressed a while ago and crossed well over into gobsmacked."

Dash laughed. In the meantime, Leira had maneuvered the Swift into the path of a second Harbinger; its chest-cannon fired, enveloping the mech in a searing blast even more powerful than the nova-gun shot. Katerina gasped, but Benzel just watched her face.

She was grinning as the Swift burst out of the plasma cloud, residual energy streaming from its shield. "Let's see how easily this one dies," she said, and opened fire, raking the Harbinger with two blasts from her own nova-gun. The Golden mech began tumbling, spiraling out of control, leaking plumes of frozen gas and trails of sparks. She turned the Swift hard, punched out two missiles, and ended the fight as the stricken Harbinger shattered into scrap.

The two remaining Harbingers had taken advantage of the Archetype and Swift being engaged to close on the *Snow Leopard*. Upgraded as she was, she was far from helpless; still, taking on two of the damned things was asking a bit much. Benzel fired a spread of missiles then ordered combat overpower to the recently installed shield.

"Dash, could use a little help here," he said. "We'll hold 'em, but it'd be nice if you could help finish 'em."

"On my way!"

The Harbingers' point-defense systems opened up, swatting away most of the *Snow Leopard's* missiles. But two were recent versions, with upgraded AI and experimental warheads that used powerful shield generators to focus their plasma blasts like enormous shaped-charge warheads. They dodged the point-defense barrage and both detonated almost simultaneously, the full force of each blast slamming into the Harbinger like colossal blowtorches. The Golden mech's shield was immediately swamped with discharge and died, letting the rest of the blasts sear deep into its armor. While it's fellow maneuvered, it just plowed on in a straight line, following its last trajectory, either incapacitated or outright dead.

The *Snow Leopard* shuddered as the last Harbinger closed, pumping missiles at the ship faster than its own point-defense could keep up. It then drew itself up, lining up a chest-cannon shot. Benzel glanced at Katerina.

"You might want to hold on. This could hurt."

Something erupted from the Harbinger's chest alright—the

flickering point of a power-sword. The Archetype yanked the sword out then swung it, decapitating the damaged mech.

Benzel relaxed. "Thanks, Dash."

"No problem."

He turned to Katerina. "So, what did you think?"

Katerina said nothing at first. She just turned to Benzel and stared. Finally, she managed to croak out two words.

"Holy shit."

Benzel laughed. "Yeah, that about sums it up, doesn't it?"

"And you get into fights like this often?"

"Eh, not often, I'd say. Maybe once or twice a week."

"A *week*?"

He nodded. "Full time job, this saving the universe stuff."

THEY'D SECURED the biggest chunks of the ambushing Harbingers and brought them back to the Forge for scrap feedstock—a midsection and leg of one Harbinger by the Archetype, and the shoulders, head, and part of the right arm of another by the Swift.

"Waste not, want not, is the Old Earth saying, I seem to recall," Dash had said as they retrieved the wreckage.

Now, finally back at the Forge, Dash was able to rejoin Benzel and Katerina. Standing in the docking bay, she had, Dash thought, *that look*—the look that everyone had on their first visit to the Forge. It was a mix of surprise, awe, a bit of fear.

"How do you like the place we call home?" he asked her.

She turned, stared, then shook her head. "I—" She looked around, then tried again. "I'm not sure what the right words are. I'm just glad I didn't try to shoot Benzel. You really would have brought that factory down around my ears, right? And not even broken a sweat."

"Yeah, I would have. But you didn't, so I didn't. Anyway, let me formally welcome you to the Forge, the capital—and mostly every other part, too—of the Cygnus Realm. We're just heading to the Command Center for a debriefing. Want to come along?"

"I—yes. Sure. Why not."

"I'll bring her along, Dash," Benzel said. "I'll take the scenic route."

With a broad smile, Benzel made an elaborate gesture for Katerina to accompany him and led her away.

Leira stepped up beside Dash, both of them watching Katerina depart. She glanced at Dash. "I'm not sure I trust her."

Dash looked back at Leira. "Why not?"

"She's a criminal, Dash."

"Technically, so am I. More than technically, in fact. There are a few systems that, if we ever have to go to them to deal with the Golden, I will also have to deal with a few warrants." He gave a sly smile. "You telling me it's not the same for you?"

"That's not the point. She runs a whole criminal syndicate. Or did, anyway. Who knows what sorts of things she's done."

Dash narrowed his eyes a fraction then looked at Katerina, who was still walking away with Benzel toward the exit from the docking bay. A bit of a wicked impulse hit him.

"Have to admit, seeing her from this angle, it's kind of hard to worry about *what she's done*."

As soon as he'd said it, though, he regretted it. He turned to Leira to offer some sort of... apology? Peace-offering? But he found her watching Katerina through narrowed eyes, too.

"Hey, you know what? You're right." She turned and gave Dash a coy smile. "In fact, she's kind of hot, in a felonious way."

Still smiling, Leira walked away.

"Women and galactic diplomacy," Dash muttered. "Two things I'll never understand."

"So there seems to be some sort of connection between these skyhooks—or at least this one, that we found on Kapok—and the Shroud." Dash turned from the image of the debris they'd pulled out of the waterlogged crater, now displayed on the big holo-image in the Command Center. Everyone else, including Katerina, stood, sat, or leaned on consoles, watching his briefing. Off to one side, two duty personnel stayed discreetly out of the way, occasionally chattering softly, exchanging routine comms with a couple of small salvage ops currently underway in nearby systems.

"So the question, then, is what connection that is," Leira said. "How does a skyhook integrate, or whatever, into something like the Shroud?"

"And does the fact that some of these skyhooks seem to be stuck inside gas giants have something to do with it?" Viktor asked.

"Only some of them, though," Harolyn said. "The wreckage on that moon, and now this stuff from that crater or lake or whatever on Kapok, wasn't on a gas giant."

"No, they weren't. But both of those *were* wreckage," Leira put in.

"Yeah, they were," Dash said. "That crater on Kapok was just that—a crater. Sentinel's scans showed evidence of a hefty impact, so either the skyhook did that when it fell, or pieces of it fell in afterward."

"Not much chance of that," Amy muttered.

Conover crossed his arms. "Is there any other evidence there was ever a working skyhook on Kapok?"

All eyes turned to Katerina, who shrugged. "Not as far as I know. If that happened, it must have been a long time ago."

"Yeah, could've been hundreds, even thousands of years ago," Dash said.

Sentinel cut in. "I would point out that sediment accumulation in the impact crater does indicate it was formed between five hundred and one-thousand, five-hundred years ago. However, I'd also point out that whatever the impactor was is unclear, and it is possible that the skyhook wreckage entered the impact crater some time later."

"Wait," Conover said. "Sentinel, can you estimate how long the wreckage was in there? From the sediment accumulated on it?"

"That is unclear, because previous activity had disturbed it too much for any reliable estimate."

"Previous activity?" Viktor said. "Someone was there before you guys?"

"A few someones, apparently," Katerina replied. "That's why it was called things like *Death Hole*, or *Tomb Lake*. Several attempts to explore it ended with people dead. That includes a group of teenagers who went out there to party and dared to go swimming. They all vanished. I've seen that particular unsolved mystery on the Kapok three-V net at least a dozen times, now." She gave a thin smile. "A popular explanation was aliens."

"And it was aliens—the Golden, or more to point, that drone we destroyed," Dash said. "Although that's another question: what the hell was *it* doing in there?"

Silence. The discussion had just smacked headlong into too many blank walls of questions they simply couldn't answer.

"Yeah, I've got nothing, either. Which sucks, because I *hate* mysteries, especially when it comes to the Golden," Dash muttered.

As they'd been talking, Dash had been idly fingering the knife that Dayna, the Gentle Friends wreck-crawler, had retrieved from the skyhook wreckage. Now, for no particular reason, he lifted it and looked at it. There was something about this damned thing he recognized—or at least, he thought he'd did.

"You expecting trouble, Dash?"

He blinked and looked up. It was Amy who'd asked the question. Everyone was staring at him, though, while he held the knife and tapped a fingernail against the blade.

Amy grinned. "Never bring a knife to a gunfight, sure. But to a planning meeting? Kind of overkill, I think."

"How come you still have that, Dash?" Viktor asked. "Does it mean something to you?"

Dash glanced at the knife. "I don't know." He looked back up and smiled. "Maybe. Anyway, I'll let you know when it comes to me."

"Since you seem to have reached an impasse regarding useful discussion," Custodian said, "then perhaps you could attend to the finishing bay on the fabrication level."

"Ooh, I think I know what this is," Amy said, nudging Conover with an elbow.

Dash did know what it was, and said they'd head straight there. He turned to Katerina. "You came at a good time. Want to see something pretty amazing?"

She sniffed and shook her head. "More amazing than all this?"

"Yeah. Come on." He turned to Leira, about to ask her to come along too, but realized how awkward that would sound. She was Leira. He didn't *need* to invite her anywhere.

Leira saw Dash look confused. She rolled her eyes then smiled and walked past him toward the fabrication level.

"I KNOW I'm supposed to be really impressed by this," Katerina said. "But I'm kind of saturated. Maybe if I hadn't seen your other two mechs kicking butt the way they did…"

Her voice trailed off into silence that lingered.

Not surprising, Dash thought. It was a pretty momentous occasion, after all. They'd just seen the size of their mech fleet doubled, because the Pulsar and the Talon were complete and ready for their first flight.

The two new mechs towered over them, imposing and dramatic in their powerful lines and curves and angles. And just to amp up the awesome factor, the Archetype and the Swift stood behind them, having just gone through minor repairs from their recent battle with the Harbingers that had ambushed them.

He looked at Conover and Amy, and saw them just staring. Conover was doing his best to look nonchalant, but Amy put up no pretense. Her eyes had gone wide, her mouth hanging open, as she stared up at the new mechs.

Dash felt more like Amy looked, but not because of the mechs themselves. He'd been involved with the Archetype long enough that the awe inspired by these enormous war machines had faded. Rather, it was the increase to their capabilities this represented.

"Side-by-side like this, they remind me of the Archetype and the Swift," Viktor said, hands on his hips.

Dash nodded. The Pulsar, Conover's mech, stood big, heftier, overall chunkier, like the Archetype—although still a little smaller than Dash's mech—while the Pulsar was smaller, her lines more graceful and lithe.

"So why are they different?" Katerina finally asked. "Why don't you guys just make one standard type of mech?"

"They have different capabilities," Leira replied. "The Archetype is a frontline combat mech, built for slugging it out. That's why it has that big-assed power-sword, in addition to the heavy weps. The Swift is more about maneuver and fire support, stand-off fighting from a distance."

"Yeah, meanwhile, the Talon is a light mech, built for scouting and skirmishing, using speed, agility, and stealth. And the Pulsar is more like the Archetype, but with more focus on electronic warfare and heavy fire support."

Katerina just nodded. "Hey, I believe you guys. You seem to know what you're doing."

"Amy, Conover, are you ready to complete your final Meld with your mechs and their AIs?" Custodian asked.

"After going through the amazingly painful process of getting that interface implant?" Amy replied. "Hell yeah. That much hurt has got to be worth something."

Conover just nodded. "Yeah, I'm ready."

Both of them were still, their faces slack, their eyes blank and unfocused.

"They're lucky," Dash muttered. "At least they knew that super-painful interface part was coming. I didn't."

Leira sniffed. "Honestly, Dash, I think you were better off *not* knowing it was coming."

Both Amy and Conover suddenly wobbled, each catching their balance.

"Whoa," Amy said. "That was intense…" Her voice faded, her face took on a look of concentration, then she looked at Dash. "Wow. I…know stuff. Just know it. Like, the status of the Talon there." She gestured at the scout mech looming above them. "I just know it. Is this what it's like for you?"

"The Meld? Yeah, pretty much."

"This is really different than working with the AIs in simulations," Conover said.

"You could not be fully Melded with your AIs until your mechs were complete," Guardian replied.

Dash had been watching Katerina as the Melding unfolded. "Kind of like seeing the birth of two new people, isn't it?" he said. "Only not as messy, and a lot more direct."

Katerina shook her head. "So, with those AIs on board, all linked up to those of you who pilot these things, do you consider them alive?"

Dash was a little surprised at what was really a pretty philosophical question—one he had to think about for a few seconds himself. "As much as we are, and a lot tougher," he finally said.

"For my part, I certainly consider myself a genuine, living being, given that my taste and style are far superior to most humans," Tybalt said primly.

Katerina laughed. "Oh, okay, they're definitely alive. Only something living could be that much of an asshole."

"Thank you," Tybalt said, bowing the Swift at the waist.

"Um, don't mention it, I guess, " Katerina replied, then turned back to Dash, who directed her toward the new mechs.

"So do these new, um, pilots? Is that the right word? Do they just make themselves at home, or is it just sit down, hold on, and shut your mouth?" Katerina asked Dash as the two new mechs folded themselves smoothly forward and down with a soft hum of moving components. Amy eagerly climbed into the cockpit of the Talon. Conover was a little slower, still seemingly caught in an ongoing moment of wonder that all of this was happening in the first place.

"What do you mean?" Dash asked.

"Do they get to personalize these things, is what I'm asking," Katerina explained. "You know, like a picture of your lover, a talisman, something like that. Something to make you feel at home. Atmo jocks do it all the time, painting their ships, naming them. Sometimes they even keep track of their kills, just to make it seem like the ship is more than just metal."

A slow smile spread across Dash's face. He pulled the mysterious knife he'd been carrying from where he kept it stowed in a pouch on his belt. "You mean marks like these?"

Katerina examined the handle, where the grooves were lined up —like someone had been keeping count. She nodded once. "That's the knife you were fiddling with in that briefing. Why, what are you thinking?"

"Yeah, what she said," Leira added. Dash felt his expression hardening, changing to something more feral, at the thoughts now parading through his mind. He wasn't usually given to expressions like that; he was too carefree. But they matched his sudden realization perfectly.

"You mentioned keeping track of kills. So, trophies. The marks on this knife are trophies. Who else have we met recently who keeps trophies of her kills?"

"Sur-natha," Leira replied. "Her necklace. It was pieces taken from hulls of ships she killed." She frowned. "And that knife does look like the ones we found on all of the Clan Shirna bodies. But what are the chances this knife, that we found in Golden wreckage on a remote, lonely moon, would actually be *hers*?"

"I'm not saying it's necessarily hers, but I'd say there's a good chance it's at least a weapon that belonged to someone close to her," Dash said.

"If you have correctly discerned the intent of those marks on the weapon then it clearly does match Sur-natha's fanatical mindset," Custodian said.

"I'm starting to wish we hadn't handed her over to the STA," Dash said. "I'd have liked to confront her about this directly."

Dash had gone back and forth on that. They'd captured Sur-natha, the adopted human daughter of the Clan Shirna leader, Nathis, that Dash had defeated on the icy planet called Burrow. They'd held her on the Forge but weren't really sure what to do with her.

"Space her," Benzel had said, shrugging. "She's a murderous bitch."

That would have been the easiest choice. But, while Dash was more than prepared to be ruthless, he wouldn't be cruel. And Sur-natha had put up no resistance after being captured, so throwing her, unresisting, out of an airlock, just seemed cruel. Kai, after helping to interrogate her, had balked at the idea, too.

"She has been indoctrinated," the monk had said. "Thoroughly brainwashed. Had she never been taken by Nathis as a child, her life would have followed a very different path." For Kai, who utterly despised the Golden and their minions with all of his being, these were weighty words.

But Dash didn't like the idea of just keeping her permanently imprisoned on the Forge, either. And neither did Ragsdale, who saw the lingering presence of an enemy leader on the station a needless security risk.

A solution had presented itself in the form of outstanding warrants from the Spinward Trade Authority, or STA. They'd handed her over through the Aquarians—Dash might have had an unresolved warrant or two with the STA himself—and now she was their prisoner.

As Dash watched Amy and Conover finish the process of closing themselves into their mechs, he crossed his arms and fretted, not for the first time, that handing her over might not have been the right move. It left her as a loose end. So maybe Benzel had been right.

Curling his lip, Dash shoved his thoughts back onto the knife and let his mind roam. He sifted the odds, which were against this random knife being Sur-natha's, or belonging to anyone close to her. But the odds had also been against him finding the Archetype and becoming the Messenger. He definitely fell short of believing in some higher power guiding things, but he had started to come around to the idea that, for whatever reason, there were no coincidences in this war.

"If it *isn't* her, then it's still someone from Clan Shirna," Dash finally said. "And that means they had access to Golden tech that's far more complex than we imagined."

"Skyhooks, while uncommon—based on your records, in any case—are also hardly rare," Custodian observed. "Clan Shirna may have had access to advanced Golden technology, but they didn't need that access to develop skyhooks."

"Sure, but not the type we found on that moon—a type that we've also found on gas giants, standing up to winds that top a thousand klicks per hour and pressures great enough to squash ceramalloy like wet clay. No way. We have to assume that they've got Golden tech we haven't yet seen, and that they—or someone, anyway—was using it for something. I don't know what yet, but I do know where we have to begin looking. How long until that monofilament cable we purchased from Katerina is prepped and ready?"

"Retrofit of the most capable ship, the *Rockhound*, will take a day, at most. It is the vessel best suited to any task involving an atmospheric tug," Custodian said.

"Then we have a day to convince Katerina here to join us, and less than that to get Amy and Conover up to speed." Dash waved a hand at Talon and Pulsar. "Amy, Conover, thirty minutes, main bay. It's time for you to leave the nest."

10

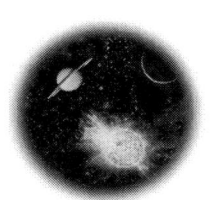

"Holy crap," Amy said, her voice bubbling over the comm. "I will never be able to sit in a pilot's seat and work a helm again. This is—"

"Amy at a loss for words?" Leira cut in. "Tybalt, mark this day on the calendar."

Dash chuckled but kept a critical eye on the Talon and the Pulsar. To be honest, and despite his being somewhat blasé when it came to mechs, he had to admit to being more than a little impressed by the array of all four mechs flying in a line-abreast formation.

"Okay, we'll try some simple maneuvers first," Dash said, then rolled the Archetype. The others followed suit.

"I just…know how to do that," Conover said. "That's amazing!"

Dash smiled again, this time at Conover's uncharacteristic enthusiasm. But it was tempered with the knowledge that, soon, Conover would have to be doing these things under fire.

Dash let out a long sigh, closing his eyes in resignation as he addressed Sentinel privately. "This war really is going to be a long one if you can see Conover in independent command of an Anchor, and everything that goes with it."

"Yes. I am sorry to say so, but you are undoubtedly correct."

He shoved the memory, and the dreary thoughts that wanted to follow it, away, and concentrated on flying, putting Amy and Conover through their paces.

The mechs rolled, spun, somersaulted, reversed, turned, and contorted themselves through all the gyrations that set them apart from regular ships in combat. When it looked like their new pilots had started to get comfortable just flying their mechs, he had Sentinel set a course to the currently closest star system to the Forge. She transmitted it to the other AIs, and they translated, popping out of reality, then re-entering it shortly thereafter just over a light-year away.

"Whoa," Amy said. "This system is weird."

"An utter mess. I don't care for it one bit," Kristen said, managing to still sound upbeat. For an AI, she had a *lot* more inflection than the first week of Sentinel's awakening.

It was indeed. The primary was a red supergiant so massive it didn't actually have a surface, as much as it just slowly diffused from star stuff to empty space. A pair of white-dwarf stars hurtled around it at breakneck speed, both trailing plumes of gas stripped away from the primary by their gravitational tug. The only intact planet was a solitary gas giant orbiting far out from the chaotic trio of stars along a slow, stately path. Anything that might have been a planet had long ago been wrenched and pulverized to rubble by the complex gravitation of the stars.

They zoomed close to the gas giant, partly because Dash wanted to give it a look-over. They already knew this one didn't contain any

Golden skyhooks, but he still reasoned that the more experience he had with the massive planets, the better prepared he'd be when it came time to dive into one. Amy and Conover both made increasingly excited noises as the huge disk loomed ever closer, until it blotted out half the starfield.

"I can't believe this," Amy said. "I mean, I've seen a bunch of these things on a view screen or holo-image, but this—hell, this is like flying through space without a ship or a suit! I *am* the ship!"

Conover said only one thing.

"Wow."

Hathaway had something else to say.

"A bit sparse on your commentary, but yes. It is a unique experience, especially for those who are new to space combat." Hathaway sniffed.

"I've had plenty of combat experience, you overly engineered coffeepot. I'm merely young," Conover replied easily.

"I'll take it under advisement," Hathaway said.

"I think the new relationship is going just great." Dash laughed.

They swept across the swirling bands of turbulent gas; Dash had Sentinel siphon up as much data as possible and add it to what they knew about gas giants. Using its gravity as a slingshot, they then raced deeper into the system, dodging and weaving their way among asteroids. Conover misjudged and clipped a good-sized rock, sending the Pulsar into a tumble. Dash braced himself to help, but he wanted to see if Conover could correct it himself.

He did, and quite handily. Dash did notice that the Pulsar now sported a gouge in its shoulder armor from the impact.

"That's going to come out of your pay," Dash said.

"But I don't get paid anything to do this," Conover replied.

"Huh, that's what everyone says. Guess I need to come up with a new threat."

"You could sing to them," Sentinel said.

"That was in *confidence*. I was testing an old drinking song," Dash said.

"I think the term song is a bit generous," Sentinel said.

"I think this relationship is simply brilliant," Hathaway gushed, and then the comms were filled with laughter as they raced on, pushing as close as they dared to the unruly trio of stars. Even from a hundred million klicks, the red giant wasn't a disk anymore; it was just a vast, incandescent wall of dull red. One of the white dwarfs was racing across it, a fierce pinpoint of searing light.

"Pretty hot here, Dash," Amy said, some of the excitement gone from her voice, replaced by a nervous tightness.

"Pretty strong radiation, too," Conover put in.

"Yeah, you'd never dare come this close with a ship like the *Slipwing*," Dash replied. "Just wanted you to see that these mechs are pretty damned tough."

"But not indestructible," Leira cautioned. "Don't get complacent about them. They do have limits. For instance, you wouldn't have wanted to do a deep dive into that gas giant back there, right, Dash?"

He curled his lip. "Generally, not without a *really* good reason, no."

"Sounds like you two are continuing some argument you started a while ago," Amy said, but Dash cut her off.

"Anyway, let's head back out. Just because we can soak up this kind of heat and rads without getting fried alive, doesn't mean we should."

"Dash?" Conover said, as they accelerated away from the stars.

"Pulsar says I can integrate my sight into the mech's sensors. I haven't tried that yet, though. I mean, last time I tried it, it didn't work out so well."

"Well, that was a Golden mech you were screwing around with," Dash replied, remembering when an attempt to hack into a captured Golden Harbinger they'd brought about the Forge, using his eye implants, almost killed him. Still, Kristen would have Conover's best interests in mind here, just as Hathaway would. That's what they were for, after all.

Besides, they might learn something useful.

"Okay, give it a try," Dash finally said. "But make sure Kristin knows to cut the connection if there's even a hint of a problem with it. Worse comes to worst, she should be able to fly the mech back to the Forge."

"Okay, just a second."

A moment passed as they raced along, the red giant once more a disk behind them, noticeably shrinking.

Another moment passed.

Another.

Dash frowned at the image of the Pulsar on the heads-up. "Conover?"

Silence.

"Conover!"

When the silence persisted, Dash said, "Kristen, what's going on?"

"Conover's fine," she replied. "Or, at least his physiology is fine and shows no aberrations that would account—"

"I'm here, Dash," Conover said. "Sorry, I was just trying to figure out what I was seeing. It can be a little confusing, being able to see across such a big chunk of the EM spectrum. You should see what the starfield looks like in radio."

"You see, I told you he was alright," Kristen said.

Dash rolled his eyes. The Unseen AIs had a penchant for pairing up mech pilots with versions of themselves that had pretty much the opposite character—so Leira's Tybalt was fussy and arrogant to her laid-back attitude, Kristen was a little flighty to Conover's more thoughtful gravity, and Hathaway was dour and self-important to Amy's free-spirited approach to life. The exception was Sentinel, which only made sense—there was no way for Sentinel to have been designed to be his opposite, because there was no way the Unseen could have known the Messenger would be him—specifically.

Or did they?

He shoved the musing aside. Sentinel and Custodian both insisted that they had no information to suggest that Dash, or anyone else, would be *chosen* as the Messenger, not without a very specific set of requirements being met.

Still.

Dash scowled at himself. "Okay, Conover, let's try something. See if you can find any Dark Metal signals using this new integrated vision of yours. Kristen has a detector, and—"

"I see some, yes. Most are a long way away, just weak, distant signals. However, there's a strong signal coming from a star system that's 6.2 light-years away. Uh, Kristen, can you send that data to everyone else?"

"Done."

Dash looked at the information that popped onto the heads-up. It was a strong signal, one they'd somehow missed detecting with the Forge. He frowned. How had they missed such a strong Dark

Metal signature from only a little more than seven light-years away? He asked Sentinel about it, concerned that there might be some flaw in their detector tech.

"It is not a flaw, as much as it is a limitation. The deep-field Dark Metal interferometer built around the Forge was designed to be as sensitive and accurate as possible. The trade-off was coverage. The portion of the starfield that would, from the Forge's perspective, hold this signal will not be scanned for another 1.7 days. Moreover, the system contains a K-class orange hypergiant star, the size and instability of which would obscure the signal because of its widely varying emissions of neutrinos."

"Huh. That is a damned big star. Make a note to bring that up at our next planning meeting, to see what we can do about it." He switched to the comm. "Okay, everyone, since we're already a light-year in that direction, let's go take a look."

A private channel almost immediately opened—just as Dash expected it would.

"Dash," Leira said. "Are you sure that's a good idea? Dark Metal signatures might mean Golden or Verity, and one that strong—"

"Makes it almost certain we're going to find something there that wants to kill us. Yeah, I know."

"Amy and Conover are on their maiden flights. I'm really not comfortable with the idea of taking them into combat."

"You know, I would *love* to be able to let them train and exercise with their mechs for another week—hell, another month. But we don't have time for that, Leira."

"Dash, I really—"

"You and I will go in first so they can hang back. And if it looks like anything that might be too tough, I'll give them orders to disengage and go back to the Forge, while we fight our way out."

"Still not happy about this."

Dash nodded. "Join the club. But here we are."

THEIR DESTINATION STAR, bright enough to rate a name on the charts—Typhoon—was easily the biggest stellar object Dash had ever seen. Even the supergiant they'd just visited, as colossal as it was, would be dwarfed by this monster.

"That is a *big* damned star," Leira said. "And, holy crap, unstable, too. Look at that mass ejection off to the right."

"Yeah, I see it. Let's stay away from that," Dash replied.

"And hope that no more such ejections occur during our presence in this system, particularly in a direction that would put us at risk. Imagine dying out here without completing a proper education," Hathaway intoned.

Dash had to smile at Hathaway's subtle insult. He made Tybalt sound like a fun guy. It must be driving Amy crazy—which seemed to be the point, because that supposedly somehow made for closer, more effective pilot-AI interaction.

Or, Dash thought, the AIs just had a wicked sense of humor.

He turned his attention back to the star. They'd only just translated into the system, and even from this far out, Typhoon loomed, a bloated, orange mass of roiling plasma so bright the heads-up had to step down its brightness. The coronal mass ejection, or CME, that Leira had cautioned them about stuck out from its flank, a titanic, bulbous protrusion of searing plasma, gas, and dust as big as a decent-sized star. Enormous blasts of charged particles poured off the hypergiant in all other directions, a solar wind that lived up to the star's name of Typhoon.

"I can't believe there are actual planets here," Leira said. "You'd think they'd never have formed around something like this."

"They are probably bodies captured by the high gravitation of this star," Tybalt said. "Even a cursory examination of their orbits shows that they do not share a common ecliptic plane. Their orbits simply reflect their trajectory when they were captured by the star."

"And for every one we see, there are probably a bunch more that just fell into the star," Conover added.

"Been there, almost done that," Leira said.

"Well, these so-called planets are really just barren hunks of rock," Dash said, eyeing the heads-up. "I mean, really barren. Not even a hint of atmosphere on any of them. That's where the stronger Dark Metal signal is coming from." He frowned. "But then there's that weaker signature, just off to the left of the star. What is that?"

"It is a toroidal structure that matches the configuration of a Golden missile platform, in close proximity to another long, linear object that has no such match in our databases," Sentinel said.

"Missile platform. That's perfect. Okay, folks, we're going to take out that platform, find out what that thing is near it, and then go check the signal from that planet."

"Why don't a couple of us take care of the platform, while the others go do the planet?" Amy said. "You know, do two things at once?"

"Because this is your first flight in the Talon, and it is going to be your first fight in the Talon, Amy. We'll do this one step at a time," Dash replied, trying to put a tone in his voice that said this wasn't open for debate.

Amy must have caught his underlying meaning. "Roger that," she replied.

Powering up the Archetype's drive, Dash set course for the missile platform, the other mechs falling into line with him.

IT WAS A MISSILE PLATFORM, all right, but it harbored a nasty surprise—a petawatt laser that rapidly, and randomly, changed its frequency from near UV to near infrared, and across the whole visible spectrum in-between. Changing the mechs' shields to make them opaque to the incoming laser energy was a challenge; even their AI's had a slight lag time.

Dash winced as the laser momentarily bathed the Archetype in searing light. Armor immediately began to glow and spall off superheated vapor before Sentinel could make the shield opaque again—by which time, the laser had shifted targets to the Pulsar. They were fortunate to have the four mechs, Dash thought, because had it only been him and Leira, each of their mechs would have taken much more of a beating from the laser. He nonetheless focused on fighting a defensive battle, so Leira could lead Amy and Conover into the attack.

"Amy, stop concentrating your pulse cannons on those incoming missiles," Leira snapped. "Use evasive maneuvers and let your point-defense take care of them."

"Yeah, but if I wasn't shooting them down, I'd have taken some hits—"

"So take them," Leira snapped. "You're not flying the *Slipwing* anymore. These mechs are meant to take hits and keep fighting."

Dash nodded approval at Leira's direction. She pulled Amy into a tight formation with her, the two smaller, sleeker mechs flew quicker and more agile than the Pulsar or the Archetype. Conover hung back, firing missiles at the platform, while also cycling through the new tricks his mech brought to the fight—electronic countermeasures.

"I just activated the anti-targeting system," he said. "Did that do anything?"

The laser flashed into space—and hit nothing. It fired again, and again, just pulsed through vacuum. "I'd say it did," Leira said. "The platform seems to have lost track of us. Amy, let's go before it adapts."

The Swift and Talon raced in, closing on the missile platform and raking it with nova-gun, dark-lance and pulse-cannon fire. As tough as it was, even Golden tech couldn't stand up long to such a sustained barrage; it defiantly loosed a final salvo of missiles, then blew apart, wreckage cartwheeling off in all directions.

"Now can we shoot down the missiles that are left?" Amy asked. "I just got hit by one, and it—that actually hurts. I mean, I actually felt it—kind of, anyway."

"Let me try something first," Conover said.

The final flight of missiles raced toward the two light mechs.

"Uh, Conover—" Amy said, but Leira cut her off.

"Five seconds, Conover, and then we're going to open fire."

"Yup—there, try that."

All of the missiles but one suddenly flipped over and burned hard, decelerating, and finally came to a stop. The lone holdout plowed doggedly on toward the Talon until the mech's point-defense destroyed it.

"Okay, that was pretty nifty, Conover," Dash said. "What did you do?"

"The Pulsar has a remote hacking system as one of its main components. I wanted to give it a try, so I used it to command those missiles to stop."

"What can I say? It is the result of a superior—" Hathaway said.

"We get it, thanks. Save the victory song for later, if you please," Dash said.

"At least I can sing," Hathaway retorted, and Leira snorted into her comms for fifteen seconds before Dash put her on mute.

"If we may?" Dash asked when it was quiet.

"Onward," Amy said, her tone betraying a smile.

Dash looked at the seven stationary icons representing the idle Golden missiles, now slowly falling into wide orbits around the star. "Well, that's great. We need to find out just what that system can do. In the meantime, though—Amy, you want to kill missiles? Kill those ones. They might be inert for now, but according to Sentinel, they're not actually dead."

"Roger that!" Amy said, returning to the job a hand. The mech swooped toward the missiles and gunned them into fragments with the Talon's pulse-cannons.

Leira came back on a private channel. "Dash, don't encourage her. I had a hard enough time keeping her focused."

"I know, and you did a good job of it. But those missiles do need to be destroyed, and Amy does need practice shooting at stuff with her mech, so…"

He switched back to their shared channel and peered at the long, cylindrical object the missile platform had apparently been protecting. It had offered not even a hint of offensive action. Instead, it simply sat there, mute, a variety of sensors and antennae protruding from it.

"So what *is* that thing?" he asked no one in particular.

"Well, it doesn't seem like it's armed," Leira replied. "Or, if it is, it doesn't seem inclined to do anything to us, at least not yet."

Amy blasted the last missile apart, swooping the Talon past the debris as she did. "A hab of some sort, maybe?" she offered.

"Doubt it. There'd have to be some pretty damned potent shielding against this solar hurricane blowing around us."

"That's it," Conover cut in.

Dash rolled the Archetype toward the Pulsar. "That's what?"

"I was discussing this with Kristen. She notes that most of those sensors on it are pointed at the star."

"So it's an observatory of some sort?"

"More like a weather station, I think."

Dash made an *ah* sound but wanted a second opinion. "Sentinel, what do you think?"

"I would agree with Conover. The effects of Typhoon extend for a great distance in all directions. Its heliopause—essentially, the outer limits of those effects—is nearly one light-year away from the star. Accordingly, being able to monitor those effects would be beneficial for ships intending to traverse that volume of space."

"Okay. Good enough for me. I guess the question is, what makes the space around this star so valuable to the Golden that they'd want to keep track of its weather?"

No one had an answer for that. Dash decided to simply send back a salvage crew to recover the weather station, or whatever the proper name for it was, and then he turned his attention to the considerably stronger Dark Metal signal coming from the outermost planet.

"Let's go see what's out there," he said. "It might just be loot."

"But it might not," Leira cautioned. "So stay ready for anything and listen for orders, *Amy*."

"Sheesh, cuz, I'm not that much of a wild card." She paused. "Am I?"

"We'll talk," Leira replied, as she shepherded the Pulsar and Talon back into formation.

"So the signal is coming from inside that planet?" Dash said. "As much as this piece of rock is a planet, that is."

It definitely wasn't much to look at it. The planet, Typhoon-3, might have been spherical once, but about a quarter of it was just gone, leaving a ragged gouge thousands of kilometers across. The rest of it, a mass large enough to have about half of standard gravity, was smooth, almost polished rock—and that was it. Sentinel noted that the smoothness was likely the result of scouring by the ceaseless gale of energetic particles from the massive star, slowly eating away the planet's substance and blowing it into space as tenuous wisps of electrically charged dust. The Dark Metal signature came from one of the few recognizable topographic features on the barren surface, a humped region of rock a few kilometers across.

"How could it be under the surface?" Leira wondered. "There's no evidence of any entrances or anything like that to an underground base."

Dash shrugged. "Only one way to find out. Amy, Conover, you're going to learn how to dig."

Dash led the Talon and Pulsar down to the surface, while Leira remained in a high, synchronous orbit on overwatch. He had

Sentinel clearly outline the limits of the Dark Metal signal, then directed Amy and Conover to start pulling away rock.

"Holy crap, I feel like a—I don't know, like some kind of super being," Amy said, lifting a slab of rock the size of a cargo pod and tossing it aside.

"Right now, you *are* a super being," Conover said. "We all are."

"Just keep in mind that even super-beings have limits," Dash said, levering up another, stony chunk and flinging it across the bleak rock-scape. "Okay, found something."

Conover and Amy both moved toward him, but he told them to stop. "I don't know what this is, or how far it extends under here. So just stay where you are, and Sentinel will share the imagery with you."

Dash gingerly moved more rock. Whatever this was—apparently the remains of a ship—seemed to have come to rest on this planet when its surface was molten. Dash furrowed his brow until Tybalt offered a likely answer.

"Based on scans from up here in high orbit, it would appear that portions of this planet's surface were relatively recently molten. However, the planet is geologically inactive, so this isn't the result of volcanic activity."

"So what melts rock that isn't a volcano?" Dash asked, but he knew the answer already. "Oh. Weapons fire."

"There was a battle here, involving weapons that could slag big volumes of rock," Leira said. "And it wasn't that long ago."

"And more to point, it wasn't us," Conover said.

11

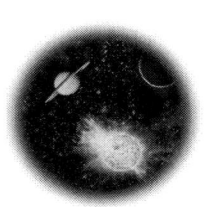

It was a ship. Or, rather, it was two ships, their wreckage intertwined. Both had clearly hit the surface at the same time, landing in a zone of melted rock that had flowed back over them, entombing them both.

"All that Dark Metal," Amy said. "Almost a ton of it. That's quite the haul."

"It is, but before we salvage it, we need to figure out what happened here," Dash replied. "We've got two ships, one Golden, and one not Golden, it seems, but something capable of actually *fighting* the Golden. Both crashed in the same spot, during a battle, at the same time. How does that happen?"

"It may be a coincidence," Conover offered. "But I doubt it."

"Yeah, so do I. I'm thinking these two ships were somehow attached to one another. So either they collided—"

"Or it was a boarding action," Leira said. "One ship was boarding the other."

"Exactly. Sentinel, it looks like part of the hull of the non-

Golden ship is kind of intact. Can you get any sensor readings about what's inside there?"

"There are no power or other emissions. Obviously, there is no atmosphere. However, there are traces of chemicals on some of the debris, which would suggest organic remains—"

Dash narrowed his eyes as Sentinel abruptly cut off. "Sentinel?"

"This is unexpected. Most of the traces are of various organic chemicals, which could have a variety of sources. However, I am also detecting traces of deoxyribonucleic acid."

"Deoxy—wait. That's DNA, isn't it?"

"It is. And it is characteristic of only one known species."

"Yeah. Us. Human beings."

DASH KEPT his pulse-gun leveled as he approached the wreckage. The Archetype towered overhead, its shield enclosing the debris and, more importantly, Dash. Without it, the ceaseless blizzard of charged particles from the gigantic star would have fried him in seconds. Even then, it wasn't a perfect defense, because the solar wind gusting off the colossal star was just so *intense*, and so *energetic*, that some of it leaked through the shield. And if there happened to an especially powerful burst, as they'd seen erupt from Typhoon several times now, and it happened to be aimed at the planet—

"Leira, reassure me that you're in position, please," Dash said.

"I'm in position. Everything looks calm—or at least as calm as they can be this close to a hypergiant star."

Leira's voice came over the comm with that slightly flat tone characteristic of comms transmitted through unSpace. In normal space, information could only travel at the speed of light, so an energetic burst from the star that had the planet in its sights would come crashing down on Dash only a couple of minutes after sensing the first traces of it. This way, the Swift would act as a sort of early warning outpost, able to detect a burst and tell Dash about it with about five minutes to spare for him to get back in the Archetype.

He glanced back at the mech then ahead of him at the wreckage. Should be no problem—as long as he didn't get stuck or anything like that, that is.

"Amy, Conover, your status?"

"We're both in position, Dash, keeping overwatch on you," Conover replied.

Dash acknowledged. The other two mechs had been deployed above the opposite poles of the planet, so nothing could approach it without them knowing about it.

The rads briefly spiked, sounding a thin beep and flashing a red warning in the heads-up in Dash's suit. It only lasted a second, but it took a couple more before his heart started beating again.

"Sentinel, what the hell just happened?"

"There are a multitude of complex and dynamic factors affecting the local intensity of the solar wind. Overall, it remains unchanged, but there will be occasional spikes."

"Great." He glanced at his total rad count. Still well below a level that would give him any trouble, but it made him move a little faster, bouncing a little higher with each step in the weak gravity.

The wreckage loomed ahead of him. The intact part formed a half-cylinder, the open end facing Dash gaping like an ominous cave. He tightened his grip on the pulse-gun. It was exceedingly unlikely that anything alive was inside there, but that didn't stop his imagination from filling the void space with lurking menace. And with the Golden involved, there might be bots—although Sentinel claimed that even the hardiest Golden bot would almost certainly have been irradiated into inert scrap in the time that had passed since this crash, which they'd put at somewhere between five and ten years ago.

Taking a breath, Dash activated low-light on his face plate and entered the wreckage.

Inside, he found a tangled strew of twisted and broken structural members, twisted conduits, and bulkheads folded and torn like paper. It was surprising, frankly, that they'd found this much intact. Again, Sentinel had offered an answer, suggesting that because the two ships had hit at such a shallow angle, in not-very-viscous magma, enough impact energy had been shed that everything simply hadn't been pulverized.

Dash picked his way among the ruin, being careful to avoid snagging his vac suit. This somewhat-intact portion of the ship was about forty meters long; Dash made it about ten meters inside before low-light imaging became useless, because there was *no* light. He activated his helmet lamp and carried on.

He'd just ducked under a hanging conduit when something caught his eye. It was—

A body. Part of a body, anyway. An arm, and some of a torso. Part of it was enclosed in the torn remains of a vac suit, but the rest was exposed. Soft tissue had been turned to what amounted to jerky by vacuum freezing, but it was still clearly identifiable as human.

"At least, I don't know any other species with breasts," Dash said over the comm.

"Human," Leira muttered. "So who were these people? Just an unlucky ship full of settlers or surveyors or something that bumbled into the middle of a battle between the Golden and someone else?"

Dash narrowed his eyes then moved to examine something else.

It was another conduit, not just intact, but looking entirely undamaged. He moved closer to it and saw why.

"This is Golden tech," he said, tapping the conduit. "I can tell Dark Metal alloy when I see it."

"So you must be inside the remnants of a Golden ship," Conover said.

But Dash shook his head. "No, this is clearly a human ship. Hell, I see a couple manufacturer's marks I recognize." He tugged at the conduit. "And it's not just a loose piece of debris, either. It's integrated right into this ship."

"A human ship with Golden tech in it?" Amy said. "So, collaborators, then."

"Maybe," Dash replied, and pushed on.

He found more evidence of Golden tech installed in what was, indeed, a human vessel. What he found when he pushed his away around a bulkhead was even more stunning, though.

He found a Golden corpse.

DASH NUDGED what had once been the leg of a Golden. The body, although still ripped apart by the force of the crash, was still much more intact than the few human remains he'd found. It must be, he thought, because of the durability of the tech that was apparently an integral part of Golden physiology.

"Probably not surprising," Leira said. "If those are Golden collaborators then it's not a big shock they had a Golden onboard."

"I only hope they saw the crash coming and it hurt like hell," Amy snapped. "Traitorous bastards…"

Dash said nothing and just narrowed his eyes. It was entirely possible that these were collaborators. Another possibility was that the human ship had been boarded. But something about this was tickling his curiosity.

"Sentinel, can you determine what parts of the debris are the human ship, and which are the Golden?"

"For the most part, yes. There is some uncertainty regarding particular fragments—"

"That's fine. Where did you scan those traces of human DNA? On which ship?"

"I detect human DNA traces on debris from both ships."

"Huh. Could that be a result of the crash?"

"It is possible, but unlikely. It is more likely that there were humans on board both ships at the time of the crash."

"How about the Golden? Can you sense any traces of them?"

"We know considerably less about their biochemistry," Sentinel replied. "So it is impossible to say if any of the other extraneous organic traces represent Golden remains. However, I can detect trace amounts of Dark Metal, which we know they incorporate into their tech augmentations."

"Okay. So are you detecting any of those on the human wreckage?"

"Besides the Golden remains you found, no."

"Dash, what are you thinking?" Leira asked.

"I don't know yet." He turned around, letting his lamp play over the smashed consoles and shattered conduits around him. He seemed to be standing in some sort of control facility—maybe even the remains of a bridge. "But there's something here."

"You are *feeling* something," Sentinel said.

"Yeah, I am." He paused, narrowed his eyes, then leaned in toward one of the battered consoles. "Hello, what's this?"

"What did you find?" Conover asked.

"A data core, I think." He pushed aside a chunk of ablative armor. "Yeah, it is. Huh. I even recognize the brand." He grabbed it and pulled. It budged slightly but wouldn't immediately come free of its receptacle.

"Dash, you'd better get back to the Archetype," Leira said.

He wiggled the core, trying to loosen it. "Why—oh, shit. An eruption?"

"Yeah. A big one. A whole coronal mass of it, almost as big as that other one we saw. It's not going to hit the planet head-on, but it's going to pass close. Tybalt says the spillover radiation is going to be way more than the Archetype's shield can handle alone."

Dash cursed to himself. "Of course. How long?"

"Five minutes, maybe."

He yanked on the core. It wouldn't budge.

"Come on," he muttered, and pulled harder. The core scraped a few millimeters then jammed again.

He glanced at his chrono, which Sentinel had set to a countdown. He had four and a half minutes left.

"Messenger, if you are not inside the Archetype when the effect of the CME arrives—"

"Yeah, I know, I know." He glared at the core. The answer to whatever had happened here might very well be contained within it. And the *feeling* he had that they were missing something had only gotten stronger.

The chrono ticked down toward four minutes. Either the core came free now, or he'd have to leave it and risk the flood of radiation wiping whatever data might be left on it.

Of course, that may already have happened.

Grabbing the core with both hands, Dash planted his feet on the console, and yanked—

Nothing. He strained and the core suddenly popped free. He flew backward and slammed into a twisted structural beam. Most of the impact was absorbed by his backpack, which was probably why his suit's temperature regulator had just gone offline.

Dash levered himself to his feet and began hurrying as fast as the obstacle course of debris allowed.

A chill began to seep into him. It was uncomfortable, but his suit was insulated enough that the heat inside it shouldn't escape before he reached the Archetype. No, the bigger problem was that the hundred meters or so of open ground he'd have to cover was exposed to the full glare of Typhoon.

It wasn't the deep chill of space that was going to do him in. It was the heat. If he could make it to the Archetype before it overwhelmed him, then the torrents of charged particles streaming toward the planet would finish what the star's heat started.

This damned star was going to kill him.

ONE MINUTE LEFT. Sentinel had already lowered the Archetype to its mounting posture and moved it as close as she dared, without counting on the broken, unstable rock around the crash site to support the mech. That still left fifty meters of barren rock, lit a dazzling orange by the glare from Typhoon.

"Damn it, Dash, get your ass inside that mech!" Amy called.

Dash huddled in the shadow of the wreckage, shivering. "Now why didn't I think of that?"

"Dash—!" Leira began, but he cut her off.

"Sentinel, I'm coming for you—now!"

He leapt into the open and began running. The temperature inside his suit suddenly shot up. The vac suit could keep him insulated for a while against the heat coming off nearly any main-sequence star, but it just wasn't designed to take what poured off a hypergiant like Typhoon. By the time he'd gone ten meters, he was already hot; five meters more, and he was sweltering.

He wasn't going to make it.

"Sentinel...I need..."

He stumbled. Sweat began to roll off his forehead, into his eyes. His vision blurred; his head swam.

"Dash, I will attempt to move the Archetype closer."

He saw the mech lift off then drop back down about ten meters away from him. As it did, the rock under its feet collapsed; only a burst of thrusters that flung debris all around Dash stopped it from toppling over.

Well, shit, Dash thought. After all this, this is what does me in.

He realized he was still running, or trying to, but it wouldn't matter, he had thirty-five seconds left, and there was no way that was enough time. The heat would knock him out cold by then.

Voices sounded in the comm, but they were just nonsensical babble. Instead, his mind latched onto his last thought—heat, knocking him out cold. He giggled.

Something massive suddenly loomed behind him, and darkness fell.

"Dash!"

It was Conover?

"What?"

"Dash, get back on your feet. Get into the Archetype."

"I...what?"

"Dash! Listen to me—"

"Yeah, yeah. Got it. Get inside the Archetype."

Wait. Get inside the Archetype. Before the rad storm arrived.

His suit had cooled down slightly. He was no longer in the direct glare of Typhoon. Something had blocked it, throwing him into shade. He glanced back.

It was the Pulsar. Conover had landed it, blocking line of sight back to the star.

Dash nodded at that. What a great move. He'd have to congratulate the kid.

Looking at the chrono on the suit's heads-up brought him back to the present. He had ten seconds left. There was no way he'd be able to mount the Archetype in ten seconds.

"Uh…yeah. Thanks, Conover. It was a good try, but I don't think it's going to be enough—"

"It will if you move fast. Sentinel and Pulsar have synchronized both mechs' shields. You've got about a minute before they're saturated and shut down."

Dash blinked up at the Pulsar. Okay, he really did have to congratulate Conover on this.

And thank him, too. Even Kristen. As long as she wasn't *too* upbeat about the whole event. He could only tolerate so much positivity in one day.

"Seventeen seconds to spare," Amy said, as the four mechs raced away from the tsunami of radiation billowing off the hypergiant star. "Hardly even exciting."

"Tell you what, Amy," Dash said. "Next time, you do it. See if you can beat my time."

She laughed, but Leira cut in.

"Dash, when you get back to the Forge, you're going right into the infirmary. You still took some rads out there."

"Yes, mom." He glanced at the data core he'd retrieved, which was now racked in a storage slot in the Archetype's cockpit. "So while I'm doing that, you come grab this core and find out what's on it. Sentinel, can you tell anything about the direction those ships were heading when they crashed?"

"Other than down, no. But the data core may help."

"Dash, are you going to share what you're thinking with us?" Leira asked.

"I'm not thinking it as much as I'm *feeling* it, as Sentinel would say."

"So what are you *feeling*?" Conover asked.

Dash eyed the data core. "Well, it's a long shot, but it's one we need to look into. Because if it works out, this could change the whole war."

"Dash, what the hell are you talking about?" Leira asked.

"Don't hold me to this, but I think there's a chance that the Golden corpse-pieces I found aboard that human ship hadn't boarded to attack them. But I also think there's a chance that those humans weren't collaborating with the Golden, either."

"So they weren't enemies, but they weren't in league with the Golden?" Conover asked. "What does that leave?"

"Only one thing I can think of," Dash said, as they neared the translation point. "That the humans and that Golden were allies, and they were fighting *against* the other Golden."

"Wait, Golden fighting Golden?" Leira said.

"Yeah. A civil war among the Golden. And if I'm right, that could change the whole damned war."

12

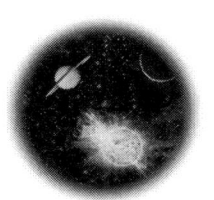

Even with their rushed departure from Typhoon, as they sought to avoid the worst of the CME's effects, they managed to retrieve almost a ton of Dark Metal among the four mechs. It had been a good haul, but as soon as Dash had been released from the infirmary with a clean bill of health—and a stern warning to avoid any further, significant rad exposure for at least a month—he headed for the Command Center. That was where the most important part of the haul, by far, had been taken: the data core.

He arrived to find Leira, Viktor, and Kai gathered around the core, which had been plugged into a port borrowed from the *Slipwing* and hardwired to Custodian's specifications. The core was now a part of the Forge's systems. Ragsdale and Harolyn hovered nearby. They were eyeing a display, watching something scrolling across it.

"What did we find?" Dash asked, bracing himself to be told that whatever data was on the core had long since become irretrievable. But Viktor looked up with a thin smile.

"Not a lot survived. But we have been able to piece together—well, take a look for yourself."

Dash peered at the display. It was replaying the tactical data for a battle between—

"Bingo," Dash said.

Human ships, augmented with what was clearly Golden tech—weapons, shields and other countermeasures—fought other Golden ships. Just as important was their recorded track as they approached contact; the joint human-Golden force had come from the direction of the galactic core.

"You were right," Ragsdale said. "Looks like the Golden are fighting among themselves."

Dash nodded. "It's a civil war. Or at least it was."

"You think the…rebels, I guess…are still alive?" Leira asked.

Dash shrugged. "No idea. But the most interesting part for me? That there could even be a rebellion. They're the Golden. They don't make mistakes like us. What does that tell you?"

Harolyn spoke first, her words slow and methodical. "There's a problem in translation."

"Translation? As in, travel from a star system?" Kai asked.

"No. From an organic body to whatever the Golden are. It's not perfect, and sometimes, the results aren't what they anticipated. Some of them still believe that life is important. That it's real and shouldn't be wasted. And, they're willing to fight to save it," Harolyn said.

Ragsdale narrowed his eyes at her. "That's just supposition."

"This is all just supposition at this point," Dash said. "I mean, there could be some other explanation for what we're seeing"—he gestured at the core and the display—"but it's a supposition we can't just ignore. The possibility of a split in the Golden is too important not to try and run down. Because, if they're still out there, then we might very well have allies."

"Not to mention, the best damned allies possible," Harolyn said.

But Ragsdale crossed his arms. "Okay, I wouldn't be doing my job if I didn't sound a warning klaxon here."

Dash nodded. "Sound away. I want everyone's input, of course."

"Well, what if you're right—but also wrong?" Ragsdale said.

"Sorry, don't follow," Leira replied.

"This looks like a—pardon the pun—golden opportunity, sure. But what if you're *meant* to think that?"

"You mean a trap?" Viktor said.

"Exactly. You meet some Golden that you think are friendly. You take them into your confidence. You plan operations together. They offer you their tech." He ended by raising his eyebrows.

"Yeah, I hear you," Dash said. "The Golden are cunning and seem to like doing things the indirect way. That's why they want to use the likes of Clan Shirna, the Bright, and the Verity to do their fighting for them."

"It would be a way of trying to sidestep our defenses," Viktor put in, rubbing his beard. "Definitely easier than trying to face us head-on."

A moment passed while Ragsdale's dire musings sunk in. Dash finally shook his head.

"Okay, we can't ignore our Security Chief's warning. But we can't just let his opportunity slip by, either. We need to follow up on this." Dash looked at Ragsdale. "I'm going to need you to scrutinize every single bit of this. If we find Golden that seem to be possible allies, I want you all over it."

"I will treat it as a massive security risk," Ragsdale replied. "Which will be easy, because that's exactly what it is."

"Custodian," Dash said. "Can you extrapolate their trajectory from the data on this core, back to its origin?"

"The data are incomplete, with many missing clusters as a result of radiation damage. This is the best estimate I can offer, and I would note that it should be evaluated with a considerable margin of uncertainty."

A lurid red arrow appeared on the star chart on the Command Center's main display. The path started at Typhoon and plunged back toward the galactic core.

"I notice it stops," Dash said. "Does that mean that was as far as you could trace it?"

"Yes. However, there are fragments of data that suggest it could also have been their origin point. It is impossible to say for certain with the available information."

Dash walked to the map, staring at the indicated path intently. When he turned around, a smile played around his lips. "Okay, first thing's first, we scout."

"And then?" Leira asked.

Dash let his smile grow wider. "Then, if we find what I hope we're going to find, we'll do what any good navy does. We recruit."

AFTER A BRIEF DISCUSSION about how they might approach the matter of rogue Golden, and their potential as allies, the others filtered out of the Command Center to attend to getting ready for what could be a very tense expedition. Dash found himself sitting alone, except for the two duty staff manning the operations station.

He gave them a thoughtful look but was interrupted by a holo-comm from Wei-Ping, who was currently aboard the *Retribution* overseeing some refits.

"Dash, I hear you want to head coreward."

"Yeah. That's why I asked to see you and Benzel. I'd like to go in a couple hours."

"Okay. Well, I looked at that initial course Custodian sent out, based on some data core or something you retrieved from a wreck-site."

Dash nodded. "And?"

"Well, your mechs may be able to stick it out the whole way in unSpace—and the *Herald* could probably manage it, too—but the rest of the fleet's going to need to drop back into real space partway, to recalibrate the navs against standard reference stars."

"Okay…"

"Well, if you're following that track, for that distance, then the calibration point is going to be somewhere around here." A window popped open on the holo-image, showing a simplified star chart and the course they'd retrieved from the data core. Partway along it, a region of space had been highlighted.

Dash leaned toward the holo-image, studied it, then shrugged. "It seems you're going somewhere with this, Wei-Ping, but—"

"That isn't exactly friendly space."

"Ah, okay. Custodian didn't have any reports of Golden or Verity activity in that region, so I gather you're talking about someone, or something else."

"Yeah, I am. The Gentle Friends weren't the only privateers in the arm. That region of space around the calibration point is the turf of the Spiral Collectors."

Dash frowned. "Never heard of them."

"You wouldn't have unless you traveled that far coreward."

"Never did." He grinned. "I didn't know you pirates—er, privateers, kept in touch like that."

"Well, it's not like we have a club. But we know about one another. People sometimes move between them. We try to stay clear of each other, but"—she smiled—"that doesn't always work out."

"Alright. So tell me about these Spiral Collectors?"

"Yeah. Pretty well established, been working for a few years now. They've got a decent-sized fleet, well-armed, mixed ships, from cutters to, I think, a couple of heavy cruisers. They're run by two sisters named Splice and Rumor."

"Splice and Rumor. Really?"

"Hey, I didn't make up the names, I'm just telling you what they are."

As she spoke, a new holo-image appeared, depicting two women. "These are the individuals in question," Custodian said. "I obtained this information from wanted postings contained in the *Slipwing's* database."

Dash studied the two images. Splice was tall and thin, with long black hair hanging over half her face, probably to cover the large birthmark along her left cheek and neck. Rumor, in contrast, was short and slightly built, with pale green eyes that seemed to stare at Dash right out of the image—the cold, empty eyes of a killer.

"Fraternal twins, too," Dash noted from the wanted message. "Mom and dad must be so proud."

"Word is, they took over the Collectors from their father—after they killed him."

"Why am I not surprised? Okay, Wei-Ping, brief Custodian on everything you know about these Collectors, and Rumor and Splice. He'll incorporate it into our mission package."

"Will do."

All of the images—Wei-Ping's, Rumor's, and Splice's—disappeared. Dash stared at the big star-map for a moment, then turned to the two duty personnel at the ops station.

"Guys, can you take a break? I need a few minutes alone here."

"Sure, Dash," a woman they'd rescued from the Verity, who turned out to have some military experience, said. "It's quiet anyway."

When they were gone, Dash turned back to the star map and stared at it for a moment longer, then he leaned back, his mind made up.

"Custodian, can you seal that door, please?"

"Done."

"Okay, I have two questions for you. These are the highest priority, but they're also utterly secret. No one is to ever know I've asked them. And the answers, of course, are for me and me alone."

"Understood."

For some time, Dash had felt questions growing in his mind—questions about things like his purpose, his larger place in the war, and what Custodian saw as the path forward, knowing what they knew after so many battles.

Despite his reservations, Dash went ahead, sketching out the issues that had bothered him for some time. When he asked Custodian for advice, there was, for the first time, a minor pause before the AI answered.

"It may take some time, but I will have the answers for you as soon as possible, Messenger," Custodian said. After another pause, he added, "I would add that I am not certain you will like them."

Dash stood but kept staring at the star map. "Oh, I don't expect to like the answers." He sighed, closing his eyes for a moment and blotting out the image of the galactic arm that had lately started to feel seared right into his brain.

"In fact, I'm counting on it."

Dash lifted the Archetype from the deck of the docking bay and launched himself into space. The rest of the strike team they'd assembled had already formed up a few thousand klicks from the Forge. They'd chosen to pack as much punch into as small a force as possible, so the team consisted of the four mechs, and Benzel in the *Herald* leading A Squadron. B Squadron and the rest of the fleet would stay with the Forge under Wei-Ping in the *Retribution*.

"Okay, folks," he said, as he slid the Archetype into formation. "You've seen the briefing. If we encounter these Collectors, like Wei-Ping thinks we will, our objective is to take them out of the fight while killing as few as possible. That means carefully aimed shots to take out drives and weapons. After all, we might be looking at some more possible allies."

"An alliance with those two psychopathic hags?" Benzel said. "I don't know…"

Leira laughed. "You know, just before we headed out to take on your Gentle Friends, I could imagine someone saying the same thing about you, Benzel."

"Hey!"

"But then we got to know and love you," Leira added, her voice syrupy sweet.

Benzel sniffed. "I wasn't worried about the psychopathic part. It was being called a hag that really hurt."

Dash let the resulting laughter linger across the comm for a moment; genuine laughter before launching on a potentially deadly op was the sound of good morale. He finally interrupted it, though.

"Anyway, kids, if we can drag our attention back to the matter at hand—is everyone ready?"

Acknowledgements came in from all mechs and ships.

"Okay, then let's go," Dash said and, because the Forge wasn't currently near a stellar mass that might inhibit translation, he flung the Archetype right into unSpace, the rest of the strike team following.

"Looks like Wei-Ping was right," Dash said, looking from the threat display to the tactical situation depicted on the heads-up. A small fleet of ships had quickly converged on them, starting almost the moment they'd returned to real space.

"Okay, no one engages until I do. I want to try talking to these Collectors first. Maybe we can actually avoid a fight for once."

"Good luck with that," Benzel said. "These are privateers. They're always going to attack as their first option, because…well, that's what we—they—do."

"Worth a try anyway," Dash said, and accelerated the Archetype, closing on the nearest of the three groups of ships approaching them.

"Hello there," he said over an open comm channel. "I'm the Messenger, the leader of the Realm of Cygnus. We're here—"

The lead ship opened fire, a heavy particle cannon lashing out and flashing against the Archetype's shield. Dash frowned.

"Listen, we're not here to—"

The ship fired again, and two more joined in. The mech's shield held but was reduced by more than ten percent. Benzel laughed.

"Wow, look at that. They shot instead of talking."

"Yeah, yeah," Dash muttered, as he targeted the dark-lance on the lead ship. He took an extra moment to line up the shot, then fired. The beam punched through the ship's drive section, leaving it coasting, its power levels dropping to emergency levels.

As soon as he'd fired, the rest of the fleet surged forward behind him, targeting the Collectors' ships and opening fire.

The battle unfolded quickly, and predictably. As powerful as the Collectors' ships were, they were no match for the Cygnus fleet and its Unseen tech. One after another, dark-lance and pulse-cannon shots disarmed and disabled their opponents. The furthest squadron, seeing the battering their fellows were taking, broke off and fled without even engaging. By then, the leading squadron, the one that had opened fire first, was just derelict ships drifting and tumbling through space, leaving trails of venting plasma in their wake.

Dash turned his attention to the second squadron. It *had* engaged, but was obviously having second thoughts, as several ships had turned and burned, racing away from the battle. Dash went after the leader, absorbing particle cannon and even missile fire with the Archetype's shield, getting in close and using the mech's power-sword to virtually sever the ship's fusion exhaust ports from the hull. A few seconds later, escape pods were flung away from the shattered hulk; Dash had Sentinel transmit their tracks to the rest of the fleet, so Benzel and his ships could round them up, then turned his attention to the fleeing ships.

"Let's see how many of these we can—"

A dazzling flash pulsed across the heads-up; EM radiation

washed across the Archetype. A second later, a plasma shockwave hit, rippling across the shield.

"Sentinel, what the hell was that?"

"One of the Collectors' ships just suffered a failure of anti-matter containment."

"Damn it, I didn't want to actually destroy any of them."

"That ship had not been engaged or fired on, and had taken no damage."

"Oh. So, was it an accident?"

"Possibly. Or it may have been deliberate, a ship being scuttled in such a way as to obscure the withdrawal of the remaining ships."

Sure enough, the fleeing Collectors' ships had vanished, their translation presumably timed with the explosion.

Dash did see escape pods, though, so the crew hadn't killed themselves. That was good, because if they had, it would have meant they were facing a far more fanatical enemy than he'd expected.

It also meant that the battle was over.

Dash called up the fleet's status and scanned it. Minor damage only. He gave a satisfied nod at that. Since the Collectors' had chosen to be hostile, he didn't want to leave them, an active enemy, behind them as they pushed on along the course leading them closer to the galactic core. That meant they still had a fight ahead of them, deeper into the Collectors' home space.

BENZEL'S FACE appeared on the heads-up. "Dash, I have someone I'd like you to meet." The image drew back, revealing Benzel standing with a group of heavily armed crew from the *Herald*, their weapons trained on a scruffy group of people.

They could have been more of the Gentle Friends, actually, just from their looks. But Dash was immediately struck by the woman Benzel had pointed out.

"This is Splice. Splice, meet Dash. He's the Messenger, the leader of our happy little band of people who just kicked your ass."

Splice gave Dash a hard look. "I don't know who you people are, but when it comes to asses getting kicked, yours is hanging out totally bare."

"Well, first, thanks for that image. Second, you should have just stood down when we offered to talk to you."

"Ain't our style."

"I see that. Seems your style is more like *losing*."

"You!"

"Don't bother," Dash said, cutting her off. "Benzel, take Splice here to a comm so she can talk to her charming sister and get her to stand down."

"She won't," Splice said.

"Oh, I think she will. You guys are no more interested in getting completely beaten up than we're interested in beating you. If I've learned anything from Benzel, it's that you folks tend to be pragmatic."

But Splice shook her head. "She won't stand down, not even if I tell her to."

Dash raised a brow. "Why? You saw what our ships and mechs did to you. Why would she keep trying to fight?"

"She just will."

Splice said it with a flat certainty that Dash actually believed. She was absolutely convinced that Rumor wouldn't back down—

and that even she, her sister and comrade-in-arms, wouldn't dissuade her.

"I have analyzed their trajectories and would suggest that the Collectors have translated to the next system core-ward," Sentinel said. "Which also happens to lie on our primary course. We can allow the ships of our fleet to complete recalibrating their nav systems here, and simply translate past them, if you wish."

Why the hell would Rumor and the Collectors keep trying to fight a battle they should *know* they couldn't win?

"I want to see how this plays out," Dash said. "Benzel, show your guests there to their new quarters then come back to me on a closed channel. Sentinel, loop Leira, Amy, and Conover into it."

"Acknowledged."

Benzel stepped away from the Collectors he'd taken prisoner. "What's up, Dash?"

Dash shrugged.

"That's what I want to know."

13

Dash swept his eyes over the tactical display and scowled. "Damn, that's a big force."

The Archetype's heads-up displayed more than two-dozen Collector ships that were backed up by layered minefields and toroidal missile platforms. The latter made Dash narrow his eyes in suspicion. The Golden tended to favor toroidal designs, but there wasn't any evidence of actual Golden tech here. Still, together with the unwillingness of the Collectors to simply give in, it made him wonder if there was more going on here than met the eye.

So they were outnumbered by more than three to one. But, unless something unexpected happened, the Cygnus strike force still vastly outgunned the Collectors.

"Okay," Dash said. "Simple plan. We go in and take them out."

"Same as before?" Benzel asked. "Emphasis on disabling, not destroying?"

"Yeah. But no one is to put themselves, their mech, or their ship at unreasonable risk just to preserve the lives of these people. We absolutely come first."

"Got it."

The strike force powered up, the four mechs, in line abreast, leading A Squadron in a wedge formation, with the *Herald* at the tip.

Missiles erupted from the platforms and streaked toward them. At the same time, small objects came tumbling out of the platforms and accelerated hard in the wake of the missile barrage.

"Sentinel, what are those?"

"They appear to be drones. Their power utilization suggests that they are not intended to be recovered and reused."

"Suicide drones, then. Basically, big missiles." Dash thought for a moment. "Leira, these things can't have very sophisticated AIs running them. Think we can confuse them?"

"Sure. Fire missiles at them on very different trajectories, but timed for a simultaneous attack."

"Sounds good. Okay, everyone, let your point-defense systems deal with their missiles. Meantime, we'll fire two salvos back. Benzel, have your squadron track your missiles on longer, slower trajectories. The mechs will fire on faster, shorter ones. Let Sentinel and the other AIs work out the details of the timing."

Acknowledgements rattled in, and Dash gave the order to open fire.

Missiles raced away from the *Herald* and her squadron-mates, immediately swinging onto wide, looping trajectories. A few moments later, Sentinel prompted the mechs to fire; their missiles flashed away.

"Okay, Amy, you're with me," Dash said. "Leira, you pair up with Conover. Both of you stick close to us. Targets of opportunity, and try to disable, but if things get hairy, feel free to just blast the Collectors into debris."

The mechs accelerated and split into pairs, aiming to flank the Collectors, while A Squadron drove straight at them. The Collectors' missiles quickly zoomed into point-defense range—and just as quickly died, their guidance systems no match for the predictive capabilities of the AIs running the point-defense batteries on the Cygnus vessels. The swarm of suicide drones fared no better, desperately trying to dodge inbound missiles that not only stayed one step ahead of them but communicated among themselves to optimize their attack. Explosions rippled through space, with only clouds of debris emerging from them. Not a single drone had survived, but several missiles had, and they acquired new targets among the Collector squadrons.

Now, small, fast corvette-sized ships raced out of the enemy line to engage the Cygnus fleet. Petawatt lasers pulsed out, their formidable energy immediately being absorbed by the mechs' shields, and just as quickly radiated away. Closer in, they opened fire with rod-guns, essentially large chain-cannons that spat out hypervelocity streams of inert metal rods. It was a weapon that Dash, back in his courier days, feared; rod-guns had an almost mythical aura of menace among couriers and anyone else who flew for a living.

Compared to the likes of the Archetype, though, they were little threat. Sentinel could track and destroy them with the point-defenses, despite their extreme velocity. The few that did make it through the barrage slammed into the shield, to an almost dead halt.

Dash pulsed out shots from the dark-lance at the onrushing Collector ships. One by one, they died, their drives turned to slag and wreckage by the relentless fire from the Archetype. Amy nimbly dodged around Dash, snap-firing the Talon's pulse-cannons at whatever Dash wasn't shooting at. In less than a minute, the two mechs had slashed through the Collectors' line, leaving derelict ships spinning in their wake.

"Leira, how goes it?" Dash asked.

"Fine. We're out of targets, actually, so we're heading in after the most missile platforms."

"Sounds good. Watch out for those mines."

"Actually, Conover has shut down most of them, at least over in this zone. Have to admit, the Pulsar—um, Kristen—gives us some damned useful capabilities."

DASH KICKED at the Collector ship and slammed it hard to one side. Spinning, he slashed at it with the power-sword, decapitating its fusion exhaust ports and leaving it dead, tumbling in space.

He kept spinning the Archetype, taking in the aftermath of battle. Only one of the Cygnus ships, the light cruiser *Grand Slam*, had taken significant damage; a missile had fluked through a storm of point-defense fire to strike her flank, penetrating and blowing a chunk out of her side. She was still spaceworthy, but it had killed three of her crew and taken one of her two pulse-cannon batteries permanently offline.

The Collectors hadn't fared so well.

Their ships—derelict, dying, or dead—spun and tumbled through space amid debris and silvery clouds of frozen atmosphere. It had been the most one-sided fight he'd ever seen. Twenty-seven ships reduced to hulks or wreckage.

Why had they so doggedly insisted on fighting? After their first encounter, when they captured Splice, it should have been as clear as a laser beam to the Collectors that they had no chance against the far more powerful Cygnus mechs and fleet. It was supremely unlikely it had been some fanatical ideology; according to both Benzel and Wei-Ping, the Collectors were privateers, motivated by profit. Losing all your ships sure as hell wasn't *profitable*.

Dash looked for the Talon and found it closing back up with the Archetype after Amy had deviated to take out a corvette.

"Okay, Amy, with me. Let's go join Leira and Conover to help them take out those missile platforms—"

"Actually, Dash, we're pretty much done here," Leira said. "We've got…looks like two more platforms still operating."

"We'll come join you anyway," he said. "Benzel, once you're done picking up survivors, come join us."

"Will do," Benzel replied.

Dash powered off toward the Swift and the Pulsar, Amy in tow.

It didn't take long to bring the four mechs back together. By the time Dash and Amy had caught up, only a single platform remained intact. The Swift and Pulsar seemed to be hanging back from it, but it likewise showed no sign of any hostile action. It just hung there in space, apparently inert.

"Is there a reason you guys aren't blowing the hell out of that thing?" Dash asked as he decelerated the Archetype to a dead stop a few klicks away from the Swift. "Or are you saving it for me and Amy?"

"You're giving us a missile platform?" Amy said. "Aw shoot, guys. You shouldn't have."

"Don't get too excited, cuz," Leira replied to Amy. "It's not actually a missile platform."

Dash frowned. It looked no different than the other, now-demolished platforms surrounding it—except for the complete lack of missiles or other weapons fire, that is. "If it's not a missile platform, what is it?" he asked.

"That's what we're trying to figure out," Leira said. "Or, what Conover's trying to figure out, anyway."

"Could it just be a missile platform that's defective? It malfunctioned and never opened fire?"

"No," Conover replied. "Kristen's detecting nothing to suggest there are any warheads aboard it. In fact, there's nothing to suggest the platform's even armed at all, except for some point-defense."

"I do not like this assembly. Analyzing now." For Kristen, that was as close to cussing a blue streak as any of them had heard.

"Huh." Dash scanned the data being repeated from the Pulsar on the Archetype's heads-up. "So what the hell is it, then?"

"Like I said, not sure—" Leira began, but Conover cut her off.

"Got it. It's a communications platform. It seems to be set up to relay comm traffic in and out of deep space."

"Where in deep space?" Dash asked him.

"Not sure. Kristen's hacking into it, but she's not finding much. There are no comm logs, and any data, like receiver coordinates, is encrypted."

"She should have no problem breaking the encryption used by a bunch of pirates," Leira said.

"No, she wouldn't. But this isn't routine encryption. She says it's a Golden encryption scheme."

There was a moment of silence, which Amy broke.

"The Golden? What the hell are they doing here?"

"I don't know," Conover replied.

But Dash narrowed his eyes at the image on the heads-up. "I do. I know what they're doing. They're pulling the strings."

14

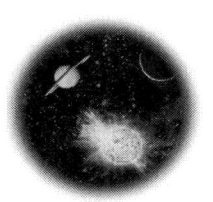

"Dash," Benzel said over the comm. "We can confirm that four Collector ships got away. All four were damaged—one popped into unSpace and went who-knows-where, but the other three dropped into orbit around the third planet's moon."

Dash called up the astrogation data for the star system they were in—four planets, three of them rocky worlds, the fourth a middling-sized gas giant. The mechs had already determined there were no Dark Metal signals from the gas giant, and the other three planets were just hunks of rock—airless, or nearly so. The third rocky planet indeed had a habitable moon, though.

While Benzel and A Squadron kept watch over the moon and approaches to it, Dash led the other three mechs into orbit. Scans of the planet revealed it to be rugged and heavily forested, with cloud-shrouded, rocky highlands looming over vast stretches of low-lying marsh and swamplands. The wetlands gave way to a pair of shallow, stagnant oceans roughly centered on each pole. There were hints of volcanic activity, too, probably from tidal stretching of the planet, the gas giant every time it swung past in its own orbit, and the primary star."

"Sentinel," Dash said. "Can you detect any lifeforms down there?"

"A multitude. In this hemisphere alone, not counting vegetable life, there are between one time ten to the—"

"That's fine. Human lifeforms is what I meant."

"I know."

"You know?" Dash smirked. "Were you—"

"Yanking your chain again? Yes. It seemed appropriate after a battle, as a means of relieving tension."

"You know, Sentinel, there are times I really regret that I can't buy you a drink."

"I nonetheless appreciate the sentiment. In any case, to answer your original question, I have determined where the shuttles from the orbiting Collector ships have landed. Two have touched down in the highland region indicated on the map. The third made a high-velocity impact in the southern ocean and was destroyed on impact."

"It crashed."

"I believe that's what I said."

Dash grinned and rolled his eyes. "Okay, everyone, I want to go take the Collectors down there alive—as many as we can, that is."

"Dash, are you talking about chasing in these mechs, or on foot?" Amy asked. "Because once we dismount, our butts are kind of hanging out in the open."

"Especially in that terrain," Conover said. "It's all rugged jungle, streams, waterfalls…"

Dash nodded at Conover's words, partly because they were quite true, but also because he knew there was more to it than that. It had been on another lush jungle planet that he, Dash, and Leira were pursued by some of the indigenous people when Conover fell into a pit-trap that almost dumped into an underground river and oblivion.

"That's okay. To be blunt, Conover, you and Amy aren't exactly the warriors-in-the-jungle types, and that's not what I want you to do anyway. I want you guys to head down into atmo and scare the living shit out of those Collectors. You're going to herd them right into Leira and me. We'll be outside our mechs, ready to take their surrender."

"Why don't you just stay inside your mechs?" Amy asked.

"Because they're more likely to surrender to a human face," Leira replied. "Let's face it, if you're being chased from above by something like the Pulsar and the Talon, and then you run into the Archetype and Swift, what are you likely to do?"

"Keep running," Amy said. "Got it. Okay, you guys just have to be really careful, okay? I worry about you enough, cuz, flying around the Swift like you do. Rounding up hostile people in the jungle—let's just say, it's not going to be any safer."

"I know, Amy," Leira said. "Don't worry, I'm *always* careful these days."

"Amy encouraging Leira to be careful," Dash said, shaking his head. "That's a switch. Anyway, yeah. I want to take at least some of these bastards alive, because we need to know who, or what, is at the other end of that relay link."

"I thought it was the Golden," Leira said. "Unless you're having another *feeling*."

"These days, I'm always having *feelings*, Leira. Always."

Dash offered a hand to Leira to help her step off one ledge and onto another. He studiously avoided looking down into the depths of the crevasse they were crossing. Water foamed along at least thirty meters below, although bashing against the sides on the way down would probably kill you before hitting the rocks at the bottom.

Once across, she pressed herself against the cliff. "Good thing I'm not afraid of heights, huh?"

"You're afraid of heights, aren't you?" Dash asked.

She looked at him with bright eyes, then nodded. "Damned right I am."

"Okay, so let's go this way," he said, gesturing along the ledge. "It should lead us up into those trees over there, which should put us smack across the path our friends seem to be following. Unless they've changed course, that is. Amy?"

Her voice hummed out of the comm hooked to Dash's tactical vest. "Nope. I've been flying back and forth across their path, kind of nudging them toward you. They don't seem interested in veering aside."

"I wonder where they think they're going," Conover said. He'd been holding the Pulsar at a higher altitude to keep a broad watch across the region against anything unexpected. "Once we chased them out of that bunker, I figured they'd just give up."

Dash glanced back along the ledge. The Collectors had originally taken refuge in a tough, well-concealed bunker they'd obviously constructed on this moon as a ground base. A single pulse-cannon burst from the Talon had persuaded them to exit it, though, and they'd been running this direction ever since. Amy was making a big show of looking for them under the tangled tree canopy; in fact, the Talon was more than capable of tracking them whether they were in sight or not. But as long as they thought they might have a chance to get away, they seemed determined to try.

And, he thought he knew where they were headed. They'd seen some caves back along the first ledge they'd followed, which would be much deeper in solid rock than their bunker.

Dash kept his senses at high alert. The Collectors weren't behaving at all the way he thought privateers would. Even Benzel was put off by their behavior, and that made them all the more suspicious.

Dash needed to know *why*. There was at least one connection with the Golden here, and there might be more.

Pulse-guns slung, he and Leira slunk along the ledge, which got progressively wider as it angled up the cliff-face. By the time they reached the top, it was a good two meters wide—and Leira was looking much happier about it. They crossed a short stretch of tall, sawtooth-edged grass that scraped at their body armor, then they stopped at the edge of a thick treeline. There they crouched, drinking from their water bottles, while Leira pulled a data pad out of a belt pouch and tapped at it.

"Here's the data repeated from the Talon," she said, angling the pad so they could both see it. "Looks like they're still a good five hundred meters off."

Dash nodded. Four white dots were coming steadily closer to their own location, which was marked with a green icon. The Archetype and Swift were about four hundred meters behind them now, hunkered down in the bottom of a steep-sided river valley, which was the continuation of the ravine they stood near.

"They're not moving very fast," he said, capping his water bottle and sliding it back into its belt case. He glanced at the treeline, an almost solid wall of foliage, massive ferns curling beneath umbrella-like trees with bark the color of blood. A scent of green rot hung in the humid air, while incessant hoots, howls, and shrieks sounded from unseen forest animals.

Wiping sweat off his nose, Dash added, "Not that I blame them, really. That jungle looks nasty."

Leira pointed at a spot on the data pad's display about two hundred meters ahead of them. "This ravine we just followed seems to turn that way, and it hits these contour lines—see, right here. There's got to be a waterfall or something there. And these Collectors do seem to be generally following this watercourse."

Dash nodded. "Good call. They'll be vulnerable coming down this cliff face where your waterfall would be. Let's go collect some Collectors." He hefted the pulse-gun and led the way into the jungle.

Leira rolled her eyes as she followed. "Collect some Collectors? Really?"

"I'm hot, sweaty, tired, and about to walk into a firefight. Give me a break, here, Leira, you're lucky to get anything even resembling wittiness out of me in the first place."

Dash found a fire position facing the waterfall just in time for something to snap through the undergrowth to this right. He flinched and ducked, then peered through leaves at the scene ahead of them.

Sure enough, the water that sluiced along the ravine behind them tumbled down a steep, rugged cliff with a ceaseless rattle and splash. Three figures were picking their way down the cliff face; the fourth, wherever they were, must have been keeping overwatch and noticed Dash.

"Amy, can you see anyone at the top of that cliff?" he said over the comm. "Hiding in the jungle, probably—"

"Yup, got him. He's about five meters to the right of the biggest rock at the top of the waterfall."

Dash focused his attention where she'd indicated but saw no one. "Leira," he hissed. "Do you see—?"

A pulse-gun shot rang out from his left, striking rock at the top of the waterfall. Leira adjusted her aim and fired again. The hidden sniper fired an instant later, but his shot went wide, passing above Dash and to the right.

Hers didn't.

Dash saw a body tumble out from behind a mound of rock then bounce down the face of the cliff. The other three immediately opened fire, spraying the jungle in Dash and Leira's general vicinity.

Slugs snapped and whined over and around them, and ferns and leaves shook as they were struck. One round hit close to Dash, spraying him with splinters of rock that clattered against his armor. He rolled once to the right and looked beneath a fallen log festooned with lurid yellow fungus, then he saw a shot and took it. His pulse-gun burst hit one of the Collectors, and the man dropped.

Two of the four were down, but the survivors still seemed determined to fight it out to the end. They dove into cover at the base of the cliff then began firing harassment rounds at Dash and Leira.

Dash wiped sweat from his eyes and cursed. "Just give up already!" he shouted. "We don't want to kill—"

Rounds cracked in around him, drawn by his voice. He scrambled backward, out of contact, then headed off to his right, away from Leira. Behind him, her pulse gun opened up, a quick series of shots that provoked a scream from one of the two remaining Collectors.

Dash crept forward again, using a fat, multi-trunked tree for cover. More sweat rolled into his eyes. As soon as he looked in the direction of the direction of their opponents, he saw bushes move, followed by a rapid-fire barrage of slug-shots toward Leira. Dash bit back a sudden, sharp pang of alarm at her lack of any return fire, then he raised the pulse gun, sighted through its scope, and fired three shots.

The incoming fire stopped.

"Leira, you okay?" she shouted

"I'm alive, if that's what you mean," she replied.

Dash waited a moment then shouted, "Cover me!" He ran forward and dove into a hollow behind a log, where he crouched.

There were no shots. No sounds, except the burbling rush of the waterfall, and maybe a faint moan.

"My turn. Cover!" Leira shouted.

He lifted the pulse-gun into the ready position and scanned for targets, the hot, damp air like syrup in his lungs. Leira crashed through the foliage then went still again somewhere off to his left.

There was still no return fire.

They pushed forward this way, one covering, the other one moving, until they found the first Collector, the last one Dash had shot. From the amount of his head that was missing, they assumed he was very much dead, and pushed on.

Eventually, they found all four. One, probably the first one Dash had shot, sprawled among rocks beside the rushing water, groaning. While Leira watched out, Dash approached him, pulse-gun raised, finger touching the trigger.

The man's eyes rolled toward Dash as he approached then

crouched beside him. He looked mid-forties, tough, but dying from a wound seared into his chest.

"Hey," Dash said. "I honestly don't know if I can save you. I'll try, but you have to tell me who's behind all this. Who the hell was making you guys keep fighting?"

The man looked at Dash, his eyes bright as glass. Dash frankly expected the man to be beyond coherent speech, or to just tell him where he could go and what he could do once he got there. But as Dash pulled a hypo out of a pouch on his belt and touched it to the man's neck, his mouth worked, bright red blood flecking his lips and scruffy beard.

"Her name—" He winced and groaned again.

Dash leaned closer. "Her name. Her. Was it Rumor?"

The man shook his head. "No. She…ran. Got away."

"Who is she?"

"Name…is—" He coughed, spitting up more blood. "She's—Sur—Sur-natha."

Dash stared.

"Sur-natha? From Clan Shirna? Are you sure?"

The man nodded, coughed again, then fought to speak, pushing the words out with terrific effort. "She…she hates. Hates light. Loves darkness. The Golden—they promised. Promised us. Promised her. They promised—"

He winced again, then gasped and tensed up. Dash touched another first aid hypo, but he hesitated. One should have helped stabilize this man, but he seemed to be getting worse, instead. A second might just be wasted, and he and Leira only carried three each.

To hell with it. He yanked out the hypo and touched it to the man's neck. After a few seconds, the brittle glassiness in the Collector's eyes softened, and he breathed a little easier, his breath not rasping quite so much.

"They promised…power. Tech. Whatever we…wanted. Sur-natha…wanted it all. Pledged herself to…to the Golden. Convinced Rumor—and Splice—to pledge, too."

"Where is Sur-natha?"

The man shook his head. "Don't know." He looked at the expended hypo, still in Dash's hand. "Trying…to save me."

"I am. Or—" Dash shrugged. "I tried. I don't know if it will—"

"Doesn't…matter." The Collector grabbed Dash's arm. "You're trying to…to save me. Not what Sur-natha said…you'd do."

"No, she kind of hates us—especially me."

"Got to stop her. Bring her into the light. Nothing makes her more furious. Nothing more than…daylight. Black of space. It's all she…loves. She fills it. With rage. Like an endless night. The others—the Golden, Sur-natha—all of them. We're just…things. Tools. That's what…what the Golden do, I think. What they did to her. Turn us into hate. Creatures of…of perfect hate. We're not people. Just things. Make us into…into things that rage in—" The man's eyes flew wide.

"—in the *night*."

He squeezed Dash's arm once, then his fingers went limp, he slumped back on the rock, and his eyes went dull and dark.

Dash blew out a long breath.

"Sur-natha?" Leira said. "How the hell did she—"

"Escape from the STA? Good question." Dash stood. "Believe me, someone is going to bloody well answer it, too."

15

Dash scanned the heads-up. All four mechs were back in orbit; the *Herald* and the rest of A Squadron prowled about a million klicks away, keeping a wary eye on the margins of the system for any relief forces that might be rushing to the Collectors' aid. But there were no hints of intervention.

"How the hell did Sur-natha get away from the STA?" Benzel snapped over the comm. "I thought they had the toughest jails in the arm. That's the line we were spun in the Gentle Friends, anyway."

"It might just be marketing," Conover offered.

"More likely some corruption in their ranks," Dash replied. "Their jails are pretty tough—a half-dozen, entirely separate habs scattered across four systems, no way on or off without a ship. And you can bet they screen the hell out anything arriving or leaving."

"Sounds like you might have some experience there, Dash," Amy said.

"Fortunately, no. Let's just say, though, that I always *knew* I could end up spending some time in one of them, so I did my homework. What it told me was there was no realistic way of escaping from them without inside help—and that meant greasing the right palms in advance."

"The Golden might have helped her escape, too," Conover said. "I doubt that you're, uh, security audits of the STA's jails took advanced alien tech into account, did they, Dash?"

"Funnily enough, no, it didn't."

"How she escaped isn't really the burning question right now anyway, though, is it?" Leira put in. "We can worry about the STA and their failure to keep Sur-natha locked up another time. Right now, the more pressing issue is, where the hell *is* she?"

"Right on point," Dash said. "That, and what the hell is her next move going to be, now that we've basically taken the Spiral Collectors out of the picture?"

"I may be of some assistance there," Sentinel said. "I have been conferring with Tybalt, Hathaway, and Kristen regarding the data we were able to retrieve from the comm relay platform and may have gleaned some useful information from it."

"Did you crack the Golden encryption?" Dash asked.

"No. That remains a significant challenge, one which Kristen continues to pursue."

"Have to admit," Amy said. "Knowing these AIs talk among themselves kind of gives me the creeps."

"Get used to it," Dash said. "Frankly, they do some of their best work when they're not slowing themselves down to deal with we imperfect humans."

"*Imperfect* is a most apt description," Hathaway said. "I mean that, of course, in the most complimentary way possible."

"How is imperfect ever a compliment, *Doctor* Dorkaway?" Amy shot back.

"It's Hathaway, you ingrate, and I'll have you know the honorific comes from—"

"Look, guys, work out your domestic problems on your own time, the way Sentinel and I do. Right now, what I want to know is what she and the other AIs have come up with about Sur-natha."

"While the contents of the comm traffic remain stubbornly encrypted, the message metadata log, used for error-checking transmissions, has proven much easier to decrypt," Sentinel replied. "The data it contains is much more limited in scope, and is much more repetitive."

"Okay, and? What does it tell us?"

"Before each transmission, the station must handshake with the one receiving its signal. We have been able to determine there are a total of nineteen transmitting sources that have been in contact with the relay station, at least as recorded by the metadata log."

"Yeah, but those nineteen stations could be anywhere," Leira said, echoing Dash's immediate thought.

"True," Tybalt replied. "But by cross-referencing them with known transmission sources, we have identified in other data logs collected from various sources—wrecked enemy ships, for instance—and we have been able to assign twelve of them to known locations that are unlikely to be Sur-natha's current location."

Suddenly intrigued, Dash leaned forward in the cradle. "Okay, so that leaves seven that are unidentified. And they could still be anywhere, right, because these aren't directional transmissions, are they?"

"Not, they aren't," Sentinel replied. "Of those seven, though, two account for seventy percent of the remaining message traffic."

"Moreover, by comparing the time stamps for the incoming and outgoing handshake signals, we can estimate the amount of time that it took for a round-trip message," Tybalt said.

"So you can estimate the distance the other station is from the relay," Conover said. "That's clever."

"Sure, I believe you, it's clever as hell. So what does that tell us?" Dash asked. "A distance gets us halfway there, but we still need a direction, right?"

"That is true," Sentinel answered. "By superimposing circles corresponding to the calculated distances on the star chart, we are able to discern which volume of space, or star systems, they pass through."

Dash felt like the AIs were just trying to build to a dramatic reveal. He was impressed at their resourcefulness, but right now, he just wanted to know what their next step should be. "Okay, guys, when we're back at the Forge, I promise I will sit through an hour-long presentation about all this stuff. Right now, what's the bottom line?"

"There are three candidate star systems likely to contain the two transmission sources in question," Sentinel said. As she spoke, the star chart appeared on the heads-up, with three systems highlighted.

Dash stared for a moment. "Oh. Wow. Okay, that's good work." He studied each system; none of the three really offered anything to set it apart from the other two, at least in any obvious way that might help them find Sur-natha. "Any chance we can narrow this down further, or do we just need to visit all three?"

The voice of a bubbly young woman came on the comm. Dash immediately thought it was Amy, but he quickly recognized the less familiar voice of Kristen.

"I think we can!" she said. "You see, this one here is currently the source of intermittent comm traffic, on channels close to the one used by the relay platform. That suggests something right there, doesn't it?"

One of the star systems lit up.

"Okay, let's hear whatever's coming out of that system," Dash said.

"Currently, there are no transmissions—" Sentinel began, then paused. "Correction. There are new comm transmissions."

The comm channel suddenly rattled with a harsh voice. It spoke in a clipped, almost frantic way. A constant rumbling rush of interference made individual words hard to make out—Dash thought he caught *attack*, and maybe *withdraw*. But it didn't matter. The tone was absolutely clear.

"That's a distress call," Dash said. "Someone in that system is calling for help."

DASH WATCHED INTENTLY as the *Herald*'s stealth-drone, deployed into the system while the Cygnus strike force remained well apart, began sending back telemetry. The system itself was nothing special, just a run-of-the-mill F-class star, with a half-dozen planets—two gas giants and four rocky worlds. None of the latter were habitable, one being too close to the star, leaving its surface a searing hellscape, the others too far away and just frozen, airless hunks of stone. But it wasn't the celestial bodies of the system itself that immediately caught Dash's attention.

It was the debris.

After a moment of silence, as everyone in the fleet took in the data pouring back from the drone, Amy spoke up.

"Holy crap. There was one *hell* of a battle here."

Dash nodded. Indeed, there had been.

A vast debris field sprawled through the system, mostly between the orbit of the gas giant and the next rocky world out from the star. Sentinel highlighted components amid the wreckage that were recognizable: fragments, hull plates, and structural members clearly of Golden manufacture; a drive section torn off a Verity frigate, still trailing a stream of glowing plasma; battered hulks that had once been Golden and Verity craft, along with a few others not immediately recognizable. Some of the debris was organic—body parts and frozen dollops of blood and other fluids.

"This was recent," Conover said. "In thermal, a lot of this debris is still warm. Some of the reactors are still hot."

"Yeah, and there's some unexploded ordnance drifting out there, too," Benzel put in. "We're counting—oh, at least a dozen missiles that either lost target locks and went inert, or just burned through their reaction mass."

"Like Amy said, one hell of a battle," Dash replied. "The question is, who was fighting who? Because it wasn't us."

"All of this wreckage appears to be of Golden manufacture," Sentinel said. "Or related to the Golden in some fashion. Some of it is unidentifiable, admittedly, but clearly not of human origin, or any other known source in the inhabited portion of the galactic arm."

"More evidence of a civil war within the Golden," Dash said.

"It would appear. However, there is a small chance that this was a single Golden fleet, which was attacked and destroyed by another force that took essentially no damage whatsoever."

Dash narrowed his eyes at that. "If that's true, and there's someone else out here that has no problem blasting apart a fleet of

Golden and Verity ships without taking any hits themselves, then they'd better be friendly, or we're just as screwed as they were."

"True, but as I said, the chance is small. I would not suggest giving it serious planning attention."

"I wasn't going to." Dash felt a frown crowd his features. There was a *lot* of salvage here for the taking. But the idea of just dropping into a system that had seen one—or two, or maybe even more— fleets utterly obliterated gave him a chill.

"Benzel, you keep your squadron back here. I'll lead the mechs in. If there's something truly dangerous or powerful in there we're not seeing, or it's some sort of elaborate trap, we'll come right back out. And if we can't, and we get stuck in a messy fight, you can come in and rescue us."

"Got it," Benzel replied. "Just be careful, Dash. Even if there's nothing big and bad lurking out there, that debris and all those unexploded missiles are still pretty dangerous."

"Everyone tells me to be careful. Do I have a reputation for *not* being careful, somehow?"

"Not anymore, you don't," Leira put in.

Dash could hear the teasing tone in her voice, but he heard—or *imagined* he heard, anyway—a hint of genuine worry too.

The teasing made him smile. The worry made him smile even more.

ASIDE FROM SOME dormant missiles that came to life—and were promptly destroyed as the mechs approached-- nothing else stirred amid the wreckage. It all just grimly whirled on in a multitude of stately orbits, a new debris field that would last thousands, perhaps tens or even hundreds of thousands of years.

"Okay," Amy said. "I have to admit, this is giving me the creeps."

"I hear that," Leira replied.

Dash nudged the Archetype aside, working around the shattered remains of a Verity cruiser. A large chunk of hull had been blasted out of its port quarter, revealing ruined compartments never meant to be exposed to space. Given what they'd found on other Verity ships, he couldn't help wondering just what sort of things had gone on in those cold, airless rooms. He didn't wonder about it for very long, though.

The smashed Verity ship fell away behind the Archetype. Ahead and to his left, another missile suddenly came to life, target-locking the mech and accelerating. Dash flashed it to fragments with a burst from the dark-lance. The other mechs occasionally snapped out shots, destroying lurking missiles, or even just blasting chunks of wreckage out of their way.

The debris field began to thin. They were reaching the innermost boundary of the battle.

"Okay," Dash said. "That seems to be most of it. We've got this one belt of wreckage that spans, what—about a quarter of an orbit around the star? And then a few more patches here and there, probably running fights between ships that broke away from the main battle—"

"Dash," Sentinel cut in. "I've detected a power-emissions signature, location on the heads-up now. Surveillance scanners have gone active. So has a high-power targeting system."

Dash looked at the source. There, in a tight orbit around the hellish, innermost planet, something had come to life.

"I'm activating countermeasures, Dash," Conover said. "I'll see if we can scramble their sensor returns."

"You do that. Meantime, Amy, you're with me. Leira, stay back out here with Conover. Cover him, but get ready to cover us, too."

As acknowledgements came in across the comm, Dash flung the Archetype onto a new course, boring straight in at the source of the active scans. Whatever it was seemed to be taking advantage of the planet's fiery soup of an atmosphere to at least partly conceal itself.

For a moment, the interference cleared, and Dash nodded. "It's another Golden missile platform. A big one, too—" He paused as a stream of new contacts broke away from it and began racing toward him and Amy.

"Incoming missiles," Sentinel said. "I am also detecting numerous small objects in the vicinity of the platform. They are accelerating themselves into higher orbits."

"Mines," Dash said. "Yeah, I see them. Amy, we've got about forty inbound missiles. It looks like Conover has managed to mess up the tracking on about, oh, say, ten of them. You fall behind me, cover my flanks, and I'll do most of the heavy lifting here."

"Roger that."

The Talon fell back from the Archetype until it was in a trailing position behind the bigger mech. Dash opened up with the darklance, taking out a missile with each shot. As soon as he did, another salvo of missiles launched from the platform. Then another.

"Dash, that's too many missiles for just the two of you to handle by yourselves. Conover and I are coming in."

Dash's gut instinct was to tell Leira to stay back, but he caught himself. Just because he'd developed some feelings—because that's what they were—toward her, he couldn't start treating her differently. A big part of what attracted him to her was her cool competence and unflinching willingness to dive into danger. They also couldn't afford to keep the Swift out of combat.

Most of all, Leira would be livid with him if she thought he might start coddling her, and rightly so.

"Roger that. Glad for the help," he answered, then forced his attention back onto the oncoming swarm of missiles fired by the automated platform.

It was a numbers game. The Archetype and Swift could only destroy the incoming missiles so fast. Sentinel predicted that between five and ten would get close to getting off damaging detonations.

The two mechs drove on anyway, pounding away at the missiles with dark-lance, distortion-cannon, pulse-cannon batteries and, eventually, point-defense systems. One missile managed to catch the Archetype in a nearby blast, doing minor damage and briefly knocking a few, non-critical systems offline. As for the Talon, though—

"Amy, you've got two missiles at your three o'clock!" Leira shouted as she powered her mech toward the battle.

"I see 'em!" Amy shouted back. One missile vanished under a barrage of pulse-cannon fire; the other jinked through a storm of point-defense shots—

—and slammed squarely into the Talon, the mech briefly vanishing in a dazzling flash and an expanding cloud of shimmering plasma. When it cooled and faded, it revealed the Talon spinning awkwardly, glowing fragments of ablative armor drifting along in its wake.

"Amy?" Dash said.

No answer.

"Dammit, Amy, are you okay?" Leira put in.

There was still no answer—and then there was a low groan.

"Oh, wow. That really hurt," Amy croaked.

"Amy, what's your status?" Dash asked. She mumbled something back, so Dash turned to Sentinel. "Contact Hathaway. Find out if Amy needs help."

"He reports moderate damage, including a temporary loss of primary stabilizers. The backups are now coming online."

Sure enough, the Talon righted itself. As it did, Amy cleared her throat.

"Okay. Yeah. Still in one piece. Anyway, guys, I'm okay," she said. "So that's what it feels like to take a solid hit, huh?"

"Yeah, welcome to the Meld," Dash said, letting his tensed-up muscles relax. "Hathaway okay as well?"

"I am irritated by the interruption but otherwise unscathed. I'll need a good buffing," Hathaway said.

"Well, I can do without *that* again," Amy replied. "How's that missile platform doing?"

"No more salvos, but it might be waiting for us to get in closer," Dash replied. "So, change of plan. Amy, you stay back and work with Talon to sort your mech out. Leira, let's you and I finish this platform off. Conover, you've got overwatch."

They acknowledged, and Dash resumed his charge at the missile platform, Leira racing in behind him.

DASH STUDIED the wreckage of the missile platform. Its cunning concealment in the uppermost reaches of the inferno planet's atmosphere meant it also needed constant boosts and corrections to its orbit to offset drag. Now dead, it had begun what would be a terminal fall, ending in the hellscape of the incandescent atmo.

"That was both easier and harder than I thought it would be," Leira said. The two mechs had found themselves with a fight on their hands, mainly because the platform had been both bigger and more heavily armored than others of its type, so it took longer to kill. But kill it they did, finally braving the minefield to get in close and pummel it once its missiles had obviously been expended.

"Yeah," Dash said. "We're going to have to study that battle recording when we get back. If this is a new type of Golden missile platform, it's going to be a lot tougher to deal with, especially in multiples. The immediate thing, though, is trying to salvage what we can from it."

"Dash, we've got way, way more wreckage in the rest of the system than we could possibly salvage already. Why don't we just let this one go?"

"Because it was alive, after everything else here was already dead. It might have data aboard that we can use."

"Tybalt gives the platform only about ten minutes before aerodynamic drag rips it apart. There's no way we could get aboard, find any data cores, then retrieve them and get back off in that time."

"I know. So, we'll have to do this the hard way. Leira, stay here, but be ready to come if I call you."

"Wait, what are you going to do?"

Dash answered by accelerating the Archetype directly at the platform. He hit atmo almost immediately, drag forces pulling the mech one way, then another. Sentinel began firing the thrusters in rapid succession, a sequence intended to keep the mech stable. The derelict platform now loomed ahead. It shuddered as the thickening atmosphere yanked at it, pieces of debris being torn off and flashing past the Archetype as it closed. By the time Dash reached it, it had begun to trail fitful wisps of flame that quickly grew in intensity.

"Okay, Sentinel, your best guess where the data cores might be," he said. "I'm thinking that central hub."

"Based on the remains of previous missile platforms we've encountered, that is a reasonable assumption. However, this is a new type, and potentially different—"

"Doesn't matter. We've got about one minute to get what we're going to get, so to hell with it. Central hub it is."

Dash applied power and slid across the outer ring of the toroidal platform. Fragments of debris banged and clattered against the Archetype's armor; now it, and the platform, had become wreathed in a corona of fire. Dash could feel the mech shuddering as the aerodynamic forces piled up.

He reached the central hub. Without hesitating, he grabbed the uppermost part of it, braced the Archetype's feet against the hull, and *pulled*.

Structural members strained, popped, and failed. All at once, the upper third of the hub ripped free. The sudden, massive shift in the Archetype's center of gravity, combined with the thunderous rush of air now getting as thick as water, flung the mech into a wild tumble. Dash fought grimly for control, wincing as the mech's legs slammed into the toroid, which began breaking apart around him. Desperately, he applied full power to the drive, lifting the mech and its prize back out of the blazing heat of the planet's soupy atmo.

Slowly, he gained altitude. But the enormous drag continued to tear at the mech and the remains of the hub. Dash realized he might have to give up the wreckage and just let it go, because he wasn't lifting fast enough. And even the Archetype, as powerful as it was, wasn't indestructible.

Something banged into the Archetype, and then the mech began to rise fast. He saw the Swift hanging onto his mech's torso, throwing its acceleration behind the effort. A moment later, the buffeting roar eased, then died as both mechs rose back into clear space. Far below, Dash saw the rest of the platform continue its plunge, a string of dazzling beads trailing long tendrils of flame—and then it was gone, vanished into the murky inferno.

"Well, that was something," he said.

"Were you actually prepared to let go of that damned piece of the missile platform, or were you going to let it drag you down into that furnace down there?"

"I would have let go. Eventually."

"Remember what you said when Benzel told you to be careful."

"Yeah."

"Listen to it again," Leira said, then she released the Archetype and backed the Swift away.

THEY LUCKED out and managed to find a single data core in the wreckage. While Benzel and the rest of the fleet began scavenging among the wreckage littering the system, Dash retrieved it—a leisurely task, compared to other space walks he'd done lately—and brought it back into the Archetype. The mechs had been outfitted with adapters that should allow almost any data core to be jacked in; they'd also physically isolated them from the mechs' critical systems to avoid contamination by alien software. Nonetheless, before accessing it, Sentinel erected a succession of firewalls, digital barriers that should be more than enough to prevent any shenanigans from the Golden core.

In the end, though, it didn't offer much up. This particular core seemed to be used for archival purposes only, so it contained nothing that would shed light on the massive battle fought here.

Dash examined the data as Sentinel summarized it on the heads-up. Most of it seemed to be largely uninteresting records of the missile platform's operating functions. He was about to shut it down and just leave it for Custodian to pore over, when something caught his eye.

"Sentinel, that entry there—the one I've just highlighted. Is that a reference to a Shroud?"

"It appears to be, yes. A cursory examination suggests that it describes a modification to the basic Shroud design. However, it will require some—"

"Dash," Benzel cut in. "I sent a message back to the Forge, like you said, to get more ships out here doing salvage."

Dash nodded. He still had serious misgivings about conducting a large-scale salvage op so far from the Forge, but there was just too much useful stuff here to pass up. "Okay," he said. "Thanks for the update—"

"That's not why I was calling," Benzel said. "We just got a burst of comm traffic that sounded like someone in trouble—another distress call, it seems. We're sending the data over to the rest of the strike force in case it comes up again."

"Roger that. Sentinel, did you detect anything?"

"No. However, Benzel is currently further away from the system's star, so he may be free of gravitational interference with long-range comms."

"Okay. Benzel, if you—"

An abrupt explosion of comm traffic, repeated from the *Herald*, cut him off. It was just gibberish, underlain by a harsh, rattling squeal. Dash immediately recognized the high-pitched racket.

"That's Golden machine language," he said.

"It is," Sentinel agreed.

Dash still had no real understanding of what seemed to pass for language among the Golden—and yet, ever since his experience aboard the crashed Golden ship on Gulch, he did. He couldn't actually translate it but, thanks to the strange "Meld" that had taken place with the wrecked ship's systems, he could still understand it—on some level, at least.

"They're under attack," Dash said. "The Golden ship transmitting this is under attack."

"Good," Benzel snapped. "Hope they get their asses thoroughly kicked."

But Dash just frowned at the heads-up, not seeing it, but seeing *through* it.

"I can't believe I'm saying this out loud," he finally said. "But let's go help those Golden."

A series of replies tumbled back over the comm.

"Seriously?"

"Are you crazy?"

"What the hell?"

"I've got a feeling," Dash replied. "This isn't one big happy family anymore. If I'm taking bets, I'd say we're seeing an ugly little war, and everyone involved is related."

A moment of silence was broken by a markedly disgusted sigh from Leira. "And I thought I couldn't stand my sister."

16

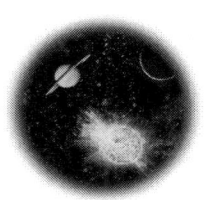

Dash scrutinized the heads-up as the Archetype dropped out of unSpace. He immediately saw the Swift about a thousand klicks off to his right, and nothing else in the immediate vicinity. Further off, the display showed pulses of energy discharge that spiked, then died, then spiked again.

"That's weapons fire," Leira said.

"Yeah, it is. Looks like three ships attacking a fourth. That must be our Golden friends."

"The three attacking ships match the configuration of Verity vessels," Sentinel said.

Dash nodded. "And there we go. That's confirmation—there's some sort of rift within the Golden."

"Looks good on them," Leira snapped. "If we're lucky, maybe they'll just all kill themselves off."

"Or one side wins, and we lose what could be a window of opportunity to gain some *really* useful new allies."

"Unless both sides are still determined to exterminate us, and they're just disagreeing about how to do it."

"Well, there's only way to find out. Let's go help that Golden ship against the Verity."

Dash powered up the drive and charged toward the combat, and Leira fell into formation with him. He heard her sigh, but she didn't raise any other objections.

He'd decided to leave the rest of the strike force, including Amy and Conover, salvaging wreckage and gathering intelligence back at the huge battlefield they'd found. Dash would have liked to have the extra firepower, especially from the other two mechs, but part of him was also relieved to not have to ride herd on Amy and Conover as they became accustomed to flying the alien constructs. It was a distraction; Leira, on the other hand, seemed to know his mind, and vice versa, so he could just leave her to do whatever needed to be done and concentrate on the fight.

"The Verity vessels have detected us," Sentinel said. "Two of them have broken off their attack on the Golden ship and are now moving to intercept us."

"I see that," Dash said. "Nice of them to come to us like this."

The Verity closed to missile range and launched a salvo, followed by streams of long-range pulse-cannon fire. Dash responded with dark-lance shots that struck one of the Verity ships, damaging it. He then had to turn his attention to the inbound missiles; by the time he and Leira had destroyed them, the Verity ships had turned and burned away, breaking contact and fleeing into unSpace. The third one made a final pass at the crippled Golden ship, then it also broke off and fled at the approach of the two mechs.

"Yeah, you'd better run," Leira muttered. "Damn cowards."

Dash gave a grim chuckle, then he and Leira closed on the damaged Golden vessel. A quick scan revealed that its translation drive had been damaged, which had prevented it from escaping. It also revealed no apparent signs of life on board.

"They're all dead?" Leira asked.

"Or they escaped," Dash replied, but Sentinel cut in.

"The escape-pod ports are still closed. If they escaped their vessel, they did not use the pods to do so," she said. "It is more likely that none have survived."

"Shit. Then I guess we'll have to—"

Another squeal of commotion erupted across the comm. Dash winced.

"Another Golden ship, and it's also under attack," he said. "Holy crap, there's a lot of fighting out here."

"Yeah, and we weren't invited," Leira said.

"I have determined the source-location of the transmission," Tybalt said. "Displaying now."

A window popped open on the heads-up, showing the nearby volume of space. This newest distress call came from only a light-hour away.

"Okay, well, we've come this far," Dash said. "Sentinel, mark the location of this Golden ship. We're going to help this one. Calling now. Let's hope we get there in time to actually do something useful."

This time, they detected only a single Verity ship in close proximity to another Golden vessel. There were no weapons-discharge signatures this time; Dash suspected that the nearness of the two vessels meant that one side was boarding the other.

"Well, let's go and see if we can help," he said. "Unless it's the Golden boarding the Verity, in which case—"

"The Golden vessel is heavily damaged," Sentinel said. "It is likely incapable of defending itself further."

"So the Verity are boarding the Golden ship," Leira said. "That's strange."

"All of this is strange," Dash replied. "But we need to know what's going on. Let's go."

They raced in toward the paired ships. As they did, another pair of Verity ships dropped out of unSpace. They began to close on Dash and Leira, while the third detached from its Golden victim and accelerated away.

"I want that damned Verity ship, the one trying to escape," Dash snapped.

"Well, we're going to have to fight our way through these two assholes first," Leira replied, just as the Verity ships loosed successive salvos of missiles.

It galled Dash to do it, but he and Leira slowed their approach, giving themselves some more time to deal with the oncoming waves of missiles. He gritted his teeth as the third Verity ship translated away. He couldn't stop thinking that the answer to all this was aboard that ship—the explanation as to what, exactly, was happening between these Verity and the Golden. One side, at least, had to be a breakaway faction.

He had to turn his attention back to the cloud of missiles racing toward them. "Know what? I don't have time for this shit."

He fired the distortion-cannon, targeting the missiles, wrenching them off their trajectories, then followed up the dark-lance, slamming hits into one of the Verity ships. At the same time, Leira punched out blasts from the Swift's nova-gun, then loosed a missile barrage of her own. Once the mechs' point-defense batteries opened up on the surviving missiles, Dash and Leira concentrated their fire on first one of the Verity ships, then the other.

A quartet of missiles made it through the close-in fire of the point-defenses; one detonated close to the Swift, sending Leira momentarily spinning before she regained control. The other three had locked onto the Archetype; Dash ignored them, letting the shield absorb the blast energy of two of them, and the third just detonated against the armor.

He cried out as the shock of the blast rattled through him, but he gritted his teeth and bored in. The relentless passage of time grated on him like a scrolling chrono, each second meaning the Verity ship he wanted to run down slid further away through unSpace.

"Screw it," he finally snapped. He decelerated the Archetype and powered up the blast-cannon.

"Dash, if that thing misfires, you could be left—"

"Dead in space. Yeah, I know. I'm just going to have to take that risk."

Pulse-cannon fire flashed against the Archetype's regenerating shield. At the same time, the wing-like accumulators that charged the blast cannon spread, then they began crackling with energy spillover. The shield finally died, and pulse-cannon shots crashed into the Archetype's armor—

And then the blast-cannon fired, a full charge that engulfed both Verity ships in a colossal explosion, like a new and fleeting star. The weapon traded an abysmally slow rate of fire and a chance of knocking the Archetype offline for a truly stupendous amount of damage.

"Now that's a *boom*," Dash said.

One of the Verity ships came tumbling out of a searing cloud of plasma so energetic it washed the space around it with hard x-rays; its entire port side had been laid open, hull-plating and structural components reduced to glowing slag. The other Verity ship was further from the epicenter and emerged mostly intact, albeit heavily battered.

Dash's eyes swept across the Archetype's status display. A few systems had gone offline and were rebooting, but everything else still showed green. Without hesitating, he deployed the power-sword and closed on the damaged Verity ship, which responded with fitful bursts of pulse-cannon fire. Dash dodged and wove his way in close, then slashed out with the sword, carving chunks out of his quarry. Leira joined him, punching the Swift's fists through hull plates, then wrenching them free. In less than a minute, they'd reduced the Verity ship to scrap.

"Okay," Dash said, watching the remains of the two Verity ships drift slowly away. "That's that. Now let's go get that bastard who wanted to get away. Remember, though—I want to take that ship as alive and intact as we can."

BY DRIVING the mechs hard and risking damage to their translation drives, they were able to catch up with the fleeing Verity ship. They dropped out of unSpace, the two mechs well apart, to take their target in a pincer attack, forcing it to split its fire. It didn't. Instead, it concentrated its pulse-cannons and missiles on the Swift, which the

Verity must have perceived as the weaker of the two mechs; Leira nimbly dodged and jinked, avoiding most of the fire, but otherwise keeping the Verity busy. It was a tragic mistake, leaving Dash a free hand.

He again deployed the power-sword, and raced in to attack, eyeing the Verity ship as he closed and deciding where to strike to cripple it. Just as he began to line up his final attack run, though, the Verity ship abruptly exploded.

The flash and plasma-blast washed over the Archetype. The shield absorbed most of the energy, with only enough leaking through to cause minor damage to the mech's armor. Dash swore and pulled the Archetype up short of the expanding cloud of gas and debris.

"Damn. So much for getting any info out of these assholes," Dash snapped. There'd be no salvage, either, but that seemed like a much lesser concern right now. "They either had critical damage already that we didn't detect, or there was something aboard that ship they didn't want us to know about."

"At least the cloud is pretty," Leira said.

"Silver lining and all that, yeah." Dash sighed. "Well, we've still got two disabled Golden ships back there. Let's return to them and see what they can tell us."

THEY CLOSED on the stricken Golden ship, which coasted along on its last trajectory, apparently dead. According to Sentinel, it would reach the nearest star system in about eleven thousand years.

Dash studied the lifeless ship. "Kind of eerie, actually. Like a tomb. In the black."

"Yeah, have to admit, I'm not keen to board it," Leira said. "Oh, and not just because of the creepy factor. We don't know what's going on in there."

"Sentinel, anything suggesting anyone's left alive on board?" Dash asked. He expected the answer to be no, as it was for the first Golden ship they'd found, but Sentinel's answer surprised him.

"This time, I am detecting signs of life," she said. "The scans return combined biological and technological signatures."

"Huh. I guess those could be Golden *or* Verity."

"Given that there are two distinct types of signal, I would suggest both," Sentinel replied. "A majority of Verity, and fewer Golden."

Dash scowled at the ship drifting along on its long, *long* journey to the nearest star system. Like Leira, he didn't relish the prospects of boarding it. There were just the two of them, and so much could go wrong once they were on foot, protected only by body armor and vac suits.

"To hell with it," he finally said. "Leira, let's just crack this nut open and see what's inside."

"Works for me," she replied, sounding distinctly relieved.

Dash powered the Archetype to one flank of the Golden ship, while Leira approached the other. Dash didn't bother with the power-sword this time, he just slammed the Archetype's massive fists through the hull plating and ripped it free. A brief gale of venting atmosphere engulfed the mech; Dash saw the Swift likewise vanish behind a shimmering cloud of fog that quickly dispersed. Debris shot out of the stricken ship, gusted along by the rush of escaping gas, and bounced off the Archetype.

Some of it was bodies—Verity. Probably what remained of a boarding party that had been left behind when their ship fled. And

Golden. Dash grabbed one of the latter and carefully placed it in one of the Archetype's leg compartments. Pockets were handy, even on a giant robot.

"Their data cores might tell us more of what we want to know," Dash said. "But we already know they're hard to decrypt. Maybe this body will reveal something. For that, though, we need to head back to the Forge."

He called up Benzel and gave him instructions to organize a massed recovery of salvage from the battlefield, as well as the skirmishes he and Leira had just engaged in. Then he set course back to the Forge, determined to get the Golden's body under the proverbial microscope.

There was one sure way to tell if the Verity and the Golden were fighting, and the corpse he'd recovered might just reveal it.

He hoped so, anyway, because it might make fighting this war a much less uncertain thing.

17

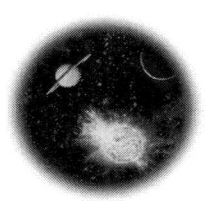

It turned out Dash was right, and it didn't take a microscope, or even complex scans, to tell that.

He stared down at the Golden corpse, which was sprawled in a sealed compartment near the Forge's infirmary. Like the few they'd seen previously, it was an unnerving fusion of primate-like organic body and dark, sleek metallic components, forming what amounted to a suit of some sort, or even a set of armor. Their newest and most capable doctor, a former refugee named Saddiq, had officiated over analyzing the body. Dash had called ahead as they were translating back to the Forge, warning Custodian about the body they'd recovered and conveying his urgent need to have it investigated; Custodian had, in turn, informed Saddiq, who had pulled the Golden corpse they'd retrieved from the crashed ship on Gulch and taken time to study it, to prepare himself to examine this one.

"Not that it takes a great deal of detailed analysis to say that a big chunk of its skull is missing," Saddiq said, pointing at the Golden's head. "I mean, I could compare it to the one you already had in storage, but a piece of missing head and brain is—well, I'd say the probable, proximate cause of death."

Dash shrugged. "Yeah, I'm not even a doctor and could probably have worked that out for myself." He narrowed his eyes at the repulsive spectacle of the Golden's damaged head. "It doesn't look like it was blown open, though. That looks too neat."

"That's because it isn't just a wound from a weapon," Saddiq replied. "Or, at least, if it is, it's a unique weapon, one that leaves very straight, clean edges."

Leira curled her lip. "This was surgical, wasn't it?"

"I would say so, yes," Saddiq replied.

"So this Golden was, it seems, having its nervous tissue harvested by the Verity," Dash said. "That's pretty ironic."

"And also kind of sad," Leira added. "Which actually floors me, the idea that I'd ever feel *sorry* for one of these monsters."

Dash nodded. "Yeah. But if we look past the sad irony, what we've got here is the evidence I was hoping we'd find. The Verity—at least some of them, anyway—have turned on the Golden—or, again, at least some of them."

"So who are the rebels?" Saddiq asked. "Is it a breakaway faction of the Verity, or has an element within the Golden gone rogue?"

Dash narrowed his eyes at the corpse. "Not sure. If I had to guess one way or the other, I'd say the Golden are probably the rebels in this scenario. The fact the Verity were collecting their nervous tissue suggests to me that they haven't changed their ways."

"Plus, the Golden were putting out distress calls," Leira said. "It was in their machine language, but they broadcast it omni-directionally and must have known it might get picked up by us. So they weren't just looking for help from other Golden, were they?"

Dash shook his head. "No. Or at least I don't think so, but we don't know for sure. I mean, they may have been desperate and just didn't care who picked up their transmissions." He rubbed his chin. "But let's work with the assumption there's some sort of rift within the Golden, and some of them have turned against the rest. So…" He looked at Leira.

"Well, then I guess we need to try and make some sort of contact with the rebels. They might still be hostile to us—after all, just because they're breakaways from the other Golden doesn't mean they're going to want to be friendly with us."

Dash nodded. "True enough. The enemy of my enemy thing only goes so far." He sighed. "Well, I guess this means we have to—"

"Excuse me for interrupting," Custodian said. "I have completed scans of the Golden corpse and thought you may be interested in the results."

"Go ahead," Dash said.

"While there are specific differences between this particular specimen of the Golden race and the one you previously returned to the Forge, in a general sense, they are quite similar. However, this particular individual has an anomalous Dark Metal signature emanating from the bottom of its right foot."

Dash glanced at Leira and Saddiq, who both shrugged. Saddiq retrieved a scalpel from a nearby instrument tray and they all turned their attention to the foot in question.

It was one of the few fully organic parts of the Golden, a narrow foot covered in tawny fur, with long, prehensile toes. Custodian opened a holo-image of the foot, showing the location of—whatever it was. Using that as a guide, Saddiq made a careful incision in the bottom of the foot then extracted something the size of Dash's thumbnail.

"There's no scarring, or anything else to indicate that this was ever implanted," Saddiq said, studying the area of the incision. "How they got it implanted in there, I have no idea."

"Not surprising, doc," Dash said. "You are, after all, saying that while standing aboard an enormous space station that's nothing but super-advanced tech run by super-advanced AIs."

Saddiq smiled. "True enough. Anyway, what is this?" He held up the object, gripped lightly in a pair of forceps.

Leira narrowed her eyes at it. "Looks like a data chip, or processor chip, or something like that."

"You are correct, Leira," Custodian said. "It appears to be a data storage device, a micro-core."

"So, I guess we should plug this into a reader somewhere and find out what's on it," Dash said. "Custodian, do you have a port for something like this somewhere?"

"There is a compatible interface in the Command Center. I will prepare it for use."

Saddiq dropped the chip into a specimen bottle and handed it to Dash.

"So this is implanted in the bottom of this guy's foot," Leira said, looking at the bottle as Dash held it up. "Sounds like someone was trying to hide something so they could—what? They were stealing it? Smuggling it?"

Dash shrugged. "Only one way to find out. Join me in the Command Center?"

"Right behind you."

Dash asked Custodian to assemble everyone—except for Wei-Ping, who was supervising recovery ops at the massive battlefield they'd found—in case whatever turned out to be on the micro core was important.

"Might be a bunch of the guy's favorite recipes or something," Harolyn said, prompting brief laughter. But Dash could feel the tense anticipation among his key officers, his Inner Circle. If this had been retrieved from a rogue Golden, and it somehow helped give them a window of opportunity to get engaged with said rogue Golden, it could mean a dramatic, even decisive turning point in the war.

Or, it could be recipes.

Dash avoided touching the micro core; he'd experienced direct contact with the Dark Metal-infused substance of Golden tech aboard the crashed ship on Gulch. It had leveraged his capacity to Meld with the Archetype to *communicate* with him—and it wasn't something he was anxious to repeat. He'd already warned Leira, Amy, and Conover to be similarly wary of directly handling Golden tech. He let Viktor do the honors instead.

Even so, when Dash dumped the micro core into Viktor's hand, Dash braced himself. Viktor just stared at the little device resting on his palm.

"Viktor?" Dash asked. "You feel anything?"

Viktor glanced around at everyone staring at him. "Yes, I feel a little self-conscious about everyone looking at me, thanks."

Dash grinned and gestured at the port Custodian had prepared. Before Viktor could insert it, though, Ragsdale spoke up.

"Aren't we worried about plugging Golden tech directly into a Forge system? I mean, I know the firewalls and everything are probably amazing, but they're still basically on par with the Goldens' capabilities."

"I have isolated the system in question from the rest of the Forge," Custodian replied. "It is entirely quarantined."

"Physically quarantined? As in, no hardware connections to the Forge's network?"

"If you wish to disconnect the physical connections, you will have to do so manually."

Ragsdale looked at Dash, who shrugged. "I've learned that when it comes to matters of security, I'm almost always better off deferring to you and your paranoia."

"When everyone really *is* out to get you, paranoia is just another name for smart thinking," Ragsdale replied. Custodian walked him through the process of opening an access panel on the terminal in question and physically disconnecting it from the Forge's network. Custodian even activated an internal backup so the power connection could be pulled, too.

When he was done, Viktor inserted the micro core into the reader. Dash frankly expected to find it encrypted, meaning they'd have to find another secure way of accessing it—maybe aboard one of the Silent Fleet ships? But the display immediately lit with data.

Viktor scrolled through it. It didn't take long.

"One diagram? That's all this contains?" Dash asked, peering over Viktor's shoulder.

"That's how it appears," Viktor replied. "This diagram, and nothing else. The rest of the storage is just empty." He shrugged. "I suppose there could be hidden data, but if there is, it's hidden."

They stared at the diagram. It depicted a construct of some sort, several symbols in the Golden language, and a series of coordinates.

"That looks like it's supposed to be a sky hook," Conover said. "A schematic, or something similar."

Dash nodded. "Yeah. Except this is the plan for a complete one, I think."

"What are these other symbols?" Ragsdale asked. "And these coordinates?"

"Since this thing is cut off from the rest of the network, I'm assuming Custodian can't actually read it," Benzel said. "Does he need us to read these out loud for him?"

"That will not be necessary," Custodian said. "I am able to discern the data through visual means."

"So that means Custodian doesn't just overhear us, he sees us, too?" Amy said. "Looks like I'm going to have to start showering with a bathing suit on."

"That is also not necessary," Custodian said. "Your physical form is of no interest to me, Amy."

She made a *hmph* sound. "I'll take that as, well, not a compliment."

"Incidentally, you should have infirmary personnel examine that mole on your—"

"That's enough of that, you," Amy snapped. "We do not discuss my moles in public."

Dash grinned, but it faded into a thoughtful frown as he studied the Golden characters. "That has something to do with…space-flight. No, wait. Translation." He pointed at the symbols. "Yeah, translation through unSpace. But not just star-to-star. This is talking about translation inside a star system. No, it's even more specific." He let the residual memories of his interface with the Golden ship just play through his Meld. "It's describing a way of translating into a planetary atmosphere—" He stopped, his eyes going wide.

"What is it?" Leira asked.

Dash just stared as it all came together. It was as though someone had handed him a key to this diagram that explained it all.

"Those coordinates are star systems with gas giants," Dash said, still staring at the display.

"That is correct," Custodian replied. "I was just about to portray them on the main display."

"Go ahead," Dash said, without taking his eyes off the image. "There's a skyhook like this one inside each of those gas giants. Each of those skyhooks is being used to store Q-cores. They were put there by translation, through unSpace, right into the planet's atmosphere."

A long moment of silence followed. Dash finally blinked and looked away from the schematic to find everyone just staring at him.

"What?" he asked.

Viktor looked at the others then spoke up. "Dash, that's not possible. Everything we know about the physics of unSpace translation precludes you from safely doing it too deep inside a gravitational field."

"And when the strength of that field gets high enough, it isn't possible at all," Conover added. "The amount of energy required becomes infinite. That's what the math tells us, and that math is pretty well understood."

"And I'd say that inside the atmosphere of a freaking gas giant is deep enough in its gravity well that translation just isn't possible," Viktor finished.

Dash nodded. "I know. It sounds insane. But that's what this schematic is showing us. In fact, there's a whole bunch of information buried in this diagram of the skyhook." He pointed at what looked just like different components. "There's stuff encoded in every measurement, angle, and ratio in this diagram. I mean, it's beyond me to work out the math involved, but it's there."

Leira bit her lip in thought. "Well, we do know that the Unseen have the ability to skirt unSpace—you know, kind of ride the boundary between it and real space, the region they call the Darkness Between."

"Sure, but we looked at that," Conover said. "And the mathematics of translation allow it, because you're not actually crossing that boundary. As soon as you do, though, the math just falls apart and you end up with results that are either infinite or entirely undefined."

Viktor gave Conover a curious glance. "What were you mathing that out for? Some idea you had?"

"No, just because I was interested in it."

Leira smiled. "So, for fun."

"I guess so, yeah."

Amy snorted a laugh. "You're weird, Conover. Good thing you're cute."

Conover gaped at her for a moment then turned progressively deeper and deeper shades of red.

Dash smiled at that but turned his attention to the main display. "There are Q-cores hidden in each one of those gas giants Custodian's highlighted up there. At least, there were. They were placed onto the skyhooks by a system—a capsule of some sort, I think—that translated them there directly."

"Okay," Benzel said, crossing his arms. "Why? What was the point?"

Dash shrugged. "Not sure. They were storing them, maybe, or they were using to power something we haven't figured out yet."

"Or something they meant to build but just never got around to," Leira said.

Dash nodded. "In any case, that's what this is about. And that makes me believe even more that there's a breakaway faction of the Golden. The body we retrieved had had this micro core implanted in its foot, suggesting it was meant to be retrieved by someone, at some point. I can't imagine he just liked the idea of body modification. Anyway, that suggests he was hiding it, which meant he was hiding it *from* someone."

"And he was taking it *to* somewhere," Harolyn said, picking up the line of thought. "Or at least *away* from somewhere. From Golden home space, maybe."

"And bringing it to us?" Amy said.

Dash looked back at the diagram. "Maybe. To anyone who wasn't able to read this, it would just be a picture of a skyhook, some coordinates, and some symbols. They could probably work out the stuff about the skyhooks somehow being related to these gas giants eventually, but that would be it. But to someone who's Melded with Golden tech and had it inside their head—"

"Like you," Viktor said.

"Yeah, like me—it's a lot more. We *have* to make contact with these rogue Golden."

"In the meantime, Messenger, I have given my attention to the issue of the translation into a strong gravity well," Custodian said. "Conover is quite correct in that the fundamental physical properties of space and time normally preclude it. However, there is a—I believe you would call it a *loophole*."

Dash glanced at the others. "And that *loophole* is…?"

"Time."

Dash winced. He was afraid of that. He and Amy—him in the

Archetype, and her piloting the *Slipwing*—had a truly bad experience with a wonky translation right before a battle that had given him a glimpse of a terrible future, one in which the Swift had been destroyed and Leira almost certainly killed. They'd been able to effectively undo it and return themselves to the correct timeline, but it had left him deeply unnerved. He still sometimes dreamed about it and would come awake gasping, sweaty, and wondering if they'd actually prevented that future from happening—or if there was now an alternate timeline, in which Leira had died and the war might have been lost.

"Time is a variable in the math," Conover said. "But it's always a positive number. The only way it would make the math work out for translating into a gravity well is..." He went quiet, his tech-enhanced eyes distant. "You're talking about time being a negative number, aren't you?" he finally said. "If it is, then the amount of energy is never infinite. In fact, the more negative it is—"

"The *less* energy it would take to translate," Viktor said, but then shrugged. "But, so what? Time doesn't run backward."

"It can, however, as a byproduct of this form of translation," Custodian said. "The schematic presented here allows for it."

This time, the silence in the Command Center was what Dash would call stunned. Even the duty ops personnel had stopped to stare.

"Are you saying we can travel backward in time?" Dash finally asked.

"Yes. In fact, it is an inevitable side effect of this translation method."

"That's—crazy."

"It is," Leira said. "The potential for screwing things up is... well, enormous. I mean, what if you go back and just by being somewhere you originally weren't, you change the trajectory of some dust particles and end up completely rewriting history?"

"That would be extremely unlikely as the behavior of the vast majority of dust particles in the universe has little bearing on events at the macro scale," Custodian said. "However, your point is sound, Leira. The potential for harm to the timeline is significant, whether inadvertent or deliberate."

"I think we should just delete this schematic and call it a day," Amy said. "This is just too—" She stopped, fumbling for a word. "It's too crazy. Too dangerous."

Dash just stared at the schematic.

"Custodian, if we put a lot of energy into this translation, then we don't go back very far, right?"

"That is how the equations resolve, yes."

"Okay. And this is meant to be installed in some sort of capsule, with limited power, right?"

"Yes. I would estimate that the maximum power generation of the capsule described would result in a time shift of several hours to several days."

"Enough time to really screw things up," Leira said.

"Yeah, and am I pissed that the Golden are able to do this," Dash replied.

"Well, if it makes you feel better, they're probably just as keenly aware as we are of the potential to really mess up history," Harolyn said.

"Yeah." Dash rubbed his face, thinking. "But what about the power available to the Archetype? The singularity that powers it is generating way, way more energy than we need, mainly because the mech doesn't have all the power cores and things in place to use it all yet, right? But if there was a way to tap into that full power potential and use it, then how small would the time-shift be?"

"It could be reduced to seconds," Custodian replied. "As long as the time variable is a negative number, its magnitude is irrelevant."

"Dash, I'd really think long and hard about this before you—" Leira began, but Dash raised a hand.

"Custodian, I'd like you to see if the Archetype can be rigged up to do this. If we can retrieve a bunch of Q-cores, we would get a dramatic power-up for the Forge, our mechs—everything. Even better, we can deny them to the Golden."

Dash saw the look on Leira's face, and he smiled. "If this is feasible, it will only be used for the Archetype, and only by me. The schematics will be locked away in the most secure part of the Forge's data stores, subject to immediate deletion if there's even a hint they might be compromised." He shrugged. "We have to explore this, Leira. It's too valuable an opportunity to pass up."

Leira glanced at the others, then a *to hell with it* expression spread across her face. "Dash, we're risking you and the Archetype on something that could really screw up everything."

Dash didn't miss the slight emphasis on the *you*.

"I'd also point out that, if this works, you're also talking about translating deep into the atmosphere of a gas giant," Viktor said. "Even the Archetype has its limits, Dash."

"Okay, believe me, I've got no death wish here, folks," Dash replied. "If the risk seems to outweigh the benefit, then we'll shelve this and move on. But I want Custodian and the other AIs to at least take a crack at it and see if it's feasible."

A sullen silence fell off the end of his words. Dash saw glances being exchanged and knew at least some of them were looking for reasons to object. But he'd already run through all the objections he could think of and still couldn't find a reason to not at least give this a try.

And that was despite the fact that he actually wished he had thought of a deal breaker. But he hadn't, and apparently neither had anyone else.

Amy finally broke the grudging quiet. "If this does work, can I pop back to my seventeenth birthday? There are a couple of things I did that night I'd *love* to be able to not have done."

Conover shot Amy a quick look. "Like what?"

Everyone laughed, but it faded quickly. As the group broke up to go to their various duties, Dash couldn't help noticing that no smiles remained on their faces, just a somber thoughtfulness.

That was what war did. It stole everything from you. Even the ability to laugh, if only for a second.

DASH WATCHED as another component for the atmospheric translation unit—and they really needed a better name for it than that—was extracted by robotic arms from a mold and moved in the direction of the final assembly bay. He'd asked Custodian to prioritize its assembly, but also to take no chances. He had Custodian banish everyone except him and Leira from the fabrication plant while the device was being assembled, whereupon the schematics would be moved to a heavily protected part of the Forge's data stores, deeply encrypted, and subject to an immediate and irrevocable wipe if the station was ever threatened with being compromised.

Dash wanted to ensure that no one could ever get their hands on what amounted to a time machine. Leira agreed, but still didn't think this was enough.

"Dash," she said, as they walked after the component toward the assembly bay. "I'm going to ask you again to not do this. Even allowing something like this to exist is dangerous. We should just delete the schematics for this thing and forget they ever existed."

"I actually agree with you, Leira," Dash said, stopping near a Dark Metal conduit and sticking his hands in his pockets. "Believe me, I had one little taste of being displaced in time, and I never want to experience that again. But we're in the middle of—"

"A war. Yeah, I know. The trouble is, we can use the whole *we're at war* thing to justify pretty much anything we want."

"So maybe the big test for us is the awful things we *could* justify but choose not to. Or we do choose them, despite how awful they are, because the alternatives are even *more* awful." He pulled his hands out of his pockets and crossed his arms. "It gets even worse, of course, because we'll probably end up facing those types of choices over and over again. So, enabling a way of traveling backward in time is bad, yes. It can lead to no end of trouble. But doing it gives us a chance to retrieve Q-cores, which will give us a better chance of ending this war and doing it sooner rather than later. Before, say, Conover ends up being our age and still fighting the damned thing."

Leira laced her fingers behind her head and sighed. "Both you and Amy have made it pretty clear that whatever you saw when you slipped in time before that battle was pretty bad."

Dash remembered the sight of the shattered wreckage of the Swift. He'd never told Leira any details of it, and he'd sworn Amy to secrecy as well. He wasn't even sure why. The Swift hadn't been wrecked and Leira hadn't been hurt or killed—in this timeline, at least. But he just couldn't bring himself to reveal it to Leira. He finally just nodded. "Yeah, it was."

"So you might be making it possible for someone else to do something similar."

He nodded. "I know. I might. But if it's that, or facing the extinction of everyone, I'll take the risk."

Leira nodded, admitting defeat. "Okay. I still think it's a bad idea, but if this is what you want to do, then you need to make me a promise."

"What's that?"

She met his gaze and held it. "You must never use this thing for anything but slipping a few seconds back in time and retrieving those Q-cores. No matter what happens to anyone or anything, you can't go back and try to undo it. And I mean anyone."

She kept holding his gaze. He knew what she was saying here.

"I get it."

"Promise me, Dash."

He nodded. "I promise."

She kept her gaze locked onto his a moment longer, then she let it go and continued into the assembly bay. The device—time slipper? Core diver? They definitely needed a name for it, anyway—sat mostly assembled in a cradle that let it be turned to any orientation. It wouldn't add much bulk to the Archetype, fortunately, and could be installed under armor, deep inside the—

Dash stopped and stared at the device.

"Wait. I've seen this before," he said.

Leira gave him a sharp look. "Where? When?"

"Custodian, show us the schematic for this." A holo-image of the diagram they'd retrieved from the Golden micro core appeared.

"Okay, now show us the schematics for the Shroud right next to it."

A second holo-image appeared. Dash studied them both.

Leira just let him, but after a moment, her curiosity got the better of her. "Dash, what is it? What do you see?"

"Just a second…" He glanced from one, to the other, letting the two schematics come together not just in his mind, but in the Meld—

"There. Right there." He pointed at the Shroud plan, and then the diagram from the micro core. "This component in the Shroud is basically the same as the guts of this new device."

"They don't look all that similar to me," Leira said.

"I would agree with Leira," Custodian added. "Those two components are—"

"The same. They do much the same thing. The difference is that the one in the Shroud is integrated right into the other systems." He gestured at the other diagram. "What this does is show how to separate it out, turn it into an independent unit, to allow these skyhooks to do what they do."

Leira kept frowning, but Custodian spoke up. "Interesting. You are right, Messenger. That is a correlation I had missed. Those components appear to be related to other systems, but when taken together, they do indeed allow for translation into gravity wells."

"Oooh," Leira said, impressed. "You got one over on Custodian."

"Yeah, you can probably thank that Melding I did with the crashed ship on Gulch for that." He scratched idly at his nose, eyes unfocused. "So, why? Is the idea that you can make cores with the Shroud and then send them directly to a skyhook for storage?"

"That, or to a base, an outpost—anywhere you want, really," Leira said. "You wouldn't need to carry them there."

"A way faster and more secure method of moving cores around as they're completed? Hell yeah," Dash said, then raised a finger as

Leira opened her mouth. "I know what you're going to say, that this just makes the whole potential time-travel thing more complicated—"

"Dash, Benzel here."

Dash raised an eyebrow at Benzel's voice coming over the comm. The man had said he was going to actually take a break and get some downtime. "Benzel, what the hell are you doing awake—or sober?"

"I just got a call from the duty ops folks in the Command Center. They lost telemetry from the *Venture* a couple hours ago. They've been trying to raise her on the comm, but nothing."

Dash looked at Leira. The *Venture* was a frigate-class patrol ship they'd modified from a heavily damaged Verity ship. She'd been patrolling coreward and spinward of the Forge, Dash recalled, and had departed about a day earlier.

"Do we have any other ships nearby?" Dash asked.

"No. The closest asset is a drone we've got scouting for Dark Metal a few light-years further coreward of the *Venture's* last reported position. She sent a routine message that she was translating, and that's it. We've got the drone redirected to take a look—it should be close enough to do some decent scanning in about an hour."

"Okay—" Dash started, and was about to go on, but the sudden, unexplained disappearance of one of the ships—especially one operating closer to the galactic core—made a thrill of worry flutter up his back.

"Benzel, I don't want to overreact here, but how long would it take to deploy the fleet?"

"The whole fleet?"

"Yeah."

"Uh…a day, maybe? Maybe half that if we forego some maintenance tasks we'd planned?"

"How big is the *Venture's* crew?" Dash asked.

"Sixteen total."

Dash looked at Leira again. "I'd hoped we'd have a few days to get the fleet marshalled and ready for its next fight. I don't think we do."

"They might have just suffered a comms failure," Leira replied. "Or some other failure. And even if we've lost them, it might have been an accident. We have been pushing these ships pretty hard, and even this alien tech isn't perfect."

"Yeah, you're right. It might be an accident or something innocent. But it might not." He curled his lip and thought for a moment. "Benzel, get the fleet ready to move on…let's say four hours notice."

"What the hell, boss? We're going to have to pull everyone off the Forge, get them aboard their ships, cancel a lot of maintenance —" Benzel said, his voice rising with strain.

"I know. And it might just end up being a big pain in the ass for nothing. But I'd rather be safe here than sorry."

"You're the boss. I'll get right on it."

"One other thing," Dash said. "I'd like you to make sure that all of our translation-capable ships are ready to deploy. And I mean all of them. Even any shuttles that can translate."

"Dash, is there something you're not telling me here?" Benzel asked.

"It's more a *feeling* than anything else. But we know that Surnatha's out there, and if I was her, my main goal would be to attack and destroy us. Not because she's a Golden puppet, but because of what we did to Clan Shirna."

"Wipe them out, you mean," Leira said.

"Yeah. So if this turns ugly, it might turn *really* ugly. I want to make sure we're ready for it."

"Once again, you're the boss. I'll get right on it and keep you updated. Benzel out."

Dash looked back at the translation unit, now complete and ready to install in the Archetype.

"Looks like this is going to have to wait, too," he said. "Custodian, do you have a smelter you're not using right now?"

"Smelter five is currently on standby, waiting for a run of Dark Metal alloy to be prepared."

"Good. Hold off on that and move this translation unit into the smelter and keep it there instead. If it looks like there's going to be any threat to it, scuttle it."

"Understood."

Leira's face displayed her deep concern. "Something's really got you on edge, Dash. What is it?"

He shook his head slowly. "It's Sur-natha. She's making me realize something I haven't faced since I had to deal with her father, Nathis."

"What's that?"

"That as bad as the Golden, the Bright, and the Verity are, they're just faceless enemies to me. With Sur-natha, just like it was with Nathis, it's personal. And if she's anything like her dad, she's not going to let this go until one of us, either her or me, is dead."

18

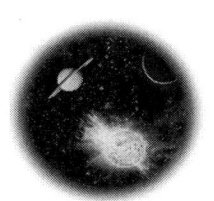

Dash gritted his teeth as the telemetry from the probe they'd diverted found no traces of the *Venture*. The complete lack of even a speck of debris meant that the ship had either been taken intact, by someone, or something, or it had translated to its next patrol objective.

"Where was she headed next?" Dash asked.

Benzel walked up to the big holo display in the Command Center and studied it for a moment, then he reached out and touched a particular star system, which lit up. "Here. A system called…um, Jabberwock?" He turned and looked back at the others. "What the hell's a Jabberwock?"

"The name is taken from the human star charts. It refers to a mythical creature from your own mythology, similar to what is known as a dragon," Custodian said.

"Dragons—they breathe fire, right?" Leira asked.

"They do," Benzel replied. "And that probably explains why this system is named that. According to this, it's an orange giant-white dwarf pairing that occasionally explodes."

Dash joined Benzel at the holo-image and studied the system called Jabberwock. Indeed, gas pulled from the orange giant by the white dwarf's gravitational tug accumulated on the latter's surface, getting compressed more and more, until it spontaneously underwent nuclear fusion and erupted in a colossal explosion, a so-called nova. Whoever had named the system had obviously put that together with some ancient story from Old Earth.

"So, based on this, Jabberwock explodes every—what, one hundred years? That's pretty damned fast, isn't it?"

"Most novae of this type have a period of one thousand to ten thousand years," Custodian said. "So this particular example does have an unusually rapid period, yes. It is not unprecedented, however."

"So when is it supposed to blow up next?"

"It last exploded ninety-four years ago."

"So, soon," Dash said.

"It's period of one hundred years is plus or minus ten years," Custodian replied.

"Oh. Right. Of course it might explode any minute," Dash said. "That means we're definitely going to end up having to go there, I know it."

"I have diverted a second drone to do a long-range scan of Jabberwock," Custodian said. "Its telemetry should be available momentarily."

Dash turned to Benzel. "The fleet?"

"Ready to move whenever you give the word. We've marshalled everything that can translate and has a weapon mounted on it—and a few that are unarmed but can still shove mines or missiles out of their hold and launch 'em."

"Good. Now hopefully we'll find the Venture happily checking out this nova that's about to explode, and we can just stand everybody down—"

"The telemetry from the second probe is now available," Custodian said.

A window popped open on the main display. Dash and Benzel had to step back to be able to see it properly. Dash saw the paired stars, one a diffuse, orange-yellow splotch, the other a fierce pinpoint of white light. A spiraling trail of gas connected them, wrapped almost a complete turn around the bigger star's equator.

"The probe is detecting multiple Dark Metal signatures in the system," Custodian said. "It would appear that a considerable number of ships are present, along with mines and defensive platforms."

"It's Sur-natha," Dash said flatly. No one asked him how he knew it was her. There was no need.

"Any sign of the *Venture*?" Benzel asked.

"I am still analyzing data from the probe. One moment, please."

They waited. Dash found himself gritting his teeth again.

"The probe has detected debris," Custodian finally announced. "It corresponds to the materials used in the construction of the *Venture*."

"They popped out of unSpace and right into the face of that damned fleet," Benzel said, his voice a quiet growl, and all the more ominous for it. "They never had a chance."

"They were never *given* a damned chance," Wei-Ping snapped.

"Benzel," Dash said, his eyes locked on the imagery. "Send an alert out to the fleet. We're departing for Jabberwock in four hours."

Thrusters flared, brief pulses of light punctuating the blackness beyond the docking bay's gaping opening. Dash watched them for a moment then turned as he heard footsteps clumping on the deck. Amy and Conover approached together.

"You wanted to see us, Dash?" Amy said.

"Yeah." He glanced at their mechs, the Pulsar and the Talon, looming over them in the bay. "I wanted to talk to you guys before we go into battle." He looked each of them in the eyes. "Training's over, I'm afraid. As of now, you're full-fledged pilots."

Amy glanced at Conover. "Um, yay? Don't we get a graduation ceremony or something?"

She smiled, but it wasn't her usual, casual, devil-may-care smile. This one left her eyes narrow and hard. Dash knew what was going through her mind, because the same thing went through his every time he strapped into the Archetype.

What if this is the last time? What if this time I get in the mech, but I never get out?

But they didn't have the luxury of giving her and Conover more time to get adept at using their mechs. Dash had wanted to make the transition to mech-pilot easier on them, but the war wasn't going to wait. Sur-natha and her fleet were only twenty-nine light-years away, so it was either attack them or wait for them to attack the Forge.

"If I could, Amy, I'd have a graduation ceremony, a big dinner, and have you guys do a flyby," Dash said. "Hell, I wanted to take a few more days, even a week, to get the fleet ready for its next battle. But the bad guys aren't giving us that option." He took a deep breath. "Bottom line here is that you guys are on your own. I want you to fight together. Amy, your mech is light, fast, and stealthy; Conover, yours is bigger, tougher, but slower and more cumbersome. I need the two of you to work out how you're going to fight, take advantage of the strengths of your mechs, while covering your weaknesses—your own and each others'."

"Got it, Dash," Conover said. "Amy and I have already been talking about this. We know that you and Leira work better together, so we've figured we should start trying to do the same."

Dash nodded. "Yeah. You guys belong together." He left it at that.

Amy glanced at Conover, smiled, and nodded. "Yeah, we do, the same way you and Leira do."

He took another breath. "I have another job for you guys. And it's going to be a tough one, but I need someone I can count on to do it."

"That sounds ominous," Conover replied. "What is it?"

Dash found himself uncertain how to proceed. Finally, he just took another breath and started talking.

"We've fought Golden, Bright, Verity, Clan Shirna—lots of battles, some of them quite hairy. So I find myself wondering, why should this one be any different?" He shrugged. "But it is. Like I told Leira, this isn't just another battle against some Golden or Verity fleet. Hell, as far as we're concerned, we could have been fighting robots when we fought them in comparison to what's coming. They were enemies, true but they were just that—enemies. This is different."

Amy frowned. "Where the heck are you going with this, Dash?"

"What makes this battle different is Sur-natha."

Conover gave a puzzled frown. "Why? Do you have some reason to believe she's a brilliant tactician or something?"

"She might be, but that's not what keeps nagging at me. I killed her adoptive father, Nathis. I've led the forces that have repeatedly fought her adoptive people, Clan Shirna, and basically all but destroyed them. She's literally one of the very last, and maybe even *the* last member of Clan Shirna. She's a true believer—a zealot—and she's *pissed*."

Conover's frown remained, but Amy said, "Ah, okay." She nodded. "Gotcha."

Conover glanced at her, then back to Dash. "I don't."

"Dash is saying that this one's personal," Amy said to him. "We might hate the Golden and the Verity, but we're not like Kai, who *genuinely* hates them. The way we hate them is more, um, abstract, I guess. But this is—" She looked at Dash. "This is real, personal, in-your-face, screw-you-sideways hatred."

Dash nodded. "And on top of that, Sur-natha really doesn't have much left to lose. I can't help feeling that her hating us—hating *me*—is pretty much all that motivates her now."

Conover gave a slow nod. "So she's going to go out of her way to beat us. But how's that different than any other enemy we've faced?"

"Sur-natha's human," Dash replied. "I know the sort of raw hatred humans can have for one another. She's not going to give any quarter, and she's not going to give up. It's going to be like our battle against the Spiral Collectors. They kept fighting us, even long after it became clear they had no chance. I'm not sure what Sur-natha has on them, or how she kept them going as long as she did, but she did it—she persuaded or coerced or somehow got the Collectors to fight us pretty much to the death."

"So that's what we need to expect from this battle," Amy said. "A nasty, bitter fight to the end."

"Yeah, we do," Dash replied. "And that brings me to the special job I have for you guys. If it looks like things aren't going well, that we're facing a catastrophe, I want the two of you to immediately bug out of the battle and come straight back here, to the Forge. Your mechs would have to be the core of whatever new fleet Custodian can help you cobble together."

Amy and Conover just stared for a moment. It was Amy who finally spoke up. "Dash, you're telling us to run away?"

"Yes, I am. That's exactly what I'm telling you. If I give the order—or if you think things have gone through a tipping point and our side is screwed—you have to cut out instantly. That means no heroics, no back talk, you just immediately haul ass back here." He sighed. "Look, I'm not a *this is an order* type of guy, but this is an order. More than that, it's me asking you to promise me you'll do this."

Amy looked at Conover, at her feet, then back up at Dash. "Orders I can disobey. Promises to you, I can't break. So if you want me to promise this, I will. But I'm not happy about it."

"Same goes for me, Dash," Conover said. "I'll do this, but I don't want to."

"Hey, it may very well not come to that anyway," he said. "It just makes me feel better knowing that the war will be in good hands no matter what happens out there."

On impulse, he put a hand on a shoulder of each of them. "I'm really damned proud of you guys. You've both come a long way since we first met." He looked at Conover. "You're not a kid anymore." He turned to Amy. "You're still a flighty goof—"

"Hey!"

Dash smiled. "That's not necessarily a bad thing. But you do have to learn to be more, um, let's call it discrete. Circumspect, maybe. Aggressive is good. Reckless is bad."

"I know," she said. "Hathaway tells me the same thing. Between him and Conover, they're keeping me in check."

"Good." He squeezed their shoulders then let go. "Okay, that's the pep talk done. You guys can mount up, and we'll see you outside."

Without warning, Amy suddenly threw herself at Dash and hugged him. "And after that, we'll see you right back here, once this is all done."

Dash returned the hug. "You can count on it."

A SHORT WHILE LATER, Dash and Leira walked past an empty bay holding the Archetype and Swift. The *Slipwing* would normally have been here, too, but Viktor had already taken her out and was joining up with the rest of the fleet. It left him and Leira alone in the vast, echoing compartment.

They took a moment to walk to the exit port, stopping a few meters short of the invisible force field that maintained atmospheric integrity. Just that force field would be a technological wonder back in what Dash had come to think of as "human" space. Before becoming the Messenger, he would have been knocked flat on the deck by the marvel of seeing such a huge opening in the side of a space station, covered by a field strong and reliable enough that its designers wouldn't even bother with doors.

Most of the fleet was, in theory, visible, but aside from a few restless specks, Dash could make out nothing distinct from the starfield. As they watched, though, a pair of shapes appeared, moving quickly away from the Forge. The Talon and Pulsar were close enough to make them out as distinct shapes flying a few klicks apart, but they soon dwindled to specks, too, as they moved to their places in the formation.

Only Dash and Leira, the Archetype and the Swift, were left to launch.

"Dash, I have a question," Leira said.

"Shoot."

"What did you see? When you slipped in time, before that battle. You saw something that shook you pretty badly. Amy didn't want to talk about it, except to say, 'ask Dash, it's his question to answer, not mine.'"

He turned away from the fleet. "Leira, it really doesn't matter what I saw, because it didn't happen. It might as well have been in a story—"

"No," she said, shaking her head. "That's not true. It *has* happened, in here." She tapped his forehead. "It's been with you ever since."

"If you're worried about it affecting me—"

"That's exactly what I'm worried about." She looked into his eyes. "I know it was something about me."

Dash frowned. "What did Amy say?"

"Nothing, really. But that's the problem. I've known Amy since we were kids. Hell, we were practically sisters. My dad died in an accident aboard a freighter when I was young, and my mom was a pilot, so she had to keep flying to keep things together, food on the table, that sort of thing. I lived most of my childhood with my aunt, Amy's mom."

"Well, I now know more about you from those two or three sentences than I ever have."

"Yeah, well, it's to say that I know Amy. She and I practically have a Meld of our own—or we did, anyway, but there's enough of that connection left that I can usually tell what she's thinking or feeling if I put my mind to it. But not this time. She's been careful to keep everything about what happened when you and she went forward in time completely closed off from me. And I can only think about one subject that might make her do that: me."

Dash looked back out at the fleet. The Talon and Pulsar were now just two more distant specks. He sighed. "Let me ask you something," he finally said. "Why do you want to know what I saw? It didn't happen, so it doesn't matter."

"Custodian says it's possible that it might have happened, though, but in a different timeline, one that branched off from this one." In answer to Dash's glance, she shrugged. "I was curious, so I asked him about it. It seems to be one of those big questions that even the Unseen couldn't answer."

"Because they knew better than to screw around with freaking *time*," Dash said, and he sighed again.

"Dash, if you really don't want to tell me, that's fine. It's not that I'm just curious about it, though. I'm worried that it might be affecting you. That it might cause you to make a decision that isn't the right one." He saw her take a breath. "That it might end up affecting *us*."

Dash finally turned to face Leira. He looked up from her, at the Swift, and recalled the awful mental image of the mech, battered and blasted, slowly rotating, dead in space.

"I saw the Swift," he said. "It had been destroyed. I guess what I saw was the future, if Amy and I hadn't joined the battle. You and the rest of the fleet got ambushed by the Verity lurking in that globular cluster, and the Swift, at least, got taken out."

Leira nodded. "So you saw that I had died."

"I'm not sure of that. I mean, I didn't see anything but the Swift. But given how beaten up it was—"

He ended on a shrug.

"I thought it was probably something like that," she said, nodding, then looking into his eyes again.

"It might yet happen, Dash. I might end up dying. Hell, we're fighting a war here, and I'm on the front lines of it. There's a good chance it will happen."

"I know that. I just—"

"Dash, I'm worried that it's going to change things—how you approach situations, what decisions you make. I'm worried you'll end up deciding to save me instead of doing what needs to be done."

"I think I've already done that. We kind of shrank a star to save you from getting killed aboard the *Slipwing*, remember?"

"I do, and it was a stupid, irresponsible thing. It could have gone so disastrously wrong." She shrugged. "To be honest, if that happened again, I wouldn't have used the Lens to fiddle around with that star."

"And wrecked my ship? Wow."

She gave him a fleeting smile. "Dash, you have to promise me that if it comes down to a choice of saving me, or potentially losing this war, you'll make the decision that's right for everyone."

"That's going to be tough."

"I know. And if that means that it isn't *us*, it's just you and me, like it's always been—then that's how it will have to be."

"Is there an *us*?"

"There could be. But not if it gets in the way of fighting and winning this war."

Dash met her eyes. On impulse, he took her hand and squeezed it gently. "I promise that I won't let this get in the way of doing whatever needs to be done."

He leaned down and his lips brushed hers. They broke apart, both a little surprised…and pleased. Another ship, a minelayer, swept by the docking bay, a latecomer to the fleet bristling with the need to fight.

"So I guess that means there's now an *us*," she said.

"I'd say so."

"Alright, but don't forget that promise."

He smiled. "It seems to be a day for promises." In answer to her puzzled look, he went on. "I made Amy and Conover promise to bug out of battle if it looks like things are going badly for us. Then they could come back here and rally what's left at the Forge. I was going to have you promise me the same thing, so you could take over leading everyone."

"Dash—"

"I'm *not* going to get you to promise me that, though, because you're right—part of it would be for selfish reasons. I am going to *ask* you to do it, if it seems like the smartest, most sensible thing to do. We're stronger with you there, flying at my side, but I want you to give me the same consideration—do what needs to be done, Leira, even if it's not what you want to do."

She grimaced. "Of course I will." Then she lifted one shoulder in frustration, her lips pursed. "Anyway, after all this dramatic talk, there's a good chance we'll both be fine. After all, when it comes to fighting this war, we kick ass."

"That we do. But, if the worst thing happens, then we've had that kiss. For now, it's enough."

But Leira shook her head, pulled Dash to her, and kissed him again. It was a longer kiss, charged by meaning that grew with each second their mouths touched. When she finally pulled back, she nodded, then touched her lip with a fingertip, like she was making a memory.

"*Now* it's enough." She let go of his hand. "And now, let's go kick some of that ass."

DASH PORED over the telemetry from the stealth drone they'd deployed. Golden and Verity ships were arrayed in two broad groups, one forward, orbiting well away from the paired stars that were the system's primaries, and one further back in a closer orbit. The farther group was centered on a truly massive ship, a type they'd only previously glimpsed. It was a carrier, a spaceborne base for a flotilla of small fighters. It added another dimension to the battle, forcing them to confront not just the massed firepower of the enemy's capital ships, but also the elusive, hit-and-run tactics of dedicated and nimble fighters.

Dash was still pondering that when the drone suddenly sent back an alarm and started into a series of wild evasive maneuvers. He saw that one of those very enemy fighters, apparently patrolling away from the enemy fleet, had detected the drone and given chase. The drone's AI was good, but not good enough, and after two close misses with pulse-cannon fire, the telemetry abruptly went dead.

"The drone has been destroyed," Sentinel announced.

"Yeah, kind of worked that out for myself," Dash replied. "Benzel, is the fleet ready?"

"Just waiting for your orders."

"Okay. Benzel, I want you to translate the entire fleet, except for the four mechs, in on the flank of that forward group, and engage immediately. You need to put everything, and I mean everything, into doing as much damage as you can, without getting decisively engaged. And then I want you to translate the whole fleet away again, out of the system, and wait for my orders to come back in."

"And what are you going to be doing?"

"I'm going to lead the four mechs into the closest translation point we can manage, which will put us between the two parts of the enemy fleet. The fighters from that carrier are going to launch en masse once you translate in. We're going to be in their way. We're going to kill as many as we can to try and take them out of the picture so they're not a factor when you come back."

"So you're going to translate back out of the system with us, right?" Benzel asked.

Dash took a slow breath. "No. We're going to stay and fight."

A moment of silence lingered. Dash could imagine Benzel staring at the comm, stunned.

"Dash, it'll be just you and the other mechs against that entire fleet until you bring us back. I hope that's not going to be very damned long."

"So do I."

"Dash, not that I'm objecting, but what's the point of this?" Leira asked.

"It's about Sur-natha. She obviously knows I'll be aboard the Archetype. If she sees a chance to finish me off, she's going to throw every last thing she has into doing it. I'll become the absolute focus of her attention. She's pretty single-minded about beating her enemies, after all—hell, she wears trophies of her victories around her neck. And I'm probably the single biggest, baddest enemy she's ever had."

"So you want to get her to concentrate her fleet entirely on you," Benzel said. "All due respect to you and that amazing mech of yours, but even the four of you together, as strong as you are, you're not going to be able to take the focus fire of all those ships for very long."

"It only has to be long enough to get it all focused on us. That should give you a big advantage when you translate back into the system."

A private channel opened. It was Leira, and he saw, also Amy and Conover.

"Dash, we're absolutely prepared to do this with you," Leira said. "That's not even a question. But we—and I'm including Amy and Conover in this because of the promise they made to you—we're all pretty worried that this is going to force us to face that promise pretty quickly. I mean, if it's just the four of us, and we're taking a shit kicking from Sur-natha's fleet, that's going to look an awful lot like things going bad."

"You might be forcing us into a position to leave you, Dash," Conover said. "Or else break that promise to you."

"Look, I hear you guys. That's not my intention here at all. Ideally, Sur-natha will get so fixated on killing me it'll pull her fleet out of position and leave her open to Benzel's counterattack." He glanced at the tactical display on the heads-up, showing the situation at the moment the stealth probe's telemetry had stopped. "In case you hadn't noticed, we're pretty badly outnumbered, here."

"What if Sur-natha doesn't fall for it?" Amy asked. "We shouldn't count on her doing what we want, right?"

"No, we shouldn't. But we can't ignore her psychology, either. If worse comes to worst, we—"

"There is an inbound transmission," Sentinel cut in. "Broad

spectrum and omnidirectional. It is originating from the enemy fleet."

Dash narrowed his eyes. The Cygnus Realm fleet had dropped out of unSpace far outside the system's Oort Cloud, too far from Sur-natha's forces to be detected unless they were deliberately searching the entire volume of space around them for Dark Metal signatures—and Dash knew that would take the Forge hours to do with its dedicated detectors. It would take ships like their own, or those of the Golden and Verity, days.

"It's Sur-natha," Dash said. "She wants to talk to me."

"You are correct," Sentinel replied. "She is addressing you directly. Intriguing—you seem to know her mind well."

"Yeah, I do. I hate to admit it, but that's because she and I aren't all that different in the way we think."

"That gives you an advantage, then, as long as you don't become predictable to her."

"That's what I'm hoping."

"Dash, are you actually going to talk to her?" Leira asked. "It's just going to let her get a fix on where you are."

"I know. And of course I am. It would be rude not to. Sentinel, open that channel."

A window popped open on the heads-up, revealing the bridge of a big capital ship—probably the massive carrier. Sur-natha stood in the middle of the image, clad in body armor, a cold expression on her face. A single fragment of alloy hung from a cord around her neck. In her hand, she held a silver-grey cable, which was connected to—

A Golden. The cable vanished into the creature's head.

And it was alive.

Dash smiled. "Hey, Sur-natha. How goes it?"

"It goes well," she said. "I'm about to win this battle against you, and that will open the way for the Golden to assume their rightful place as the rulers of the galactic arm—actually, the whole damned galaxy."

"Let me guess. In this new galactic order, you're going to be powerful, right? Maybe ruling over a big chunk of it yourself, like a governor or something?"

"The Golden reward their loyal subjects, yes. As for those who are *disloyal*, the rewards are considerably less pleasant—even if they're doing it to their own kind." She tugged the cable, and the Golden winced, its eyes fluttering. "I should add that the Golden consider you and your little Single Realm quite disloyal."

"*Cygnus* Realm."

She shrugged. "It doesn't matter. Whatever you call it is going to be soon lost to history, anyway."

Dash tipped his head back, drawing a calming breath like he was speaking to an unruly child. "Sur-natha, did you call just to monologue at us? Because, if so, I've frankly got better things to do, starting with kicking your ass." Dash put on a smugly deliberate smile. "Just like I did to your dad—what was his name again? I've killed so many Golden and Bright and Verity—oh, and lots of Clan Shirna—that I've kind of lost track. Was it…Mathis? Nasty? I just don't remember, sorry."

As Dash spoke, he kept a close, sidelong gaze on Sur-natha, gauging her reaction. He saw her eyes narrow and, even though it didn't seem possible, become harder. Around her mouth, lines became even more pronounced, and her body grew rigid as if she was barely holding herself back from lunging at the screen.

Perfect.

Her voice had become a rough hiss. "You are not worthy to speak his name—"

"Whatever it was."

Without warning, she yanked on the thin cable plugged into the Golden's head. The creature wobbled, its eyes fluttering.

"What I have done to this pathetic being, I will also do to you, and every one of your wretched followers. You'll all just become more nodes in my computer network, useful for something at last. I think I'll make sure you're the last one to be lobotomized, though, so you can see it being done to each one of them—starting with that woman, Leira."

"That *bitch*," Amy spat over the private comm.

Leira, though, just chuckled. "You said it, cuz. Although I am kind of flattered she knows my name."

Dash ignored them, as well as Sur-natha's insidious attempt to rattle him. "Hey, wow, you're generous compared to the Golden, then. They just want to exterminate all sentient life—and I mean *all*, including you. Oh, didn't they mention that during the sales pitch? Eh, it's probably buried in the fine print somewhere."

Sur-natha bared her teeth. "They said you would try to claim that—that the empty propaganda of the failed and long-dead Unseen was true."

"You know what, Sur-natha, I would *love* to keep talking to you, but I've got a war to win. I will do you a favor, though."

"Oh? What do you think you have to offer that could possibly interest me?"

"I'm going to give you a chance to be reunited with your dear dad...er, Natter? Nutbar?"

Dash closed the channel, cutting her off.

"Nothing like poking the Kirian spider-wasp nest there, Dash," Benzel said. "I'm assuming you were trying to rile her up."

"Damned right. Angry people make mistakes."

Leira came on a private channel. "Just don't let her get to you, Dash. I mean, she did know my name."

Dash paused a moment, swallowing a sudden slug of fear. Sur-natha could have found out Leira's name any number of ways, but hearing the vile woman actually say it—

"Don't worry about me," he said. "I have this."

"I know you do."

Leira's simple statement of faith made Dash smile.

"Okay, everyone, let's do what we came here to do. All ships, this is the Messenger. Weapons free, *attack*."

Dash watched as Benzel translated the fleet, almost all at once, then reappeared in space and opened fire on Sur-natha's forces.

"And, here we go again."

19

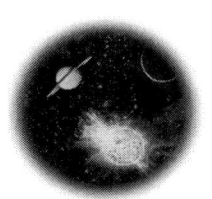

Dash flipped the Archetype end-over-end then reversed hard and fired the dark-lance at the fighter that had been tailing him. The enemy craft, small and nimble, dodged, and his shot missed—but Leira's didn't, her nova-gun blast erupting right where both she and Dash knew their target would be. What had been a sleek fighter became a cloud of tangled wreckage.

More shots slammed into the Archetype, flaring against its shield. Dash spun around and saw another wave of fighters racing in. He punched out dark-lance shots at the leaders, sending one spinning out of control and slamming into one of its fellows; it gave him about twenty seconds of lull before the rest swept into range.

"Amy, Conover, status," he said.

"Still in one piece—" Amy began, then made an *ooph* sound as pulse-gun shots raked the Talon. "Sorry, just a sec."

Dash saw her weave the Talon around the bigger, more lumbering Pulsar, chasing a fighter that had looped behind

Conover's mech. The Pulsar had become a sort of firebase, a tough, durable target that was proving even harder for their enemies to hit, thanks to Conover's clever use of electronic countermeasures. But *harder* wasn't *impossible*, and Dash could see damage starting to pile up on the other two mechs.

Kristen's voice came to life over the main channel. "We're taking damage. Nothing critical at this point, but it's ruining my mood."

"You have moods?" Conover asked her.

"Of course. And these idiots are ruining it," Kristen replied, as if it was obvious.

"Allow me to help with your stress then," Amy said. Everyone could hear the growl in her voice over the open channel.

Amy's pulse cannons erupted with searing blue bolts, a stream of them slashing across the fighter and blasting debris off it. For an instant, it stopped its wild maneuvering, but an instant was all it took. Conover fired a hip shot from the Pulsar's nova-gun, turning the fighter to vapor and slag.

"We're holding up, Dash," Conover said. "But that other half of Sur-natha's fleet is starting to get pretty close. Kristen estimates they'll be in range in just over ninety seconds."

"Got it," Dash replied. "Just hang in there for now."

He scanned the threat indicator, and then the tactical display. Per the plan, Benzel had led the bulk of the Cygnus fleet into an attack on the more forward portion of Sur-natha's forces, loosing a barrage of missiles and weapons fire that crippled three ships outright and damaged two more. They'd lost one ship, a frigate, and taken hits to four more before breaking contact and translating away. Now they waited for the word to return.

That left the four mechs alone against the entirety of Sur-natha's fleet.

As he'd hoped, she'd gone all-in on taking the mechs out, trying to tie them down with swarms of fighters launched from the big carrier, while maneuvering her capital ships in from both sides, like a massive set of closing jaws. Sur-natha left a small reserve force to guard against Benzel's return, so she wasn't completely overtaken by her rage at Dash; besides, taking out the four mechs would devastate the Cygnus Realm's ability to wage war, and she knew it, and so did her Verity allies.

It meant that he, Leira, Amy, and Conover would have to brave the full fury of her fleet long enough for Benzel to be able to deliver a knock-out blow to her reserve then attack Sur-natha from behind. But that needed another few minutes of staying decisively engaged with essentially every ship Sur-natha could muster.

It wasn't going to be pretty.

The onrushing fighters raced into range and, as one, opened up. Pulse-cannon shots poured in at the mechs, flashing against shields. And now more powerful weapons joined in as the capital ships also found the range—missiles, heavy pulse-cannons, and petawatt lasers lashing out in a dizzying display of raw offensive power.

Dash and the others flung their mechs through wild, evasive spins, turns, spirals, and reversals. Amy proved especially adept at maneuvering her mech, an apparently innate sense of movements intended to dodge and weave through enemy fire turning her mech into a whirling dervish of avoidance and return-fire. Conover, on the other hand, leaned on the Pulsar's formidable electronic warfare capabilities, painting multiple images of all four mechs on the enemy's targeting scanners, or simply showing them where they weren't.

But the weight of fire grew. Dash desperately threw the Archetype back and forth, up and down, side to side. The mech's shield kept darkening as searing beams of laser energy swept across it. He snapped out shots from the dark-lance and nova-cannon as targets flashed by; fighters zoomed in at the mechs, firing as they came, then flew on past as tumbling wreckage.

"Leira, to your left, watch out!"

"Got it—on your six, Dash!"

He somersaulted and found a fighter less than a klick away, then he charged at it, fists extended and together like a battering ram, and crashed into it headlong. The Archetype recoiled hard, but the tough mech absorbed the impact; the fighter simply flew to pieces of wreckage.

Dash recovered, looking for a new target, just as a petawatt laser caught him full on.

The Archetype's shield went black—stayed black—then flashed brightly as it died, its accumulated energy erupting like a small nova. The laser beam enveloped the mech, its furious radiance brighter than a star, turning armor to vapor and making Dash yell out.

"Dash!" Leira called. "Dash, are you—?"

"In pain? Yes." He groaned, "Yes I am." He slammed the Archetype into a hard deceleration; the laser kept tracking his last trajectory, sweeping away. He reversed course, reorienting just in time to see paired streams of pulse-cannon shots from a Verity heavy cruiser converge on the Swift, burying it in a staccato series of dazzling blasts. When it cleared, Dash saw the mech's left arm come whirling away, blasted right off the Swift's shoulder.

"Leira!"

"Yeah, that hurt," she groaned back. "A lot. Can't scream, though. Kinda busy!"

Dash didn't have time to chat anyway. He dodged a pair of missiles, then fired at a fighter that flashed by, made a tight spin and fired again at a light cruiser that had charged in among the mechs. He saw both Leira and Conover's mechs pour missiles, as well as dark-lance and nova-gun fire into it, blasting chunks out of its hull. But it struck back, hitting the Pulsar squarely with a petawatt laser that momentarily turned Conover's mech into an incandescent beacon.

Dash lined up a shot on the laser mount and fired, the dark-lance slashing through the weapon array, which exploded in a shower of glowing debris. He didn't have time to gloat, though, as another laser swept over the Archetype, at the same time a missile slammed into its right knee. The combined effect left Dash momentarily reeling, the mech spinning out of control, its lower right leg blasted away.

"They all hate my feet," Dash muttered.

"What?" It was Leira.

"Lost part of Sentinel's leg. It's like the Golden and their servants have something against my legs."

"Better that than your face," Leira said, teeth together as she spun into a wild evasive curl.

"Gotta protect the moneymaker."

"You do that, pretty boy. Now *fight*."

Grinning, Dash righted the mech and hunted for a new target. There was no shortage of them. But he spared a moment to glance at the tactical display to see how the battle had evolved.

"Catastrophic damage to the right leg," Sentinel said. "Moderate damage to upper-starboard thruster array, left foot actuator, secondary inertial dampers—"

"I get it, we're taking a beating," Dash snapped. He wanted to hold off a little longer before calling Benzel back, but the fire was just becoming too intense, the mechs taking too much damage too quickly.

"Dash," Conover said over a private channel. "This isn't looking good. Even when Benzel comes back, I'm not sure it's going to be enough."

Dash had already come to the same conclusion. They might have bitten off more than they could chew here. And that meant Conover was asking Dash a question—a crucial one, that would probably decide the battle in Sur-natha's favor.

You wanted us to promise you we'd leave and go back to the Forge if it looked like things were going wrong. And things seem to be going wrong, so…

Should we stay, or should we go?

Dash saw another missile crash into the Swift. A stream of pulse-cannon fire tore at the Talon. The petawatt laser that had been reaching for the Archetype like a groping hand found him again, boiling away more armor.

Call back Benzel and fully commit?

Or send Amy and Conover away, the Archetype and Swift staying to cover their withdrawal?

He had only seconds to decide.

I'll make sure you're the last one to be lobotomized, though, so you can see it being done to each one of them—starting with that woman, Leira.

It was as though Sur-natha's sneering tone actually came across the comm again and didn't just ring in his mind.

The entire Verity fleet now unleashed its fury on the four mechs.

Dash's strategy had been flawed, wrong, and this could only end one way.

He opened his mouth to say, *Amy, Conover—Leira, too—go, leave now, I'll cover you and follow when I can—*

But something raced past the Archetype, almost close enough to touch. On instinct, Dash made to lash out with a shot, but he checked himself when he realized it was his own ship, the *Slipwing*, tearing past.

"Dash," Viktor said. "I'll take some heat off you. Stand by."

He could have been describing an interesting new piece of tech to Dash, for all the inflection in his voice. But that didn't stop him from throwing the *Slipwing* around like a fighter; any lingering doubts Dash had about Viktor's abilities as a pilot evaporated in a puff of satisfaction as he watched his old ship nimbly slip among reaching streams of pulse-cannon shots and flashes of laser fire. She landed hit after hit, and then more weapons fire followed as the rest of the Cygnus fleet, led by the *Herald*, came charging in from above the ecliptic plane.

"Got tired of waiting, Dash, sorry," Benzel said. "We were starting to worry you were going to hog the victory today all for yourself."

Dash opened his mouth to protest Benzel deciding to decisively engage with the fleet, but he closed it again. Wasn't that why he'd eagerly surrounded himself with people like Benzel? To make the right decisions and generally be damned good at what they do?

"No problem, Benzel," Dash replied. "I was getting a little tired of winning the battle all by myself, anyway."

Benzel laughed, then the *Herald* opened fire, pouring shots into the Verity ships.

Dash turned back to the tactical display. Benzel had elected to ignore Sur-natha's reserve—probably a good move, but it left her with something to yet influence the battle, while the Cygnus Realm was now fully committed. But then Dash saw that Benzel had just officially earned the title of wily; a group of minelayers, led by the *Horse Nebula*, raced between Sur-natha's reserve squadron and the rest of the battle, spewing mines as they went. It was insanely brave, and also costly—of the eight minelayers, three were left derelict wrecks by fire from the Verity ships, while all the rest took at least some damage. But it stopped the reserve in its tracks, isolating it from the greater battle, at least for now.

Dash turned his attention back to the immediate fight—

Just as something slammed into him, hard, and everything went dark.

Dash winced then almost panicked at the fact that the Archetype's cockpit was plunged into darkness, the heads-up dead. It left him briefly entombed in dark metal, something deep inside the mech damaged by whatever had struck him. But the displays flared back to life, and the Archetype powered up again, as emergency backups kicked in.

"Sentinel, what the hell was that?"

"A pair of Harbingers have joined the battle. One is—"

Another massive blow struck the Archetype.

"—nearby."

Dash spun around and found a Harbinger literally a few hundred meters away, somersaulting back toward him for another pass with its fists. Instinctively, Dash ran the Archetype up to full emergency overpower, driving the mech quickly away from the

Harbinger. The enemy mech swept its next attack through empty space, apparently surprised by his rapid retreat from combat.

"I expected you to attack," Sentinel said. "Not withdraw."

"I know. So did the Harbinger. That Golden AI is starting to get clever, so I have to get even more unpredictable."

"There is a limit to your unpredictability."

"Maybe, but I haven't found it yet—hell, I still surprise myself sometimes."

Dash raced away, two Harbingers now in pursuit. It pulled the powerful enemy mechs away from the battle, but now he needed a finisher, something to disable or destroy them. He desperately sought inspiration, because a straight, stand-up fight wasn't going to do it—they were fresh, while the Archetype now decidedly counted as *battered*.

He found himself rushing directly toward Sur-natha's reserve force, still trapped on the far side of a minefield they were desperately trying to shoot their way through.

The minefield. *Ahh.*

Dash angled the Archetype just as the trailing Harbingers opened fire. Massive plasma bolts flashed past, bracketing him as they unleashed their potent chest-cannons at their quarry. He raced into the minefield, dodging among the mines, and now taking fire from the dozen or so ships of the enemy reserve. Behind him, the Harbingers slowed, apparently unwilling to follow him any further. They knew the mines that were ignoring the Archetype would certainly attack them. Instead, they each unleashed a barrage of missiles then reversed course and started back for the heart of the battle.

Just like that, Dash found himself caught between a salvo of missiles coming from one direction, and the increasing weight of fire from Sur-natha's reserve from another.

He had maybe thirty seconds.

"Conover!" he called.

"Busy here, Dash—"

"Aren't we all! Have Kristen open a datalink to Sentinel. Sentinel, please tell me the Pulsar is close enough to affect those missiles with its ECM."

"It is."

"Good, work with Kristen. Take control of as many of those missiles as you can and use them against the enemy reserve."

"One moment."

Dash gritted his teeth and waited, pumping out shots from the dark-lance as he did. The weapon must have been damaged; its recycle time had increased, forcing him to wait almost five full seconds between shots. He did still have the satisfaction of punching a hole clean through a Verity frigate, then he turned to find the missiles seconds from impact.

If this didn't work, he was about to receive a whole world of serious hurt.

"Sentinel…"

"One moment."

"You said that a moment ago! We don't *have* a moment."

The missiles raced in—and past. Only one managed to avoid the ECM, clipping the Archetype and blowing off the mech's right hand. The rest, though, carried on through the minefield and began to detonate among the ships of the reserve.

"Good work," he said, releasing a long breath. "Even if you did leave me hanging."

"Apologies," Sentinel replied. "Would you prefer that next time I give you my undivided attention and just forget about the complex task of hacking and redirecting a whole salvo of enemy missiles?"

"Don't be smart," Dash snapped, then he took a deep breath and powered the Archetype back toward the battle. "Wait, scratch that—be as smart as you want. As long as we *win*."

DASH ARRIVED JUST as Sur-natha launched her last wave of fighters from the big carrier. By then, ships on both sides had been battered, several wrecked, and all damaged to some extent. But with Sur-natha's reserve force largely neutralized by the combination of mines and hacked missiles, the battle had been evened up.

But it was still *far* from decided, something of which Dash was keenly aware. As he closed back on the carrier, he passed by a derelict Cygnus frigate called the *Ravager*; he'd been aboard her only a couple of days earlier, visiting her crew as they'd tensely prepared for an inevitable, impending battle. He particularly remembered one young woman named Sharrah—she'd probably been in her late teens—a former refugee who'd eagerly volunteered to serve with the fleet rather than be repatriated. She had been assigned to the *Ravager*. Dash remembered two things about her: an outward façade of casual bravado, layered over an obvious core of deeper fear.

It looked like the frigate had been repeatedly struck by the searing beam of a petawatt laser, which had turned most of her starboard flank to slag. He didn't even want to think of what had happened to her crew—including that prideful, scared young woman. So he grimly fixed his gaze ahead on the heads-up, and the battle that now raged around Sur-natha's carrier. There'd be time to think about the terrible cost of all this later.

Right now, Dash had an ass to finish kicking.

He studied the tactical display. Sur-natha's fleet had fallen back, reorganizing itself into a protective bubble of ships around the carrier. The final swarm of fighters had swarmed out of the bubble, focusing their attacks on the Cygnus fleet's B Squadron; Dash saw the *Retribution*, Wei-Ping's flagship, locked in a desperate struggle with at least a dozen of the nimble little craft. A Squadron, under Benzel in the *Herald*, had swept out to the other flank, looking for a gap in the formidable array of firepower the enemy ships could bring to bear. A trio of Harbingers harried them as they maneuvered, and Dash saw that Amy and Conover were still in the thick of it, harrying the Golden mechs right back.

"Leira...*Leira*—" Dash snapped it out when he realized that, in the confusion of the breakaway to the minefield, the missile-hack, and now the return to the heart of the battle, he'd lost track of the Swift. For a wild, panicked moment, he couldn't find its transponder icon on the display, and he had a momentarily gut-wrenching vision of the Swift, battered and lifeless, just as he'd seen it in the time slip. What if he hadn't been seeing the impending battle then, and actually saw the wrecked Swift *now*.

But he couldn't fix the Swift's location because he was looking too far away. An instant after he'd said Leira's name, Sentinel had zoomed in and panned the tactical display, showing the other mech tucked in close to the Archetype's starboard rear.

Relief flooded over Dash in a welcome rush. "Oh, damn—Leira, there you are. Sorry, I lost—"

"Track of me, I know. You were busy. But I'm flying your wing, remember? You just do what you need to do, and I'll be there for you."

He smiled. "Of course you will." His relief was short-lived, though. The longer this battle went on, the more scenes like the shattered *Ravager* there'd be. They'd reached that point in the battle where he knew they needed to end it, and soon, or be ground down so badly that even a victory would just technically be *not entirely beaten*.

His smile fled. "We need a way to take out Sur-natha. Benzel, I need you to attack and break through that Verity battle line, then open a door for me to get in close with that carrier."

"We're probing for a weak spot right now, Dash, but we're not finding one. A head-on attack straight into them is going to cost us badly. But if that's what you want…"

Benzel trailed off, saying nothing more, because nothing more needed to be said.

Once again, Dash frantically sought inspiration. He found himself eyeing the nearby paired stars, the red giant and its parasitic white dwarf companion. The star stuff from the former, that had accumulated on the latter, had to be close to undergoing spontaneous fusion. Maybe they could hasten it along—use the Archetype's distortion cannon to increase local gravitation on the star and provoke it into a single burst of ultra-high energy radiation, aimed squarely at Sur-Natha's fleet.

But Sentinel shut that idea down almost immediately. "While it would likely be possible to induce spontaneous fusion on a single point on the white dwarf's surface, the heat and pressure from the fusing material would likely prompt adjacent material to undergo fusion, which would cause the same effect in material adjacent to it, and so on—"

"And the whole damned star explodes, yeah, I get it. How likely is that to happen?"

"Unknown. There are simply too many variables with values I

could only guess at. I would have to say it would be more likely to happen than not, though."

That would wipe out both fleets—a truly empty victory. Okay, so this time, taking advantage of a nearby celestial phenomenon wasn't going to be the answer.

In that case, then…

"Sentinel, if we fire every single missile we have left, in all of our ships and mechs, in one big salvo, how many missiles will that be?"

"Approximately four hundred, plus or minus one hundred, based on expenditure estimates. If you wish me to query each ship—"

"No, don't bother." Dash narrowed his eyes. Would that be enough to swamp Sur-natha's defenses long enough for them to break through?

Did they have another choice?

He quickly outlined his plan over the comm. He heard Benzel hiss in a breath.

"If that doesn't end it, Dash, we'll be left fighting this with no missiles. That's about half our firepower right there."

"This is going all-in on one last throw," Leira said.

"Hey, there's a term I haven't heard for a while," Dash replied. "A last throw. But that's what this is. The key to winning this battle is Sur-natha. As long as she's alive, she won't give up."

"Yeah, but do you really expect that, even if you kill her, the enemy fleet will just give up?" Amy asked.

"Give up? No. But she's the glue holding this together, not to mention another fanatic willing to do the Golden's dirty work for them—and I hate to admit it, but she's pretty damned good at tactics. So even if we kill her, and then withdraw, we push the Golden a little closer to having to commit themselves fully to the fight. We let her survive this, though, and we'll be right back here again in a few weeks or months, having exactly this same conversation."

"Dash is right," Leira said. "Sur-natha's never going to give up. She'll be a pain in our ass as long as she's still breathing."

A broken, choppy transmission crackled across the comm. It was Wei-Ping, aboard the beleaguered *Retribution*, which was surrounded by a cloud of Verity fighters.

"Whatever you're…to do, do it fast…hold out as long as we can, but…our asses handed to us!"

Dash could hear weapons impacts echoing behind the sound of her voice. It made up his mind.

"Okay, let's do this. Wei-Ping, just hang on a few more minutes. Keep those fighters tied up!"

"Will do…damned vacation after this, though!"

It turned out Benzel still had a trick up his sleeve. He'd brought one of their shipkiller missile platforms with them, stowed in the *Herald*'s hold. Dash had assumed he'd have deployed and expended it by now, but he hadn't, and now they had another hundred or so missiles, all trans-luminal, available to throw into the attack. Moreover, the platform itself was designed to become a single, exceptionally powerful missile, once its ordnance had been expended.

"Dash," Conover said. "I've been talking to Kristen, and we think that we can make it look like even more inbound missiles with some sneaky electronic deception. A kind of mirror effect, if you will."

"Totally doable," Kristen put in. "We'll make it look like a gazillion more missiles are coming at them."

Dash shook his head. It was hard to remember sometimes that Kristen was an AI and not some friend of Amy's.

"Do it," Dash replied, then glanced at the chrono. Benzel's squadron and the mechs had continued to prowl around the flank of Sur-natha's fleet, as though seeking an opening, all while trading sporadic weapons fire. The bigger problem was Wei-Ping, whose squadron was close to breaking under the sheer weight of attacks from the fighters.

It was time.

"Okay, everyone," Dash said. "We launch in fifteen seconds."

"Uh, Dash, we could use another minute or so—" Benzel started, but Dash cut him off.

"Wei-Ping doesn't have another minute. It's now, or we just withdraw."

"Yeah, not doing that. Let's just get this over with."

Dash turned the Archetype directly toward Sur-natha's fleet.

"And—go," he said, then he kicked the mech's drive up to half power.

An instant later, a veritable wall of missiles erupted from the Cygnus ships. They launched as fast their tubes could reload; the shipkiller, which had nudged out of the *Herald*'s hold, poured out missiles in a stream.

"Hope the bad guys never catch on to that," he muttered, watching as the trans-luminal missiles launched, burned, then vanished—

—and reappeared within a few klicks of the enemy ships, still burning at full acceleration. Explosions began to tear at the Verity forces, as point-defense systems opened up, destroying some of the missiles, while others just slammed home.

Dash ramped the Archetype's drive up to full now, following close behind the rest of their missiles as they raced toward Surnatha's fleet. The other three mechs, the *Herald*, and her consorts all followed.

DASH PUMPED out shots from the dark-lance and nova-cannon, blasting chunks out of enemy ships. A Harbinger raced in to loose a volley from its chest-cannon, but Amy zoomed up behind it, grabbed it, and spun it into the conning tower of a Verity cruiser. Torrents of point-defense shots streamed in every direction, seeking missiles to kill—real ones, and scanner-ghosts created by the Pulsar.

"Damn, this is tough going," Dash muttered, waiting for the dark-lance to recycle. "We've got to get closer to that carrier."

The big ship loomed tantalizingly close, but the intervening ships seemed determined to protect it at all costs—and the Cygnus ships were taking a beating.

At least the pressure was off Wei-Ping. The Verity fighters had mostly broken off their attacks on her and were now racing to the aid of their carrier. Wei-Ping's squadron was trying to rally, but only the *Retribution* and two light cruisers looked at all fit to fight.

A fighter flashed by, snapping pulse-cannon shots at the Archetype. Dash ignored it, just grunting as the bolts slammed into the mech's armor. He needed to find a way through.

"Benzel, where's that shipkiller?" Dash asked.

"Still have it tucked in against the *Herald*, where the enemy can't see it. Been saving it to use on the carrier once we break through," Benzel answered.

"We're not going to break through at this rate. See that heavy cruiser, the one at your two o'clock, and high? Fire at it."

"You sure?" Benzel's tone was openly doubtful.

"Yes. We need to break their line," Dash growled.

"On the way!"

The shipkiller, now exhausted of its missile-load, had been almost clinging to the *Herald's* port flank like one of the weird little deep-space creatures called vacuum limpets. It was an attempt to keep the shipkiller off the enemy targeting scanners, getting only a single return from the *Herald*. So far, it had worked, but the shipkiller had still taken a few extraneous hits. Now it thrusted away, then its primary drive lit and it drove toward the heavy cruiser.

"Leira, on me! We need that thing to get to its target!"

He zoomed in close to the shipkiller and poured power into the Archetype's faltering shield, desperate to keep the shipkiller intact until it impacted. The Swift slid into place on its other flank. This was going to be close—they had to stick near to it but break away before it detonated—

The Archetype's shield failed.

"Shit! Sentinel, get that shield back up!"

"The shield generators have suffered a catastrophic failure. Infield repairs are no longer possible."

Dash hissed in anger. Already, point-defense systems were swivelling their fire toward the two mechs and their charge. Shots began to strike the Archetype and the Swift, who closed in, doing their best to shield the shipkiller.

Which might succeed—and leave both mechs too badly damaged to carry on with the fight.

Dash took a breath and grimly resolved to just keep going.

A shape flashed past the Archetype, racing out in front of the shipkiller. It was the *Slipwing*. Again. And this time, she was traveling at a scorching rate of speed.

"I'll block as much fire as I can," Viktor said, his voice as placidly gruff as ever. "The *Slipwing's* shield and armor should be enough to—"

He broke off speaking as fire began to slam into the *Slipwing*, flashing against its shields. Dash knew her shield generator was nowhere near as capable as that of the mechs; his old ship just didn't have the power to keep it energized for long.

"Viktor, get out of there!" Dash shouted, but the same slightly dour tone came back over the comm.

"I will, in another minute or so."

The *Slipwing* wove back and forth, taking shots that would have struck the shipkiller. Now her shield died, and bolts of energy started smacking into her armor.

"Viktor—!"

"Good enough," Viktor said, and peeled away.

The cruiser was now only seconds away.

"Leira, break off!" Dash snapped, wrenching the Archetype through a hard, tight lateral acceleration.

Now point defense fire did begin to pound the shipkiller, tearing debris away from it—but it was too late. It smashed into the side of the heavy cruiser—

Then the single most powerful explosion Dash could recall ever seeing in battle blew the Verity cruiser apart.

A BRIEF LULL fell over the battle, as all combatants took a few seconds to simply gape. The shipkiller, already an enormously powerful weapon, must have managed to strike and breach the cruiser's anti-deuterium containment. The anti-matter storage was the most robust part of a ship by design; its actual failure, even in the event of the catastrophic destruction of the ship, was rare. But when it did fail, it *really* failed—spectacularly so.

A roiling cloud of plasma swept out and engulfed everything near the cruiser. Even the Archetype and Swift, already accelerating away, were brushed by the fringe of searing vapor, rocketing their hull temperatures up hundreds of degrees in an instant. Dash ignored it, though, and frantically sought out the rest of the Cygnus fleet. The unexpectedly immense blast had far exceeded anything any of them had expected; terror gripped him, that they had just managed to cripple or destroy many of their own ships, and kill many of their own people.

But the *Herald* swept through the plasma cloud, trailing vaporized armor, and drove on toward the carrier. Only two more ships— one of which was the *Slipwing*, which just made Dash shake his head —followed her, while the rest of her squadron decelerated, too spent to even contemplate fighting in-close.

But the way was clear. "Leira, we've got a run at the carrier. It's time."

"Right behind you—what's left of me, anyway."

Dash powered the Archetype through a hard turn and dove back into the now-cooling plasma cloud. When he emerged on the other side, he saw the *Herald* and the *Slipwing* raking the carrier with fire, turning her hangar bays to glowing scrap.

Dash pushed the Archetype harder. This was their chance to run down Sur-natha, but he could think of only one way to achieve it.

"Sentinel," he said. "Compare the bridge of that carrier with wherever Sur-natha was when she was on the comm. Are they the same place?"

"Almost certainly."

"Leira, don't follow me," Dash said.

"What? Why?"

On impulse, he grabbed the derelict remains of a fighter tumbling away from the anti-matter blast. "Because I'm going after Sur-natha."

"So I'll come with you!"

"The Swift has taken too many hits; this is going to be too rough a ride. Coordinate with Benzel, and find another way of boarding that carrier, as close to the bridge as you can."

"Wait—Dash, what are you planning?"

He saw a petawatt laser mount above and behind the carrier's bridge swivel toward him. He flung the wrecked fighter at it, smashing it to sparking debris an instant before it fired. Then he pushed the Archetype's arms ahead of him and adjusted his trajectory a fraction.

"This," he said, firing the nova cannon point-blank at a big set of blast doors just behind the bridge. They blew inward, and the Archetype raced through the whirling debris, then it slammed headlong into the carrier.

DASH GROANED. The heads-up had gone blank; status warnings flickered in the sudden darkness. He was still alive—more or less, although the inertial dampers hadn't offset all the energy of the collision, so he'd been slammed pretty hard in the cradle.

"Sentinel?"

"I am operating only in stand-by mode," she replied. "I have limited access to any of the Archetype's functions."

"Can you open up the cockpit?"

After a pause, she said, "That, I can still do."

Dash dismounted from the cradle, groaning and wincing, because everything was either a dull ache or a sharp pain. He grabbed and sealed the helmet of his vac suit, pulled on his tactical vest, and cradled his pulse-gun with a gesture of grim readiness.

"Okay," he said, raising the pulse gun. "Crack it open."

The Archetype's cockpit unsealed, split open, and stopped. Dash moved to the gap and peered through it. The mech seemed to have embedded itself directly behind the carrier's bridge.

"Suddenly I feel like I've been here before."

"You have, in a way, when you confronted Nathis—" Sentinel said.

"Yeah, I know. I was just making conversation. Nervous conversation." As he spoke, he scanned through the gap, swivelling his head from side-to-side. Beyond he saw nothing but a wrecked compartment, decks, and bulkheads smashed and buckled by the Archetype's impact.

A wave of déjà vu swept through Dash. He really had been here before, or somewhere much like it, when he'd faced Nathis aboard his battlecruiser, while Leira and the others aboard the *Slipwing* sank ever deeper into the crushing atmosphere of a gas giant.

Now, it was Nathis's daughter, another massive ship, and Leira and his expanded circle of friends and followers still fighting for their lives not far away.

"Wei-Ping's right," Dash muttered. "We'll all need a *long* vacation after this."

"I believe Kristen requested you all have something called *boat drinks*, although I find the idea of drinking a sailing vessel odd at best," Sentinel said.

"It's an old saying. We'll discuss it later, if I get out of this wreck."

He pulled himself through the gap and planted his boots on the deck of Sur-natha's ship, pulse-gun ready.

He looked around. The blast doors had sealed off a bay apparently meant to contain shuttles and similar utility craft, probably for immediate use by the bridge crew. Only one shuttle had been stored here, though, and now it lay on its side, flung against a bulkhead by the Archetype's catastrophic arrival. The mech had kept going, smashing through at least two bulkheads, delivering Dash into a compartment almost immediately rearward of the bridge.

He started forward, moving cautiously. The Archetype had hit the carrier just behind the bridge. Certainly, he had no guarantee Sur-natha was here—she could have fled to a different part of the ship, or even fled the ship altogether.

He carried on anyway. He had a *feeling* that Sur-natha was still here, because she wouldn't flee anywhere—certainly not from Dash.

What there wasn't was Golden, or Verity. He'd expected to encounter some, his first face-to-face encounter with one of the vile creatures. But they were nowhere to be seen. The only resistance he encountered, in fact, was a pulse-gun turret that clipped his body armor before he could destroy it, and a bot that opened up on him with some sort of electrical arc weapon. The bot had been pinned under a fallen structural member, so he'd been able to dispatch it as well. He finally did find Verity—two of them, both killed by the battering ram of debris that the Archetype had shoved along ahead of it.

He checked both quickly; they were clearly dead, but he fired a single pulse-gun shot into the head of each anyway. It was harsh, even brutal, but the last thing he needed was to find out that the Verity had some sort of reanimation function and would get back to their feet behind him. Then he moved to the final blast door leading into the bridge. He expected to need Sentinel's help opening it, but on a whim he tapped at a control labeled with a symbol he knew meant it was the door control.

The door slid open. It was so unexpected that it left Dash momentarily framed in the open doorway, a perfect target for anyone inside. He dodged quickly aside then peered back around the frame.

He saw consoles, displays, all the usual clutter of the bridge of a big ship. What he didn't see was any crew. Had the bridge been abandoned? Had Sur-natha actually left?

"You don't need to lurk out there. I'm not going to shoot you."

The voice came from somewhere inside the bridge, and to the right. It was Sur-natha.

"Yeah, sorry, Sur-natha," Dash called back. "But I'm having a little trouble taking you at your word on that."

"I didn't say I wasn't going to kill you. I said I'm not going to *shoot* you. When the time comes to finally end you, I want to feel your blood gushing over my hand."

Dash sniffed. "Still having trouble buying it, sorry. I think we both want to end this fast, and guns are the best way to do that."

"Well, unlike you, I'm no coward. But if you insist on doubting me—"

Sur-natha stepped into view. She still held the cable plugged into the head of the Golden; the creature moved with her, as though led by a leash. Which, Dash thought, in a horrible way, it was.

Incredibly, Sur-natha wore no vac suit, just loose leathers, her own body armor, and another necklace of spaceship fragments. Her only visible weapon was a brutal-looking knife, similar to the one Benzel's wreck crawler had retrieved from the debris of the skyhook brought back to the Forge. She either had absolute faith in the ability of the Golden ships' tech to maintain atmospheric integrity, or she just didn't give a shit.

She gave Dash a wicked smile. "See? I'm not afraid. Now, you can always try to shoot me, of course…"

Dash narrowed his eyes at her. Not for an instant did he take this whole, *facing each other and fighting up-close and personal because it's the honorable way* thing seriously. That only happened in stories. In real life, people like Sur-natha merely fought to win.

And so did he.

Which meant that just shooting at her probably wouldn't work. She likely had some sort of personal force field, or some similar trick in play.

"How fast can you get into a vac suit, Sur-natha?" he said. "Because I think all I have to do here is have Sentinel—that's my mech's AI—shut down any force fields between here and where we made our big entrance, and just blow the atmosphere out of here."

"You can try," she said, crossing her arms and leaning against a console, her smile unchanged. "Or maybe we can talk, instead."

"Oh, I think we're way past the point of talking this out."

She shrugged. "You know what, I think you're probably right—"

Without warning, the Golden suddenly raised a hand. Dash saw a pulse-gun and started to move—

Too slow. Sizzling bolts flew through the hatchway. One

slammed hard into Dash's shoulder armor; a second hit his own pulse-gun, blasting it out of his hand.

Sur-natha exploded into action, charging at Dash, her knife held low and close to her body, her other arm extended to block. As she ran, the cable leading back to the Golden went taut, then it tore out of the creature's skull with a spurt of gore. The Golden dropped like an empty sack.

Dash flung himself backward so Sur-natha would have to exit the bridge and turn a corner, slowing her slightly. It bought Dash a second or two, long enough for him to brace himself—

—before Sur-natha was upon him.

She burst through the hatchway, swinging the knife. It whistled through the air just a few centimeters short of Dash. He clutched at his backup weapon, a pulse-pistol holstered on his vest, but Sur-natha lashed out again, and again. Damn, she was fast—Dash only had time to dodge and dodge again. He punched out at her, and she jumped back, slashing at his exposed arm as she did. He caught the blade on his forearm armor and deflected it—almost into his thigh. It made him jump backward again and collide with a twisted bulkhead. Sur-natha lunged after him, her knife clanging against the bulkhead beside his head.

"You lied," he snapped. "You fired."

She pulled back a couple of paces and gave a fierce grin. "No, the Golden shot at you."

"Just *technically* right."

"That's the best type of right," she said, and leapt again. This time, her knife skidded off his forearm armor and cut into his upper arm.

Dash hissed. Fortunately, the tough layers of vac suit material took most of the impact, but it still let a good two centimeters of knife gouge into his flesh. Sur-natha's grin widened and she pulled the knife back, then she drove it forward again. Dash deliberately ducked into it, the blade slamming ineffectually into the impact-resistant material of his helmet. At the same time, he kicked out, catching Sur-natha just below the knee. She cursed and stumbled back.

Dash yanked out the pulse-pistol and fired, just as Sur-natha flung herself back through the hatchway and into the bridge. The shot hit a conduit, which burst with a shower of sparks and a guttering, blue-green flame. He immediately charged after her to prevent her from repositioning herself to ambush him as he came through the door behind her. She tried to anyway, spinning like a coiling serpent and striking at him—or, rather, at his pulse-pistol, which flew out of his hand.

"No more guns!" she shouted, then she laughed and drove in, trying to blitz Dash before he could get himself properly defended.

They descended into an animal state, whirling and punching like fevered beasts. She would strike; Dash would counter—each time, their bones jarring from the chaotic crash of their attacks. Dash fought desperately, pulling every trick he knew about fighting hand-to-hand out of his bag, even making up a few new ones on the fly.

But Sur-natha was an expert at this; Dash couldn't help feeling that she was, in the end, playing with him.

She jumped back, barely breathing hard. Dash felt like he just couldn't find enough breath, his lungs heaving like a bellows. He glanced at the gaping gash in his suit, thought *to hell with it*, then snapped open the latch on his helmet. He yanked it off and tossed it aside.

"Good," Sur-natha said. "Now I can look you right in the face as I kill you."

"You're not very bright, are you? Despite your suspicion and drive and courage—which is mindless, but still—you're a rube at heart."

Sur-natha had tensed, about to lunge, but a brilliant flash through the viewports around the bridge made her stop.

"I wonder, was that one of your ships exploding, or one of mine?" he said.

She shrugged. "They're not my ships. They belong to the Verity." She grinned. "See, that's the difference between us. I will do whatever I have to to win. I don't care how many die in the process—mine or yours. You're held back by your sentimental attachment to your followers. Even now, you worry that explosion was Leira, or Benzel, or one of those blind idiots who follow you with such loyalty. And, yes, I know their names. Once I've finished you off, they'll be next, one after another." She touched her necklace. "First, though, I have to get a piece of that mech of yours to add to this."

"You're delusional," Dash said, his eyes darting about, seeking a weapon, an opportunity—something. "You think you're using the Verity, but they're using *you*—"

"No, we're using each other. That's how it works. Everyone uses everyone else to get what they want."

"Your dear old dad teach you that? What else did Nathis teach you—before he died, that is—when I, you know, killed him."

It was just a move of desperation, trying to rattle her with mention of Nathis. She knew it, too.

"My father died a hero," she said. "Just as he was destined to." Her body language went taut and ready. "You won't. In fact, maybe

I won't kill you. Instead, I'll have the Verity do to you what they did to that traitor over there." She nodded towards the fallen Golden—

Which was looking at Dash.

It wasn't dead. It soon would be, but life flickered within it, still. And, with the cable jack yanked out of its head, it was no longer a mindless drone.

It met Dash's gaze, and something happened he'd have never believed. There was an instant of *understanding*.

The carrier shuddered, the deck rattling under Dash's feet. At the same time, distant clatters and bangs drifted from somewhere sternward of the bridge.

Sur-natha's eyes flicked that way. "Sounds like we're about to have company. Guess I'd better finish—"

She lunged at Dash, swinging a knife stroke that would have nearly decapitated him. He jumped back but slammed hard into a console. Sur-natha's slash missed him, but she reversed and swung a back stroke that he barely caught on his forearm. Again, the blade skidded across the armor and plunged into his bicep—and again, only the tough fabric of the vac-suit stopped a deep and serious wound.

He drove his knee up, catching Sur-natha in a way that would have left her gasping for breath if she'd been a male. It *did* shove her back far enough for Dash to sidestep and then run around another console, toward the fallen Golden.

Sur-natha reversed course and went the other way around the console, cutting him off—or at least that what she thought she was doing, preventing him from leaving the bridge and potentially joining up with whoever had just boarded the carrier. Instead, he kept going, leaping over the prone form of the Golden. Sur-natha cursed and raced after him, striking out with the knife at Dash's back—

I hope I understood what this wounded Golden was trying to tell me and it isn't just another part of her trap.

There was no way to know. Dash was literally taking this on faith, spinning in time for her knife to catch him across the chest, raking through the vac suit and then jamming down inside his body armor. Bright pain flared from the wound, which was—he had no idea how bad it was.

Sur-natha let out a triumphant yell, then she yanked the knife back, raised it for a final strike, and aimed right at Dash's face.

Then she pitched sideways with a heavy grunt as the Golden grabbed her calf and rolled, pulling her off-balance.

It gave Dash a window of opportunity, as Sur-natha cursed and fought to recover. He lunged and grabbed her, pinning her knife arm to her side and slamming her face-first into the console. She fought back like a maniac, thrashing and bucking, trying to throw him off. Grimly, he drove his weight down on top of her and jammed an arm across her throat, pulling hard, trying to squash her breath away against his forearm armor.

"Not gonna work, Sur-natha. Not today. Gonna walk away from this and gather up those Q-cores your friends thought they'd stashed away. And then, we're going to win this damned war—"

Sur-natha went berserk, driving herself side-to-side, frantically trying to shake Dash free, get her knife arm unpinned, strike back, anything, and Dash just fought with every flicker of strength he had left, desperately determined to choke her.

Sur-natha convulsed, throwing every bit of her own strength into it, one last effort to throw him off. Then something snapped, and she went still.

Gasping, Dash doubled down on his grip around her throat, but her head just flopped loosely aside. Slowly, he released her, realizing she was no longer fighting him. She fell against the console then slid to one side, toppling to the floor with a heavy thud beside the Golden.

Dash slumped back against another console and sucked in a few breaths. He had enough presence of mind to kick Sur-natha's knife away, then he just stood, catching his breath and letting his brain finally catch up to what had just happened.

"Dash!"

He turned. Leira had run into the bridge, pulse-gun at the ready, a group of vac-suited figures behind her.

"Oh, hey, Leira," Dash said. "Was wondering when you'd show up."

She lowered the pulse-gun and moved toward Dash, while the rest of the boarding party fanned out across the bridge. One of them yanked off a helmet; it was Benzel. While he shouted instructions, Leira came to Dash's side, her pulse-gun trained on Sur-natha as she did.

"I killed her," Dash said, then he gestured at the Golden, meeting its lifeless eyes. "Had some help doing it, too."

Leira pulled off her helmet and put it down on the nearby console. She frowned at the bloody gashes in his suit. "You okay?"

"Yeah. I mean, I took some cuts, but—" He looked at Sur-natha. "I killed her. Didn't even mean to. Thought I could take her alive."

"Why would you want to?"

"I—" he began, then shrugged. "I don't know. I guess I wanted her to answer for the things she's done."

"I think she has."

"Yeah." He took a shuddering breath. "Holy shit. I mean, I broke her neck. I've never done that before, broken someone's neck." He could still hear that wet snap, could *feel* it in his arm."

Leira answered by unlatching and removing Dash's gloves. "You did what you had to do, and that's all. That's the only reason you killed her. That you've ever killed anyone." She raised his hands and kissed them. "These are not the hands of a murderer, and don't you ever think they are. They're the hands of a man who's fighting a war that needs to be fought."

Dash gave her a grateful smile. Somehow, breaking Sur-natha's neck—or, more properly, her breaking it herself when she fought against his hold—had hit him in a deep, primal way. It felt like a bestial, almost irrational way to kill someone. Leira's words steadied him, though, and he finally nodded.

He pulled his hands out of Leira's and knelt beside the Golden. "It helped me kill her. It was dying, and it helped me kill her." Dash looked at Leira. "It wanted me to live. And if a Golden can want anything to live—"

"Then they're not all devoted to extermination."

Dash nodded again. "Which means we *do* have allies out there." He looked back at the dead Golden.

"Now, we just have to find them."

The butcher's bill turned out to be far less awful than Dash had feared. Two Cygnus capital ships were beyond repair and now just salvage. Five smaller vessels, four of them mine layers, had also been lost. Every other ship, and all four of the mechs, had been as badly battered as Dash had ever seen them, and a few of them worse. The *Retribution*, in particular, had taken so many hits, had so many blast gouges and splashed scorch marks scoring her armor that Dash found it hard to believe she could even still move under her own power. But she could, Wei-Ping proudly easing her ship back into the head of the squadron's formation for the trip back to the Forge.

"We have to wear vac suits almost everywhere except on the bridge and in engineering," she'd reported. "So we've got everyone messing and sleeping between her reactors, but she'll hold together for the trip back home."

Their casualties likewise hadn't been as bad as Dash had braced himself for—thirty-seven dead, and another fifty or so wounded. All in all, it had been a good day—to the extent a day on which thirty-seven people had died could be called good.

There had been one bright spot, though, that had also been an amazing coincidence. While maneuvering the *Retribution* out of the thickest part of the debris field from the battle, Wei-Ping's ship had picked up a fitful distress beacon of the type mounted on a vac suit. They'd traced it to a lone figure drifting among the tangled wreckage and shattered fragments of ships. On the wild chance it had been a survivor, they'd retrieved what they actually expected would be a body—and found, instead, someone very much alive, and even conscious.

It was Sharrah, the young woman from the *Ravager*, who Dash had remembered when he'd seen the stricken frigate. Incredibly, she'd been blown out of her ship when it was savaged by petawatt laser fire, but in such a way that she'd remained in the *Ravager's* shadow and escaped being turned to a puff of vapor. She'd then just drifted, a lone figure in a vac suit, while the battle raged all around her.

According to Wei-Ping, she'd said only one thing when they recovered her and asked her how she felt.

"I'm good now. Nice light show. Thanks for that."

And then she'd passed out.

As they rallied the fleet and prepared to return to the Forge, Dash found himself chuckling every time he thought of it—that this young woman, not yet twenty years old, had floated helplessly through space, a mere speck among howling blasts of energy and violence, any one of which would have snuffed her out like a candle by a plasma torch.

Good light show.

With people like that on our side, Dash thought, the war seemed just a little more possible to win.

20

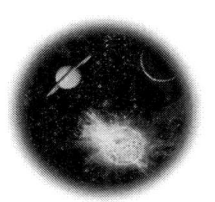

Dash squeezed between beds, crash carts, and people jammed into the Forge's infirmary. It was one aspect of the station they still had to work on, getting more medical facilities powered up and in use. Dash also made a mental note to get Harolyn working on getting them more doctors and medical personnel; their fifty-odd wounded from the battle had stretched their trauma and treatment resources *way* thinner than Dash liked.

"So that's the last of them," Saddiq said, passing his hands through a sterilizing field. "Of the fifty-two casualties, we lost one—she was just too badly injured to save. Of the rest, fifteen for sure are going to be spending some time recovering, three of those in medically induced comas."

Dash nodded then shoved himself aside as a nurse eased another crash cart of medical instruments and supplies through the throng. As he did, he recognized the young woman sprawled on a gurney against a bulkhead and moved to her side.

"Sharrah?"

Her eyes fluttered open. "Oh, Dash." She started to push herself up, but Dash put a hand on her shoulder and firmly, but gently, kept her down.

"You just stay there. How are you doing?"

"Pretty good, considering."

"Yeah. That must have been—" He stopped and shook his head. "I'd have been scared shitless."

"Oh, I made it *way* past scared shitless," she said, smiling weakly. "You know what it looks like when a missile zooms past you, almost close enough to touch? Because I do."

Dash smiled back at her. "How about we put you on duty in the Command Center for a while. I think you've earned a break—"

This time, she did force herself partway into a sitting position, propped on her elbows. "No way," she said, shaking her head emphatically. "I want to be out there. I just—" Her hard look of determination suddenly became one of sadness. "I need a new ship, I guess."

Dash nodded. "I'll talk to Wei-Ping. She kind of took you into the *Retribution*, so I think you should stay there."

Sharrah smiled. "Thanks, Dash."

He patted her shoulder then carried on, following Saddiq through the end of his briefing, then leaving the infirmary and making his way to the fabrication level.

"THE VERITY CARRIER IS BADLY DAMAGED," Custodian said, as Dash rode the elevator down to the fabrication plant. "But I have consulted with Benzel and Wei-Ping and believe it can be repaired.

However, doing so will consume considerable resources and take a great deal of time."

Dash nodded. Custodian's recounting of the spoils had been a joy to hear—the largest haul of Dark Metal, ship components, and miscellaneous scrap they'd managed yet—but it came with its own set of problems. They'd captured a dozen more ships, including the big carrier, that they could repair and repurpose for their own use. But they had to balance that against repairs to their existing ships, as well as upgrading them *and* expanding their production capacity. All of these things required time and resources, and they only had so much of either.

"Let's put fixing up the carrier on hold for now. Hell, we don't even have fighters to station on it, so it'd just be a mostly big empty ship anyway."

"That is true. I shall confer further with Benzel and Wei-Ping."

The elevator stopped and Dash stepped out, then he walked the short way to the fabrication plant.

He found Leira, Amy, and Conover already there, watching as their mechs were repaired. Benzel, Viktor, and Wei-Ping also showed up, only a moment after Dash. He gave the last two a glare as he took in Viktor's slung arm, and the bandages around Wei-Ping's neck and head.

"You two are supposed to be resting," Dash said firmly. "You know, getting better, so I can put you back to work?"

"You can put us back to work now," Wei-Ping said, frustrated. "I've got too much to do to just lie around recuperating."

"You took a bad plasma flash burn," Dash replied. "Saddiq specifically told me to give you crap if I found you on your feet. So I'm giving you crap. That treatment he used works best when you're not moving around."

"Yeah, yeah," Wei-Ping replied, waving a hand. "I know. If I don't want scarring, I'm supposed to stay perfectly still for at least a day. Well, screw that. Among the Gentle Friends, scarring just means you've been doing your job."

Dash opened his mouth, but he closed it again. Arguing with this formidable woman would be a waste of breath. So he turned to Viktor instead.

"What about you? What's your excuse for not following doctor's orders?"

Viktor shrugged—awkwardly, and in a lopsided way, because of his bound arm. "I was bored."

"How'd you get hurt," Amy asked.

Viktor shrugged again. "Turns out that, when the inertial dampers go offline, you really should have seatbelts." He turned to Dash. "There's now a dent in the shape of my arm in your ship's nav. Oh, and on a vaguely related note, the *Slipwing* doesn't have any seatbelts."

Dash shrugged back. "Never occurred to me. Good point, though. We should get those retrofitted wherever they're needed."

"Starting with the *Slipwing*," Viktor said with a winning smile.

"Sure, let's do that."

He turned back to the mechs. All four stood in the assembly bay, robotic arms slinging around newly crafted armor plates, structural components, and even whole subsystems, like the Swift's missing arm. Custodian estimated that all four mechs would be fully repaired in another day. This sort of capacity to repair damage and return mechs and ships to service fast was, Dash realized, a crucial part of the Forge's capabilities they tended to overlook. But, as he watched a new hand being installed on the Archetype, his thoughts turned to another system waiting to be plugged into the mech.

"Custodian, what's the status of the stardiver?" he asked, using the unofficial name they'd given to the specialized translation drive, the one meant to allow jumps directly into a gas giant to retrieve Q-cores and other tech stored in their murky depths.

"The stardiver system is complete and currently in storage. I had assumed that you would prioritize repairs to the fleet over installing it in the Archetype."

"And that's a plan we should stick with," Leira said, catching Dash's eye.

He sighed. He knew how she felt about the whole idea of the stardiver. Not only did it make possible the insanely dangerous journey into the crushing heat and pressure of a gas giant's lower atmosphere, but it did so by functioning partly as a time machine—and that could, itself, cause all sorts of dire effects if not used with extreme care.

He even agreed with her. But if they could retrieve working Q-cores, then they could power up the Forge more quickly and fully and get things like that additional medical capacity online.

"Custodian," Dash said. "Before you release the Archetype from its repairs, go ahead and install the stardiver in it. I want to give that a trial run as soon as we can."

He braced himself for the inevitable burst of outrage from Leira, but she said nothing. Instead, she just turned and walked away, leaving Dash standing awkwardly among the others, who all tried to studiously look anywhere else.

He would have preferred the outrage. This was actually much worse.

Dash found Leira in the War Room, the repurposed crew lounge they'd used for their planning meetings before the Command Center had come online. The big viewports offered a spectacular view of the fleet arrayed around the Forge and the deep starfield beyond.

Leira stood in front of one of the ports, arms crossed, staring in the direction of the battered *Retribution*. He doubted that was what she was seeing right now, though.

"Hey," he said.

She didn't turn and didn't speak.

Taking a breath, Dash walked up beside her. For a moment, they just stood that way, side-by-side. Finally, he couldn't take the roaring silence any longer and turned to her.

"Leira—"

"If you came here to justify this dangerously insane thing you intend to do, don't bother," she snapped. "You've obviously already made up your mind, so there's not much point talking about it, is there?"

He crossed his own arms. "Yeah, I have made up my mind. And yeah, I am going to do this. And, yeah, I still think we need to talk about it."

"Why? I obviously can't change your mind."

"Maybe you can't, Leira, but I'm willing to listen. *Especially* to you, and believe me when I tell you—if I'm wrong, I'll admit it., but there are times when you have to let me take a risk. This is one such moment."

Leira scowled and turned away.

"If it makes you feel at all better, I don't want to do this."

"So don't."

Dash kept looking at her, even if she wouldn't look at him. "So just walk away from these Q-cores? Leave them in the hands of the Golden?"

She finally turned to face him. "Custodian says we've got so much Dark Metal coming in now that we have to store most of it, because we can't refine and use it fast enough."

"I know. That's because we've maxed out the Forge's current capacity. And that's why we need those Q-cores."

Her scowl deepened. "We can *make* Q-cores—"

"Not fast enough. If we only use what the Shroud can make, it'll be weeks, probably months, before we can get to where retrieving these hidden Q-cores could get us in just days." He sighed. "I know you don't want to hear this. I don't want to say it. But you know it's true, Leira."

She looked back out at the *Retribution*. A moment passed in silence, then she turned back.

"Of course I know you're right," she snapped. "And that's the problem. I want to be able to say '*don't do this*' and give you a killer reason that makes you go, oh, you're right. But I can't. You're right, and I'm wrong, and it's pissing me off."

"Because you're wrong?"

"No, you moron! Because I don't want to lose you!"

The two of them just looked at one another in silence, then Leira turned away again, biting her lip.

Dash put his hands in his pockets. "Leira, look. I'm so glad about us. About what we seem to have. Nothing, right now, makes me happier." He glanced at the pummeled shape of the *Retribution*, at the flickering, dazzling points of light flaring from her, where repairs were being welded. "But, as good as it is, it can't get in the way of fighting this war. It can't stop either of us from doing the things that need to be done to win it. You know that, and I know that, and there it is."

She shook her head but said nothing again.

"Leira, if we can't do that, then maybe we should just—"

She turned and hugged him.

"Don't bother saying it," she said. "Because you *know* that the answer to that is going to be, 'like hell we're going to give this up before we even know what it really is.'" She kissed him and then pulled back. "You're just going to have to accept something. I'm going to worry. A lot. And I'm not going to like a lot of the things we both have to do. Again, a lot." She gave a rueful smile. "But I guess that means I have to accept the way things are." Her eyes met Dash's. "I'll be so glad when this damned war is over."

Dash made himself smile. He had to, because as soon as she'd said it, he remembered his secretive meeting with Custodian in the isolated part of the Forge meant specifically for the Messenger.

"Conover has abilities that, given time, will develop and allow him to thrive as a commander," Custodian had said. *"In fact, he may have the greatest potential of all of your current allies."*

"This war really is going to be an awfully long one, then, if you can see Conover in independent command of an Anchor, and everything that goes with it."

"Yes. I am sorry to say so, but you are undoubtedly correct."

"Believe me, Leira, there'll be *no* one more glad than me when this is all finally done and I can stop calling myself the Messenger."

Leira nodded and put her arm around Dash. He did likewise with her. Then, for a while, they both just stood that way, looking out at their growing fleet of warships.

EPILOGUE

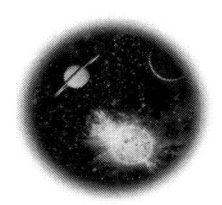

Dash took a moment to simply stare down at the roiling cloud tops of the gas giant. This was the smallest one within which they'd found clear signals of Dark Metal and, therefore, a skyhook and likely Q-cores. But *small* was relative—it was still a vast body, over twenty thousand klicks in diameter, and about fourteen times the size of a typical, terrestrial rocky planet like Old Earth. It was also absolutely beautiful, being rendered a deep, rich azure by traces of methane in its atmosphere.

"Any time you're ready, Dash," Conover said.

He looked from the planet to the tactical display. The Talon and the Swift both hung in orbit nearby. Higher above the planet, the *Herald* and the *Slipwing* likewise kept station, providing top cover for their operation against any attempts at interference from the Golden, the Verity, or anyone else.

In theory, they also represented rescue if anything went wrong. In reality, even the mechs, as tough as they were and with their shields overcharged, wouldn't survive a trip into the depths to which he was headed, much less have any chance of extracting him.

"Yeah, I'm just waiting for Sentinel. She's crunching the numbers that the stardiver needs for the translation. It's…complicated. Even for her."

"It is," Conover said. "She has to start with baseline equations and then determine ranges for the variables involved. And based on that—"

"Conover?"

"Yes?"

"That's why I have allies like Sentinel—and like you. It's so I don't need to know the details, I just have to trust the people who do. In other words, I believe you."

"Yeah—got it, Dash. Sorry."

"Don't be. Just don't be miffed when I say I don't need the details."

Actually, Dash found himself squirming a little uncomfortably in the cradle. It was taking Sentinel too long, even with help from Tybalt and Kristen, to come up with the necessary inputs for the stardiver. The fact that these super-advanced AIs were spending so much time on this problem hinted at just how complex it was. He even began to wonder if it might be too complicated and Sentinel would come back and say, *sorry, Dash, this just isn't possible.*

That would be disappointing.

And it would also, frankly, be a relief.

"We now have our best solution to the mathematical issues involved in operating the stardiver," Sentinel finally said. "I have loaded it into the system and am prepared to initiate it on your command."

Dash frowned. There was a tone he'd never before heard buried in the back of the AI's words. It was—uncertainty? Even *worry*?

"Sentinel, is something wrong?"

"Can you be more specific? Depending upon what you're referring to, there could be many things considered to be *wrong*."

"Look, we've been together long enough that I know something's bothering you—which is itself really weird—plus, you're dissembling. Is there something you're not telling me about this little endeavor of ours?"

After a pause, Sentinel said, "Yes. I am experiencing a heightened degree of concern over the uncertainties involved in many of these variables. We have established ranges of possible values for them, but—"

"Sentinel, are you *worried*?"

No answer.

Despite the gravity of the situation, Dash had to smile. "Sentinel, if you are worried, that's fine. Mind you, I didn't even know you *could* be worried. That's kind of a human thing."

"What is worry but a reaction to uncertainty?"

"Good point. But it's okay. Hell, I've come close to pissing my own pants a few times, facing some of the things we've gone through together."

"I have previously been concerned. This, however, is different. Not only must the translation itself work properly, but it must do so twice within the five seconds the Archetype can safely withstand the conditions below. And it must do so accurately, while experiencing a negative flow of time. You will be translating to and from the Darkness Between, rather than real space, to avoid having duplicates of the Archetype and yourself exist simultaneously in real space. If that is not done correctly, it is not possible to predict the ramifications that would result from such a violation of the law of conservation of energy, nor the potential damage to space-time—"

"Sentinel," Dash cut in.

"Yes?"

"I trust you. If anyone's got this, it's you."

"Your trust is based on a lack of understanding of the potentially dire implications—"

"Yeah, ignorance is bliss. Doesn't matter, because I know this could go really, really wrong. And yet, here I am, waiting for you to take us down into that gas giant."

"You truly have no reservations?"

"I sure as hell do. Tons of them." He smiled at how much this echoed his conversation with Leira, which meant he had *two* women in his life he had to watch out for. "But, like I said, here I am, ready to go when you are."

"I appreciate your trust in my abilities."

"I count on your abilities, Sentinel. And you've never let me down. So I don't expect you to start letting me down now."

"Very well. I will signal to the rest of the ships that we will translate in one minute. And—"

Dash waited.

"And thank you, Dash."

"Any time, Sentinel. Now, let's go get us some Q-cores."

Dash watched the chrono. At the thirty second mark, Leira's voice came over the comm on a private channel.

"One more try at persuading you not to do this?"

"Do you really think that's going to work?"

"No. But I wanted to say it anyway. That and—"

Again, Dash just waited. He wondered just what Leira was going to say here…

"And if you don't come back in one piece, I'm going to kick your ass."

Dash laughed. "See you in a few minutes."

"I'll be here, waiting."

"Ten seconds," Sentinel said. "I have redirected all power not allocated to the stardiver to the shield, and to scanners."

Dash just nodded as the background rumble and hum of the mech changed. There'd be no need for the Archetype's weapons, or the primary real space or translation drives.

The chrono scrolled past three, to two, to one—

To zero.

The starfield vanished on the heads-up as the Archetype entered the Darkness Between. From the perspective of real space, it, and Dash, no longer existed.

"I am initiating the stardiver now."

Dash could only imagine the fantastically complicated calculations, the framework around which the mech's colossal power would flow, shifting them to—

Somewhere else.

Blackness became a howling inferno. Warnings erupted from the mech as its shield was almost instantly saturated with energy, its hull temperature shooting up a thousand degrees in an instant. At the same time, the Archetype shuddered and groaned as hydrogen and helium with the consistency of wet plasticrete slammed into the mech, driven by energies with origins that could only be guessed at. The almost-solid wind shoved hard at the mech, pummeling it with glittering snowflakes made of metallic platinum.

The chrono ticked—one.

Dash looked at the surface upon which the mech stood, scarred rock and exotic natural alloys shot through with ponds and rivers of liquid metal.

Two.

There were humped shapes, covered by rock and what looked like metal plates, the closest near the mech's right foot.

Three.

He reached down, grabbed it, and wrenched. As he did, a heavy, shuddering groan ran through the mech, punctuated by a sharp, metallic squeal, and then an explosive crack. More warnings lit, but Dash ignored them.

Four.

The cover came away. It exposed two Q-cores.

Five.

He grabbed both, shouting as he did.

"Sentinel!"

Blackness, and silence.

"Dash!"

He opened his eyes. "What? Oh, sorry, must have dozed off for a minute."

The Archetype stood in the hangar bay aboard the Forge. People thronged the big chamber, gaping at the mech.

"Dash!" Leira called again.

"You'd better let me dismount, Sentinel, before Leira has a heart attack."

"Understood."

The mech bent forward and down, and the cockpit opened. Dash levered himself out of the cradle and stepped onto the deck.

Everyone started to cheer. The cheers only intensified when Viktor and Conover stepped away from the cargo compartment on the mech's leg, each holding aloft a Q-core.

Leira, though, pushed through the crowd, ignoring the Q-cores, the cheers, and keeping her focus firmly on Dash.

"You don't have to look so worried," he said. "I mean, we talked a bunch on the way back here."

"I know, but still." She nodded toward the Archetype.

Dash followed her gaze, then winced. He'd seen the status warnings that had erupted across the heads-up, but seeing the damage to the mech inflicted by the gas giant was something else altogether. Parts of the Archetype looked as though they'd been kneaded like soft clay, bent and twisted and malformed. Its armor sported long, deep gouges where chunks of metal "ice" driven along by the slushy hydrogen-helium winds had slammed into it at thousands of kilometers per hour.

The mech would require lengthy time in the shop before it was ready to fly again. But it had survived, and so had Dash—and they'd brought back two functioning Q-cores.

So the concept worked.

Relief finally flooded Dash. It had been absolutely terrifying, which just made what he was about to do all the sweeter.

He grabbed Leira and kissed her.

The crowd fell into stunned silence—then erupted again into a roar of approval and raucous cheers.

When Dash pulled back, Leira smiled. But he saw her also searching his face closely, seemingly looking for any sign of hurt.

"So you've avoided saying just what happened down there," she said.

He shrugged. "That was so I didn't have to tell the story a hundred times."

"Well, tell me. What was it like?"

"Meh."

"Meh? Diving into the depths of a gas giant was *meh*?"

He shrugged again. "Yeah. Meh. The usual. A power surge."

And then he kissed her again, harder. He liked that kind of power surge better.

Around them, the cheering went on.

DASH, SENTINEL, LEIRA, VIKTOR, and CONOVER will return in HEAVEN'S DOOR, coming May 2020.

For more updates on this series, be sure to join the Facebook Group, "J.N. Chaney's Renegade Readers."

STAY UP TO DATE

Join the conversation and get updates on new and upcoming releases in the Facebook group called "JN Chaney's Renegade Readers." This is a hotspot where readers come together and share their lives and interests, discuss the series, and speak directly to J.N. Chaney and his co-authors.

https://www.facebook.com/groups/jnchaneyreaders/

He also post updates, official art, and other awesome stuff on his website and you can also follow him on Instagram, Facebook, and Twitter.

For email updates about new releases, as well as exclusive promotions, visit his website and sign up for the VIP mailing list. Head there now to receive a free copy of *The Other Side of Nowhere*.

https://www.jnchaney.com/the-messenger-subscribe

Stay Up To Date

Enjoying the series? Help others discover *The Messenger* series by leaving a review on Amazon.

ABOUT THE AUTHORS

J. N. Chaney is a USA Today Bestselling author and has a Master's of Fine Arts in Creative Writing. He fancies himself quite the Super Mario Bros. fan. When he isn't writing or gaming, you can find him online at **www.jnchaney.com**.

He migrates often, but was last seen in Las Vegas, NV. Any sightings should be reported, as they are rare.

Terry Maggert is left-handed, likes dragons, coffee, waffles, running, and giraffes; order unimportant. He's also half of author Daniel Pierce, and half of the humor team at Cledus du Drizzle.

With thirty-one titles, he has something to thrill, entertain, or make you cringe in horror. Guaranteed.

Note: He doesn't sleep. But you sort of guessed that already.

Made in the USA
Middletown, DE
16 May 2020